KEEPER'S REACH

CARLA NEGGERS

KEEPER'S REACH

MIRA

MIRA

ISBN-13: 978-0-7783-1752-4

Keeper's Reach

Printed in U.S.A.

First printing: September 2015
10 9 8 7 6 5 4 3 2 1

To Jim, Maureen, Martha and Todd

1

Near Stow-on-the-Wold, the Cotswolds, England
Wednesday, 4:00 p.m., BST

Martin Hambly had expected additional visits from the FBI, but this agent was new to him. Rangy, sandy-haired, early forties. He conveyed an unsettling mix of suspicion and arrogance, with none of the humor of the agents Martin had encountered last fall.

Kavanagh. Special Agent Ted Kavanagh. That was his name.

Martin supposed it could be the case.

The American flashed his FBI credentials as he gave his name, but Martin, carrying clay pots planted with amaryllis bulbs in each arm, didn't examine them.

Kavanagh tucked his credentials back into his overcoat, a sturdy but inexpensive dark gray wool. He had intercepted Martin on the narrow lane in front of the small village church, an oft-photographed favorite with the few tourists who ventured this deep into the Cotswolds countryside.

"Mr. York isn't here," Martin said.

"'Here' meaning his farm, the village or England?"

"He's in England."

Martin shifted the amaryllis pots in his arms. He had picked them up from friends who ran a flower shop in nearby Stow-on-the-Wold. His decades-old Barbour jacket, wool cap and waterproof walking shoes were adequate for the twenty-minute walk to and from the York farm on a chilly February afternoon, but not for standing still for a long, awkward chat.

"I will tell Mr. York you were asking for him," Martin said with a deliberate note of finality.

"Okay. Thanks."

The FBI agent—if, indeed, that was what he was—made no move to continue on his way. Martin didn't notice a car that could have belonged to him, or a partner lurking down the lane or in the churchyard. In the fall, three FBI agents had arrived at the York apartment in London. Matt Yankowski, Colin Donovan and Emma Sharpe. Martin had expected Oliver to refuse to let them in, but he had instructed Martin to have the agents join him in the library. It was the same library where, twenty-nine years ago, eight-year-old Oliver, an only child, had witnessed the murder of his parents.

Martin decided not to mention the previous agents to this new agent.

"Quiet village," Kavanagh said.

"Yes, it is. Stow-on-the-Wold isn't far. It's a market town with shops and restaurants, if you need anything. Are you staying in the area?"

"Off to Heathrow and home tomorrow."

It wasn't an answer, was it?

Martin felt the weight of the pots and now regretted not bringing the car. After two days of rain, he had looked forward to a good walk.

"Why do you suppose they buried people in the churchyard?" Kavanagh asked, nodding to the age-worn gravestones, many standing crookedly, covered in white lichens. The church itself was constructed of the yellow limestone characteristic of count-less structures in the rolling Cotswolds countryside west of London. It dated as far back as the twelfth century, but, of course, had been added to and reworked over the ensuing centuries.

"It was the thing to do, I imagine. I've never thought about it."

Kavanagh grinned. "Stupid question from an annoying American?"

"I didn't say that, sir."

"You didn't look surprised when I recognized you. Then again, you're obviously a man of great self-control. How long have you worked for Oliver York?"

Martin saw no reason not to answer. "I was twenty when Mr. York's grandparents hired me."

"You're what—a valet? A manservant?"

"Agent Kavanagh, if you have a card with your contact information, I can give it to Mr. York."

"I don't, in fact." The American smiled. "Long story."

Martin doubted that. "I should get cracking. Enjoy your stay, and have a good flight tomorrow."

"Thanks." He made no move to go on his way. "You met a few of my colleagues in November. Agents Yankowski, Sharpe and Donovan. Any contact with them since then?"

So, Agent Kavanagh knew about the November visit. "We exchanged Christmas cards," Martin said, immediately regretting his sarcasm.

Kavanagh laughed. "A smart-ass under all that English formality, aren't you, Martin?" He nodded at the pots. "What color amaryllises?"

"Both are bloodred."

"Surprised I know an amaryllis bulb from a tulip bulb, aren't you? In fact, I don't. It says so on the little stick in the dirt."

Chuckling to himself, the American resumed course down the lane, back toward the village, away from the church. Martin debated finding out whether Special Agent Kavanagh was booked at the village pub, which also let rooms.

"Best not," he said under his breath.

Restless now and decidedly ill at ease, he set the pots on the low wall in front of the church. He was sixty-three and in excellent shape, but the pots were heavier than he had anticipated. A short break was in order before he continued on to the farm. He stretched his arms as he walked in the opposite direction of the FBI agent. The lane ended at the entrance to a cemetery, which adjoined the churchyard but was separate from its scatter of gravestones.

A breeze stirred, and he noticed the sun, a welcome sight earlier in the day, was giving way to a gray, still dusk. Martin watched a lone bird—he couldn't say what species it was—float above a barren field past the cemetery and disappear over the horizon, as if it wanted to get away from the dead.

His imagination, of course.

He veered off the paved walk, slowing his pace as he cut down a muddy footpath, past bare-branched trees and more graves. He had grown up in the village and had family buried here, but it wasn't their graves that drew him.

He came to a far corner of the cemetery and paused at a low stone wall that bordered the field. He pulled off his cap and felt the breeze in his graying hair as he breathed in the cool air and tried not to let emotion overcome him.

Finally, he leaned forward and touched the name carved on a cold, gray stone.

Priscilla Farley York.

He shut his eyes, his fingertips on the letters. He could feel Priscilla's bony, aged hand as she clutched his wrist, and he could see the pain in her dying eyes. She had been frail then, a ghost of the woman who had put him to work. Yet undiminished were the will, the determination and the faith that had seen her through more than any mother and grandmother should have had to bear.

Look after Oliver, won't you, Martin? He's suffered so much. Promise me you'll look after him.

Martin hadn't hesitated, although he had known, even then, it wouldn't be an easy promise to keep. He could hear his certainty and sincerity as he answered her. *I will look after Oliver. I promise.*

Priscilla had died a few hours later.

The next day, Oliver had dropped out of Oxford.

Opening his eyes, Martin touched his fingers to the names on three more York gravestones.

Nicholas York

Charles York

Deborah Summerhill York

Martin had known them all. Nicholas, Oliver's grandfather, had preceded Priscilla into the grave by eighteen months. He had loved the Cotswolds. The York farm had been in his family for generations, and he and Priscilla had relished retiring there and turning over their London apartment to Charles, their only son, and Deborah, his lovely wife.

Who could have imagined that Charles and Deborah would be murdered?

Who could have imagined Oliver, their eight-year-old son, would be snatched and taken to Scotland, then held alone in a church ruin? Shivering and hungry, the traumatized boy had escaped. No one could say how long he had wandered in the cold Scottish countryside before a priest, on a walk to the ruins, had discovered him.

Oliver's kidnappers—his parents' killers—had yet to be captured, convicted and sentenced for their heinous crimes. They'd been identified as groundskeepers the Yorks had hired, briefly, shortly before their murder, but no trace of them had ever been discovered.

When the police had arrived at the farm with the terrible

news, Martin had gone to find Nicholas and Priscilla, out with the dogs on the farm. The searing trauma of those days had undoubtedly shortened their lives. Despite their own grief, they had done their best to raise Oliver and get him whatever help he needed.

His throat tight with emotion, Martin turned back through the cemetery. He had dedicated himself to the welfare of the last of the Yorks—Priscilla, Nicholas and Oliver.

Now there was just Oliver.

Martin heard the distant cry of a bird, but otherwise the cemetery was quiet. As the church came into view again, he could see young Charles and Deborah on their wedding day, laughing as they greeted guests. There had been no question they would have the ceremony here in the village.

Martin scooped up the amaryllis pots from the wall. He needed to put aside loyalty, grief, pity and sympathy and see clearly what options were available—especially now with the bloody FBI popping into town for a visit.

He had made a promise. He couldn't falter, and he couldn't fail.

He glanced down the lane toward the village center, but he didn't see the American.

Should he call Emma Sharpe or Colin Donovan and ask them about Special Agent Kavanagh and this strange visit?

Let Oliver make that decision.

A pot in each arm, Martin set off down the lane, cutting onto a public footpath that paralleled the main thoroughfare. It was part of the Oxfordshire Way, one of the many marked walking routes in the picturesque Cotswolds. On his free days, he liked nothing better than to don his walking shoes, choose a loop and set off for the day. Oliver was fit as a fiddle, but he hated to "ramble," as he put it, preferring endless hours of solitary martial arts practice. Martin suspected his employer and friend's distaste for country leisure walking harkened back to his kidnapping, but he had never asked—and he never would. Heart-to-hearts would only make them both uncomfortable, and Martin had decided years ago that some things he was best not knowing for certain. Guessing was enough for him.

Oliver would be in from London tomorrow. Martin would have the morning to see to errands and deliveries and get the house prepared for Oliver's arrival. He was inviting a friend, he had said. An Irish priest Martin had yet to meet.

You'll like him, Hambly. He's a whiskey expert. He and his twin brother own an Irish distillery.

It was a marginal recommendation. Martin preferred Scotch.

Nonetheless, he appreciated that Oliver was making an attempt to turn over a new leaf and have real friends. Martin would be sure the guest suite was immaculate and fires were lit throughout the house, ready for their arrival.

Converting the small dovecote on the edge of the farm's main grounds into a potting shed had been Priscilla York's idea. Although the family employed a gardener, she had loved to putter with her pots and seeds. Martin had spent many hours helping her, although he didn't pretend to have her knowledge, expertise or interest in gardening.

Adding a stonework studio to the dovecote twelve years ago, long after his grandmother's death, had been Oliver's idea. He hadn't asked Martin for help, opinions or approval and went about stocking the studio with lapidary saws, heat guns, polishing wheels, hammers, chisels and various kinds of glue. Stonecarving became another of Oliver's solitary hobbies. Martin had thought no harm could come of it.

One of his more spectacular miscalculations.

He set the pots on a rough-wood worktable. Deep red amaryllis blossoms would provide welcome color before spring returned. He felt his tension and melancholy lifting after meeting the FBI agent and visiting the graves. He envisioned hillsides of daffodils, fields of bright yellow rapeseed, lambs prancing with their mothers. Truly, was there anything more glorious than springtime in the Cotswolds?

He helped himself to a bottle of water he kept on the work-table and groaned when he noticed a package by the door. He had forgotten about it. Oliver had packed it himself before departing for London late Monday. Martin had no idea what was inside and wasn't about to rip it open to find out. *Surely* it couldn't contain anything provocative, since it was addressed to Emma Sharpe, one of the FBI agents from November.

Martin noticed Oliver hadn't used Agent Sharpe's Boston home or office address, which, to the consternation of the FBI, were in his possession. Instead, he had addressed the package to her in care of Father Finian Bracken at the St. Patrick's Holy Roman Catholic Church rectory in Rock Point, Maine.

Oliver's new friend, the Irish priest.

Father Bracken was also Emma Sharpe and Colin Donovan's friend, an awkward and potentially incendiary situation in Martin's estimation.

He rang the courier service, catching them in time to pick up the package for overnight service to the United States. He wasn't surprised to discover Oliver had done a perfunctory, inadequate packing job. He added more tape before setting the package outside on the doorstep. He would wait for the courier. Then an early supper and some well-placed acupressure on his sore arms were in order.

He heard a rustling sound behind the dovecote, which sat atop a wooded hillside above a stream.

"Not the bloody ram again," he muttered.

The stubborn beast refused to stay within the fence. He liked to escape the confines of his carefully maintained pasture and romp through forbidden territory. Farm animals weren't Martin's responsibility, but he couldn't leave the sheep to his own devices. At the least, he could assess the situation and then call for help if necessary. If it was the ram and he wasn't in too big a fix, Martin could manage to get him back into his pen on his own—if grumbling the entire way.

He went around to the back of the dovecote. The ground was soft and wet, no surprise given the two days of rain. At least it hadn't been snow. He noticed with pleasure that snowdrops were in bloom, blanketing the grass around an oak tree with their tiny white flowers, a welcome harbinger of spring.

The hillside was darkened with dusk and shadows, but not so much so Martin would be unable to see a wandering sheep. Still, he saw nothing. He paused, listening, but he couldn't make out any bleating.

Perhaps it had been a fox or pheasant he had heard, stirring with the warmer weather and now on its way.

"Well, good, then," Martin said aloud, turning back toward the dovecote.

Then came a scraping sound…metal on metal…as distinct and unmistakable as his own breathing.

Now what?

It had to be the ram. He must have caught on something.

Martin decided to have another look then get a farmworker out here.

Then came a grunt, distinctly human and close.

"No!"

Martin heard panic and fear in his voice. His heart jumped, adrenaline surging painfully through him as he tried, instinctively, to dodge what he knew was an oncoming blow.

He was too late.

The blow came quickly, hard, to the back of his head, sending him sprawling down the hill. He couldn't get his footing and crashed against winter-denuded trees and brush, until finally landing facedown in wet grass and dead leaves.

He was vaguely aware of the taste of mud and the stab of a twig in his cheek as pain exploded in his head.

Bastard.

Unable to breathe, he gasped in agony, fighting to stay conscious as he sank into the cold ground and the inevitable blackness.

2

Emma Sharpe was in love with her wedding gown. Totally, absolutely in love. It was silky, simple, flattering and *exactly* what she had envisioned. She took a selfie in the fitting room of the Newbury Street shop and texted it to her mother in London, who responded immediately.

It's perfect. I'm sorry I'm not there.

Emma didn't mind. Her father was recovering from his latest procedure to help ease his chronic back pain due to a long-ago fall on the ice, and her mother was at his side. For most of the past year, they had been living and working abroad, away from reminders of the past, and of the future they had once envisioned for themselves. Their hometown of Heron's Cove, Maine, had become a trigger for emotional and physical pain.

Her parents had promised to return for Emma's spring wedding. That was enough, she thought as she eased out of the dress. It was pinned for alterations. She smiled at her reflection, her fair hair a bit flyaway from the dress and the dry winter air. From her late teens into her early twenties, she had believed she would never marry. She had been Sister Brigid then.

She thought of Colin, a hardheaded Maine Donovan, an FBI undercover agent and her fiancé since he had proposed on bended knee in early November in a Dublin pub.

She was Sister Brigid no more.

She slipped back into her jeans, sweater and boots and grabbed her three-quarter-length wool coat, hat and gloves as she exited the dressing room. She'd left work early for the fitting but had stopped at her Boston waterfront apartment to change out of her work clothes. Around the same time her parents had left for London, she had moved to Boston to join HIT, a small FBI team started and led by the senior agent who had recruited her out of the convent. Matt Yankowski had never doubted his conviction that Emma wasn't meant to profess her final vows and become a full-fledged member of the Sisters of the Joyful Heart.

We can use your expertise in art and art crimes, Yank had told her when he had visited her at her Maine convent four years ago. *Give it some thought, Emma.*

He hadn't called her Sister Brigid.

Her early expertise in art crimes hadn't come from her time at the convent. She was the granddaughter of Wendell Sharpe, founder of Sharpe Fine Art Recovery and one of the foremost private art detectives in the world.

As she ducked out onto the Back Bay street, her phone dinged with another text. Although it was from London, it wasn't from her mother. It was from Oliver York, aka Oliver Fairbairn, a British aristocrat, self-educated mythologist and international serial art thief.

Who is the FBI agent following me?

Emma stared at the screen. There was no FBI agent following Oliver. She would know if there were. She typed a quick response.

I'll call you in an hour.

Oliver responded immediately.

I'll be waiting.

Lucy Yankowski buzzed Emma into the third-floor apartment she had just rented on Marlborough Street, two blocks from the Newbury Street wedding shop in Boston's Back Bay. "Matt hasn't seen it yet," she said as she led Emma into the living room. "He'll love it, don't you think?"

"From what I can gather, he'll love anything that isn't infested with cockroaches."

Lucy shuddered. She was a small woman with dark hair cut short and edgy, something of a new look for her as she reinvented herself in Boston. She hadn't wanted to move from northern Virginia. It had taken her a year to decide saving her marriage was worth giving up her life in suburban Washington, DC. Her reconciliation with Yank—Matt, as she called her husband of fifteen years—hadn't been without drama or peril, and it didn't mean her new life in Boston was settled. For one, she was a clinical psychologist and was talking about giving it up to open a knitting shop.

First order of business, however, had been to find the "perfect apartment." As far as Emma could see, there was no question Lucy had done just that.

"I insisted on a washer and dryer in the unit, and I wanted a decent view—I didn't want to drink my morning coffee looking out at trash cans. I swear I manifested this place, but I'm not sure I believe in that stuff."

She gave Emma the grand tour, starting with the living room and moving into the bedrooms—there were two—and dining room. Although small given its upscale location, the apartment was a far cry from the cheap, roach-infested one-bedroom Yank had rented, thinking he would be there for a couple of months at most. Like the rest of Back Bay, Marlborough, one of Emma's favorite streets in Boston, had been underwater before the massive nineteenth-century project that had created the gracious neighborhood, now known for its tree-lined streets and Victorian brownstones.

"Look," Lucy said, smiling as she raised a shade when they returned to the living room. "We have a tree outside the window. Imagine it in the summer. When do you get leaves on the trees up here?"

"May for sure," Emma said. "I count on full leaf bloom by Memorial Day at home in Maine."

"Gad. It's too late to change my mind. We've already signed the lease." She sighed, gazing out at the bare-limbed tree. "I'm sure there are quirks, but I couldn't be happier with this place. Matt will freak out if he sees a roach, but it's the city. There are bound to be roaches. We sleep with a can of Raid and a flyswatter next to the bed in our current apartment."

"I can see why you're eager to move," Emma said.

She lowered the shade again. "I'm giddy. It's fun to show the place off. Thank you for indulging me."

"I love checking out Boston apartments."

"Will you and Colin stay where you are once you're married?"

"For now."

"Boston rents are insane. I'm sleeping here tonight. I brought over a few basics from Matt's place. He won't be back for a couple more days, and a sleeping bag on the floor here is more appealing than another night on my own with the roaches."

Emma laughed. "I can't say I blame you."

"Do you ever miss convent life?"

Ah, Emma thought. The real reason for her presence here. "I miss the gardens and the scenery. It's a beautiful place."

"Matt says you're heading up there for a couple of nights."

"Tomorrow after work, yes. It's a mini retreat."

"I've always loved the name of your order. Sisters of the Joyful Heart. Are they a joyful lot?"

"Most of the time," Emma said.

"Matt says your time with the sisters has served you well in the FBI. You strike me as centered, Emma. You have good command of your emotions and the ability to stay fully present. I can see how you and Colin do well together. He operates on gut instinct honed by training and experience." Lucy moved away from the window. "I'm aware Matt was Colin's contact agent on at least one undercover mission."

Emma followed Lucy to the entrance, making no comment on her assertion.

The older woman smiled. "Not going to confirm anything, are you? That's all right. I wouldn't expect you to. One learns to ferret out tidbits when one is married to a senior federal agent. The isolation, constant danger and pretending to be someone else as an undercover agent can take a toll after a while. Some personalities are more suited to that sort of work than others. There must be a high burnout rate."

"You have to know when you've had enough in any line of work," Emma said.

"Ah, how true. Here I am thinking about opening a knitting shop. I'm eyeing a spot on Charles Street. I could walk to work. That would be a first for me. A knitting shop might be a fantasy to help me with the transition to life in Boston, but if it is, it's working. I haven't been this excited in a long time."

"Maybe you needed something new."

"I wonder if that's part of why I resisted moving for so long. I didn't want to face my own boredom. Psychology is a relatively portable career, but maybe it's run its course. I thought maybe my marriage had, too. I'm glad I was wrong about that."

Emma wasn't going there. "I can see Yank taking up knitting."

"My husband's idea of a hobby is cleaning his gun."

Lucy thanked Emma again as she left, taking the stairs down to the small lobby and heading out into the February cold. What Lucy Yankowski hadn't brought up—and clearly hadn't had any intention of bringing up—was that her husband and Emma's fiancé were both in Washington, DC, likely meeting with the new FBI director about an undercover mission.

With Oliver York waiting for her, Emma grabbed a cab back to her waterfront apartment. After a quiet winter fitting himself into HIT, Colin had been summoned to FBI headquarters in Washington in late January. He'd returned several times the past month, so far managing to fly back to Boston for weekends.

Wedding or no wedding, he had a job to do.

And so do I, Emma thought, reading Oliver's text again. Wealthy, solitary and very smart, he might be a man haunted by his past, but he was firmly anchored in the present. It helped, no doubt, that he didn't fear arrest, by the FBI, Scotland Yard or any of the law enforcement agencies in the other countries where he had helped himself to valuable art over the past decade.

Oliver York was, in a word, untouchable.

When she reached her tiny apartment, Emma heaped her coat, hat and gloves on a chair and kicked off her boots. She sat on her couch in the living room and dialed up Oliver York on her laptop on her coffee table.

"Sorry I'm late," she said.

Oliver peered at her from across the Atlantic. A thick, dark blond curl flopped onto his forehead as he leaned closer to his screen. "What happened to your hair, Emma?"

"Hat head." She had no intention of telling him about trying on wedding dresses.

"It's cold in Boston?"

"Yes. Where are you?"

"My London flat."

It was a room she didn't recognize from her one visit last November to his sprawling Mayfair apartment overlooking St. James's Park. Colin and Yank had accompanied her. Oliver had met them in the library, where his parents had been murdered almost thirty years ago. Now he sat in a tall-backed red-leather chair in front of a draped window and a painting of porpoises in Ardmore Bay on the south Irish coast. Emma knew the painting, an early work by well-known Irish artist Aoife O'Byrne.

"A video chat is more intimate than a phone call, at least. How are you, Emma? It is all right if I call you Emma, isn't it? It's more informal than Special Agent Sharpe, but this is an official chat, I assume?"

"I'm an FBI agent. You're a thief. Yes, it's an official chat. But Emma is fine."

He pointed at her. "You're testier than when I saw you here in November."

That was when she had figured out that Oliver Fairbairn, a tweedy British mythologist caught in the middle of a murder investigation in Boston, was also Oliver York, a cheeky, wealthy British aristocrat with a tragic past. That Oliver Fairbairn and Oliver York were one and the same wasn't widely known. He preferred to keep the two identities separate, and Emma had no reason to announce it to the world. In fact, the opposite.

"Tell me about this FBI agent you believe is following you."

He gave an audible sigh. "Testy. Definitely testy."

She tried to resist a smile.

"I have reliable radar for FBI agents, and it went off like crazy when I spotted this man. He was in the park outside my apartment. I had just returned from an art gallery. I wouldn't be surprised if he followed me."

"Was this today?"

"Around noon, yes."

"Is the gallery the one holding the show for Aoife O'Byrne?"

"Mmm."

The Irish O'Byrne family was one of Oliver's victims—his first, ten years ago. He had made off with two Jack Butler Yeats landscape paintings of western Ireland, a fifteenth-century silver wall cross depicting Saint Declan and an unsigned landscape of a local scene, probably by a young Aoife O'Byrne herself. Her Yeats phase, Oliver called it. The porpoises had come after that, as well as a few crosses of her own, but she was known now for her moody seascapes.

At least Oliver had bought the porpoise painting instead of stealing it.

"What's the name of this agent you ran into in the park?" Emma asked.

Oliver looked surprised. "I only saw him. I didn't speak with him."

"How do you know he's an FBI agent if you didn't speak with him?"

"The suit. The look. He's one of yours. I've no doubt."

"Did you take his picture?"

He sniffed. "Of course not. I'm a mild-mannered mythologist, not Scotland Yard or MI6. This man is tall, lean, medium coloring, perhaps early forties—but that describes a lot of your colleagues, doesn't it? Not you, of course."

"Of course."

Oliver sat back, amusement lighting up his face. He was good-looking and surprisingly affable for a man so solitary, so haunted by his past. "I'm many things, Emma, but paranoid isn't one of them. I'm convinced this man is one of yours. Consider yourself alerted."

"Fair enough. Anything else?"

"I've sent you a package. Martin has, actually."

On her November trip to London, Emma had also met Martin Hambly, Oliver's longtime personal assistant. It was unclear to her whether Martin was aware of his boss's alter ego as an art thief. "What's in the package, Oliver?"

"A present for you. A surprise. You'll love it. I packed it myself when I was at the farm over the weekend. I returned to London on Monday. Then today…" He grimaced. "Today, I saw the FBI outside my apartment."

"Where did you send the package?"

"I addressed it to you at Father Bracken's rectory in Rock Point. I thought that would be simpler, but, as luck would have it, our Irish priest friend is here in London."

Emma frowned at that bit of news. "I thought he was in Ireland visiting his family."

"He joined his brother on a business trip on behalf of Bracken Distillers. I ran into Finian at the gallery. He, Declan and I are all about to have a drink together. Declan has to return to Ireland tomorrow, but I plan to invite Father Bracken to the family farm in the Cotswolds."

"I wish you wouldn't do that, Oliver."

"Why not?"

"Because you're a thief and Father Bracken is a friend of mine."

"That's plain enough." Oliver paused. "How is your family, Emma? Everyone's well?"

"Doing fine, thank you."

"Did your grandfather come home to Heron's Cove for Christmas?"

"You know he didn't. You two rang in the New Year together at Claridge's."

"Ah, so Wendell did tell you. I wasn't sure he would. He told me he'd expected to fly home to Maine for Christmas, but he didn't feel comfortable going so far with your parents here in London. The experimental procedure to help relieve your father's chronic back pain went well, but it's taken some time to recover."

Emma made no comment. She wasn't discussing her family with Oliver York.

"Chronic pain takes a toll," he added.

"Yes, it does," Emma said. Although there was a psychological component to her father's physical pain given its impact on his life, it was different from the chronic psychological pain Oliver York endured. She was convinced he'd turned to planning and executing solitary, daring art heists to provide relief. It must have worked, at least temporarily, since he'd been at it for a decade. Of course, catching him sooner would have put a stop to it.

"I gather you and my grandfather are on a first-name basis now," she said.

"I haven't seen him since New Year's. He came out to the farm for a couple of days, then went back to Dublin to pretend he wants to retire."

"You harassed him for ten years. He wants to see you arrested before he retires."

Oliver waved a hand. "Nonsense. Wendell said you spent Christmas with the Donovans in Rock Point, that gloomy yet oddly charming Maine fishing village of theirs. You two haven't been to Ireland or London since November. Perhaps I should have had you come to the farm and collect the package yourself."

"It would have to contain the last of your stolen art for me to come to your farm."

"Emma, Emma."

"We're still missing the two Dutch landscapes you stole in Amsterdam." She kept her tone even, without any hint of hostility, sarcasm or cajoling. "I would fly to England to get those works back to their rightful owner."

"I wish I could help."

"That's a start. We're also missing the unsigned landscape you stole in Declan's Cross, but I doubt you'll ever return it since it's a fair guess it's an early work by Aoife O'Byrne. You're familiar with Declan's Cross, Oliver. It's the tiny village on the south Irish coast where you launched your stint as an art thief."

"I'm familiar with Declan's Cross. It's quite a charming hamlet."

"Aoife's missing landscape depicts the three crosses on the headland in Declan's Cross where you hid after stealing from her uncle. The painting has personal value for you, but you still should return it."

Oliver peered at her. "You look happy but preoccupied, Emma. I can understand you have much on your mind. When you do come to England again, you must bring Special Agent Donovan with you. Are you two inviting me to your wedding?"

Emma smiled. "No."

"Pity. Your Colin isn't hovering in the background, is he?"

"No, he isn't. Anything else, Oliver?"

"I'm reading a new book on the early Irish saints. Would you like me to send it to you when I finish? Did you study Saint Patrick, Saint Declan and the like when you were a nun? You must have studied Saint Brigid since that was your name as a novice."

Her grandfather must have told him. She knew she hadn't. "Good night, Oliver."

"The farm is stunning in the spring, which, happily, comes to the Cotswolds earlier than it does in your part of the world. You and Colin can walk in the countryside to your hearts' content. We can all have English tea and scones together."

"Only if there's clotted cream to go with them."

"Absolutely. It will be homemade, whipped from cream from our own dairy cows. We'll have our gooseberry jam, made with wild berries picked on the farm, although not by me. Monotonous, repetitive tasks like berry-picking tend to make my mind go to other things."

"Like plotting your next art heist?"

"By all means, cling to your theory that I'm your art thief. I won't try to dissuade you." He waggled a finger at her. "Your nose is red, too, Emma." He sat back with a mysterious smile. "As cold as it is there, you'll enjoy my present all the more."

She didn't want any presents from Oliver York, but she wasn't arguing with him.

"Enjoy the rest of your evening," he said. "Shall I give Father Bracken your best?"

Emma wasn't enthusiastic about Oliver meeting the Bracken brothers for a drink, much less inviting Finian to the Cotswolds, but there was nothing she could do about it. "Please do," she said.

Oliver clicked off and the screen went blank.

He wouldn't send valuable stolen art from England to Maine, and he wouldn't send it to her.

Would he?

Emma opened a file on her laptop and brought up photographs of art stolen over the past decade by the same unidentified thief—from homes, businesses and museums in Ireland, Amsterdam, Brussels, London, Venice, Prague, Oslo, San Francisco and Dallas. After each heist, the thief sent Wendell Sharpe a small, polished stone inscribed with a Celtic cross. Emma had worked on the case even before she became an FBI agent.

There was no proof Oliver York was their thief, but there also was no doubt.

Emma wasn't unsympathetic to the torment he'd endured as a young boy and undoubtedly still carried with him, but she was careful not to get sucked into it as rationalization for his stealing and taunting—for his crimes. After she and her grandfather had figured out Oliver was their thief in November, the stolen artwork started turning up, each piece back in the hands of its rightful owner, with nothing to trace its theft or its return to Oliver York.

What, Emma wondered, was returning the art costing Oliver?

What would he do now to relieve the sense of helplessness and the terrible pain he had suffered as a child?

She let her gaze linger on the photos of the two missing Dutch landscapes, small oil paintings done by lesser-known seventeenth-century artists. They were valuable but not as valuable as a Rembrandt or a Van Gogh would have been. Oliver tended to stay away from art that would have attracted worldwide headlines. The Amsterdam museum that owned the landscapes had left the spaces empty where they had hung for decades.

Oliver needed to return them. Then Emma could think about his pain.

She shut her laptop and went into her tiny kitchen. She didn't want to go out again, but she had little in her refrigerator. She was digging out vegetables and hummus when her phone dinged.

Oliver again.

I forgot to tell you. Our agent spoke to a woman in the park.

They knew each other?

I'm certain. They looked like they were arguing.

Did you speak with her?

No. Is she FBI?

Emma resisted getting him back on the phone.

Go enjoy a whiskey with Fr. Bracken and forget about FBI agents.

Ah, Emma. I never forget about you lot.

She responded with a smile icon and resumed collecting her dinner. As she took her plate into the living room, her gaze settled on a photo of her and Colin together in Ireland last fall. Framing it had been her idea. He didn't think of such things. She set her plate on the coffee table and eased onto the couch as she touched a finger to his chin, as if he were with her. He was solid and confident, a man who relied on his instincts and his training. On Monday, he had packed his duffel bag and headed to the airport, saying he had meetings in Washington and would be in touch.

All very sudden and mysterious.

Colin wasn't a natural fit for HIT, but he'd managed to make a place for himself once Yank had shoehorned him onto his team in October. Colin contributed to complex investigations with the eye of a seasoned undercover agent and the gut instincts of someone who had faced sustained, real danger in the field.

Emma hadn't thought his meetings involved HIT until that morning, when Yank had left for Washington with no explanation beyond "meetings." It was possible his trip had nothing to do with Colin's trip, but what were the odds?

Given Colin's absence, she supposed she didn't need to spend two nights on her own at the convent. She could stay here in Boston and contemplate her life. But her current life wasn't the reason she had arranged for her mini retreat with the Sisters of the Joyful Heart.

It was her past that was driving her to return, briefly, to the sisters.

Ever since the first of the year, she kept seeing herself walking through the convent gates as a teenager, thinking she would never have another home. It was as if she were looking at a stranger, someone outside herself—a different person altogether from the woman she was now, or even the child she had been before the thought of becoming "Sister Brigid" had gripped her.

Emma wiggled the diamond engagement ring Colin had

placed on her finger in Dublin. Was he even in Washington? For four years, he had told his family he worked at a desk at FBI headquarters.

Such was not the case.

While tempting and inevitable, speculating, she knew, wouldn't answer any of her questions. She'd waited for Colin before. She would now, for however long was necessary. She had her work, and her retreat.

Not to mention lunch on Saturday in Maine with his mother.

Emma smiled and pulled out her phone again, flipping to her photo of her wedding dress.

It *was* a great dress. Perfect for an early June wedding on the Maine coast.

"Not any wedding," she said. "*My* wedding."

To Colin Donovan.

She slipped her phone back into her coat pocket. She would call him later about Oliver York. If he could talk to her, he would. If he couldn't, they would talk later.

And wherever he was—whatever he was up to—he would come back to her.

3

It took Mike Donovan a full three seconds before he realized the buzzing he heard was his cell phone. He wasn't used to having a phone. He picked it up from the counter where he'd left it while he chopped garlic. He'd been up since five, when he had pulled on jeans, a heavy flannel shirt, a vest, wool socks and L.L.Bean boots and headed outside. The temperature was in the double digits. He could get work done.

He answered his phone without checking the screen to see who was calling. Before he could get in a word, his mother spoke. "No one's hurt or been arrested," she said.

"That's good. What's up?"

She launched into something about a visitor. Some guy. Mike couldn't make it all out. The connection was weak. It was dark at his cabin on a remote stretch of the Maine coast down east of Acadia National Park. The Bold Coast, it was called, named for its dramatic cliffs and tides. His mother was in Rock Point, his hometown in southern Maine.

"You run an inn," he said. "What's wrong with visitors?"

"This wasn't a *guest*. It was one of your army buddies."

He heard the urgency in her voice. Married to a police officer, now retired, and the mother of four adult sons, Rosemary Donovan wasn't prone to overstating her case.

Mike stood at his front window. The evening air was still and dark, stars glittering on waves of undisturbed snow and the ocean, quiet and starlit past the marsh across from his cabin. He'd worked outside most of the day and had planned to spend the evening alone by the fire, reading a book. He owned a television but didn't watch it much. He liked his life but it was new to him compared to the army. Three years into it instead of ten.

"What army buddy?" he asked finally.

"Jamie Mason. Do you know him?"

Retired army, none better at logistics support. "I know him. When did he stop by?"

"Just now. I offered him coffee, but he said no, he had things to do."

"Pop's there?"

"No. I'm here alone. Your father's at Hurley's having a drink with your brothers."

Andy and Kevin, Mike thought. Not Colin. Colin had told them he was in Washington, but he could be anywhere. Their folks would like all four sons in town having a drink at Hurley's.

Mike turned from the window back to his kitchen area. "You let this guy in?"

"Of course. It's cold outside."

It wasn't that cold for Maine in February. "Just because he said he's a friend doesn't mean he is one."

"Oh, stop, Mike. I didn't call you for a lecture. He left a message for you. I wrote it down. I have it right here. Hang on a sec." She paused, and Mike could hear her shuffling through papers. He pictured her in the old sea captain's house that she and his father had converted into an inn in Rock Point, four hours by car down the coast. "Got it. He said to tell you that Reed Cooper is on his way to Maine from London. He's meeting with a small group at the Plum Tree Inn. He wants you to join them. You know the Plum Tree, don't you, Mike? It's just up the road from here. I thought it was closed for the season."

"I know it."

"What do these men want with you, Mike?" his mother asked, as if suddenly realizing she had reason to be suspicious.

"Reed has started his own private contract security firm. Cooper Global Security."

"Oh."

Mike heard the apprehension in her voice. He scooped up chopped garlic and tossed it into his frying pan. Jamie Mason wouldn't be one of Reed's operators. More likely Mason would be running the office, probably with his wife, Serena, also retired army.

"Did Mason say anything else?" Mike asked.

"He gave me a few more names. I wrote them down, too. My mind's a sieve these days. Let me see. One's a woman's name, I remember that." Another long pause, more paper shuffling. "Here we go. Buddy Whidmore, Ted Kavanagh and Naomi MacBride. Mr. Mason says he expects them to be at the Plum Tree in addition to Reed Cooper."

Mike absorbed the silence of his isolated stretch of the Atlantic coast. The snow blanketing the evergreens that dominated the woods on three sides of his cabin muffled any sounds. He could hear, faintly, the wash of the incoming tide. Sixty years ago, his grandfather, his mother's father, a Rock Point harbormaster, had built the cabin as a getaway. He had never lived up here full-time. Mike had since leaving the army.

"Mike? Are you still there?"

"Still here."

"Who are these people?"

"I knew them when I was in the army."

"Were any of them with the Special Forces?" his mother asked.

"Reed and Jamie. Kavanagh was with the FBI. At least he was then. I don't know if he's retired or quit."

"Does Colin know him?"

"I've never mentioned Kavanagh to Colin. No reason to."

A moment's silence. "What about the other two?" his mother asked finally.

Mike set his paring knife in the scratched stainless-steel sink, but he was seeing Naomi's smile. "Civilian." He tried to keep any tension out of his voice. "Buddy's a tech guy. Naomi was with the State Department."

"A diplomat?"

"I guess you could say that."

"I don't understand why they would come to Maine in February. The Plum Tree must have given them a good deal or something."

"If I knew what was going on, I'd tell you."

She didn't respond at once. He wasn't sure how well she could hear him, but he figured she wasn't going to gripe about the lousy connection. It was better than nothing. She had been after him for months to get a cell phone rather than to rely on the landline at the general store.

"I hope these people aren't a problem for you," she said.

"They're not. I'm glad you called. What are you and Pop up to this weekend?"

"Emma is heading up here tomorrow afternoon. She's staying at the convent for two nights, and I'm taking her to lunch on Saturday. She'll be on her own. I'm looking forward to spending some time with her. I've never had a daughter, and Emma will be my first daughter-in-law."

Mike smiled, despite his tension. His mother's tone said "it's about time" even if she would never utter those words out loud. He doubted she'd ever imagined one of her sons marrying a woman like Emma Sharpe. An FBI agent, maybe. But an FBI agent who was also a member of a family of renowned art detectives? An ex-nun? Mike, the eldest, had put aside his own doubts about Emma in the months since Colin, the second-born Donovan, had met her, fallen for her and asked her to marry him.

"Mike…" His mother hesitated. "This Reed Cooper…"

"It'll be fine. Don't worry. Have a good time with Emma."

When she disconnected, Mike could tell she wasn't satisfied. She might not be able to put her finger on exactly why, but she had well-honed instincts after all this time. Her four sons had been in plenty of jams—and she was well aware she didn't know about all of them and there were likely more to come. Mike was ex-army living out on the Bold Coast as a wilderness guide and outfitter. Colin was an FBI agent based in Boston. Andy was a lobsterman. Kevin was a Maine state marine patrol officer.

Frank Donovan, their father, would just tell his wife, "The boys know what they're doing."

Sometimes it was true. Not always.

Mike stepped outside onto the porch. He had his grandfather's old wooden canoe turned over on a rack. It needed work. Winter was a good time to fix things that the busy warm-weather months didn't allow time for. He had the occasional backcountry skier or snowshoe group request his skills as a wilderness guide and outfitter, but not many people were interested in a trek along the icebound cliffs of the Bold Coast in the dead of winter.

Even in summer, he seldom had company. On a cold February night, he might see a white-tailed deer or a moose, but otherwise he had his spot in paradise to himself. His clients never came to his place, winter or summer. He would meet them at the general store in the village a few miles down the road. Some of them would ask, "Hey, Mike, where do you live?" He would say, "On the coast," as if it could be anywhere on Maine's more than three thousand miles of coastline.

The sun first hit the Continental United States on the Bold Coast, and he liked to be up for it, no matter what time. It was noticeably earlier now that it was late February. That morning the ocean had glowed with shades of deep orange, red and purple. Now it reflected the night sky of sparkling stars and a quarter moon.

He breathed in the salt-tinged air and listened to the tide wash over ice, rocks and sand. He liked to tell himself this place wasn't an escape, as it had been for his grandfather. He lived here.

His mother wanted him to get a dog. *Dogs are good company,* she would tell him.

His father had been more direct: *There must be women up there.*

If his parents guessed there had been a woman during their firstborn's time in the army, they didn't say.

Mike had no photos of Naomi MacBride.

He didn't need any. Every inch of her was etched in his mind forever. He could see her wide smile and dark, wild, curly hair. He could hear her laughter—she had an indomitable sense of humor—and he could feel her skin, hot and smooth, under his hands.

He turned away from the water and walked back to his cabin.

An ancient Vermont Castings woodstove served as the cabin's sole source of heat. It had to be tended, but Mike had people who could do that for him when he was away. He might like his solitude but that didn't mean he was without friends.

He checked his phone. No texts or emails.

He put another log on the fire and went back to cooking his dinner. He sautéed garlic, ginger, green beans, ground beef, soy sauce and rice vinegar and made brown rice. The kind of meal he could eat for a couple of days.

He dumped his dinner on a plate and sat by the fire.

Should he tell his FBI brother about another FBI agent coming to Maine this weekend for a get-together with private security contractors?

Probably, but Mike didn't see any big rush. He'd call Colin in the morning.

He felt the heat of the fire and tried to remember the last time he had allowed himself to think about Naomi. Months, anyway. A year? Longer?

Not longer.

He didn't know what he would do about Reed Cooper and the gathering at the Plum Tree. He did know that nothing good ever happened when Naomi MacBride was anywhere near his life.

It was something he couldn't let himself forget.

4

The insistent crow of a rooster and the smell of rain roused Naomi MacBride from a not-so-dead sleep. She rolled onto her back and opened her eyes, trying to shake off dreams of a life and a man she had left behind years ago. She was in England, in a quiet Cotswolds village two hours west of London. It was February, and from the crowing rooster, she would guess it was morning, although it was still quite dark. She was in a double four-poster bed in a cute room in a small building located across the courtyard of a classic English pub complete with low, beamed ceilings and a huge open fireplace. She'd had a pint there last night before venturing into her room and falling into bed. It had been a long week.

Her room also had a low ceiling. She could feel its looming presence. She had never been one for squirrely places. Hence, the cracked window and her natural wake-up call.

The rooster crowed again.

He didn't sound as if he planned to give up anytime soon.

With a groan, Naomi sat up, keeping the duvet tucked around her. She could hear more chickens now, warbling outside her window. Probably hens. If she were one of them, she would organize a revolt against the rooster.

Chickens.

She sighed. "Of course the place has chickens."

She threw off the duvet and stood on a soft hooked rug that, she recalled, depicted a sheep. It was too dark to see it now. She shivered, rubbing her bare arms, wishing she had resisted the impulse to take this side trip and instead had spent her last night in England in London, where she'd had a room in a proper hotel with five-star service, a bustling lobby, a great location and no chickens. But here she was in the English countryside after a week of intense meetings.

She fumbled with the lamp on the nightstand, found the switch and turned it on. The worst part of her constant travel, Naomi decided, was locating light switches.

Nightmares about an ex-lover weren't that great, either.

It wasn't her fault she had dreamed about Mike Donovan. As much as she wanted to find someone to blame and could pick a name or two, she knew it wasn't anyone's fault. Not really.

She seldom had nightmares anymore about the dangers she'd faced in the past decade, maybe because she'd found healthy ways to process them. Post-trauma therapy had helped—or debriefing, or whatever one wanted to call it. *Naomi, you've been through hell,* her mother, blunt as ever, had told her. *You need to talk to someone.*

Naomi hadn't mentioned Mike in her sessions—or to her mother. What was the point? By then, he was just another Special Forces soldier she would never see again.

She felt the cool air from the cracked window. Her room really was adorable with its English-country-chic decor. When she'd arrived last night, the woman at the reception desk in the pub had handed her a real key and reminded her that this was a pub that let rooms—meaning she could expect noise from the patrons late into the evening.

No mention of early-morning roosters.

Not *that* early, Naomi thought as she noted the time on her phone, faceup on the nightstand. Eight twenty. She had been in England long enough to adjust to the time change but not so long that it didn't still feel like the middle of the night. It was, after all, only 2:00 a.m. at home in Nashville.

She went to the window and pulled back the curtains, letting in more of the gray light. Her rooster was parading on the edge of a stone fountain in the middle of the courtyard. He was black with white spots, or at least appeared to be. Sunlight would help. He threw back his head and belted out another crow, letting the world know he was awake and ready to take on the day.

"Well, good for you," Naomi muttered, remembering her granny describing how she would have to catch a chicken and wring its neck for Sunday dinner. That prospect didn't seem as horrifying at the moment as it had at six years old.

She noticed a handful of brown-feathered hens pecking and warbling in the herb gardens that flanked the pretty courtyard. She doubted they or the rooster were in any danger of becoming dinner. She envisioned the courtyard in spring and summer, when the dripping, winter-browned vines that trailed the trellises and the tall fence would be blossoming with clematis, roses and wisteria. The smattering of tables were all empty now, the cold, gray, drizzly morning not exactly a draw for breakfast outdoors.

With a yawn, Naomi ducked into the bathroom, stifling a yelp when her bare feet hit the cold tile floor. She spread a bath mat in front of the tub and turned on the water, letting it get good and hot while she pulled off her yoga pants and tank top, her standard sleepwear on the road—which meant her standard sleepwear, period. She opened the bottles of luxurious, locally made shampoo, conditioner and body wash. She wondered what it would be like to stay in this place for a few days for a break. A real getaway. It was appealing even now, in midwinter, with its soothing blend of English charm and sophistication and its perfect location in the heart of a small, traditional Cotswolds village.

A getaway would have to wait. She had a late-afternoon flight back to Nashville via Atlanta. She would gain six hours and be home in time to sleep in her own bed tonight.

"Preferably without nightmares."

And definitely without chickens, she thought, smiling as she stepped into the tub and eased under the steamy shower.

When she stepped out of the tub again and wrapped up in a fluffy towel, she was much warmer and smelled faintly of herbs and citrus. She dried off, combed out her hair, basic brown and ridiculously curly, and got dressed. Since she had expected to stay in London for the duration of her trip, she hadn't packed any serious country clothes. The slim, stretchy pants and wine-colored cashmere sweater she planned to wear on her flight would have to do for her morning in the Cotswolds. She did have an authentic Barbour jacket, an indulgence she had succumbed to on a long, drizzly walk in London. She never remembered to bring an umbrella with her, and that day she had bolted out of her hotel without so much as a jacket. Too much on her mind. She was good at assembling information and making sense of it, analyzing it and seeing where it pointed, but it was often a messy process that completely absorbed her.

It certainly had been that afternoon in London. She had found herself cold and wet, standing in front of a store that sold Barbour jackets. Her jacket's waxed dark green cotton and English-country look would do nicely today. Her slip-on ankle boots, at least, were good for walking, if not for a full-blown trek on one of the network of walking trails that zigzagged throughout the region. Before dozing off last night, she had flipped through a bedside notebook filled with "guest information" and had noticed mention of a medieval church in Stow-on-the-Wold whose arched door had reportedly inspired J.R.R. Tolkien when he created the door to Moria.

Wouldn't it be wonderful to prowl through an English church-yard and then relax in an English tea shop?

It wouldn't happen on this trip.

Naomi ignored a tug of regret mixed with nostalgia and lone-liness, as if she had lost something that, of course, she'd never had. Love, trust, understanding.

Someone to wander through churchyards and have tea with her.

It was the nightmare, she knew. It still had her in its grip.

What are your plans for after the army, Mike?

She could see his enigmatic smile, at the same time self-deprecating and confident—and annoyingly fatalistic. With-out saying anything, he had managed to tell her that he didn't think past the army. If he got home to Maine, he got home to Maine. He wasn't a pessimist, he would say. He was a realist who lived in the moment.

Did Mike Donovan ever imagine himself wandering through old English churchyards and having tea and scones with the woman he loved?

"Not a chance," Naomi said, grabbing her jacket as she headed out to the courtyard and the chickens.

The same man who had poured her pint last night showed Naomi into the breakfast room in the pub building across the courtyard. He offered her tea or coffee. "Coffee, please," she said, not quite choking on her words when she recognized the only other diner, a man seated on a cushioned bench, watch-ing her, his back to the wall. It was all she could do not to turn around and walk out of there. She forced herself to smile at the waiter. "Thanks."

He retreated, and she pushed back her dismay, frustration and

mad curiosity as she walked over to the table where Ted Kavanagh sat with a pot of tea. "I didn't take you for a tea drinker,
T.K.," she said.

"I've been here for an hour. I've already had coffee and a full
English breakfast." He motioned to the chair across from him.
"Have a seat, Naomi."

She didn't want to but if she sat at another table, he'd still be
here, a few feet away, annoyed and annoying. She sat, not much
distance across the little blond-wood table. "First we run into
each other in St. James's Park in London. Now here we are in
the Cotswolds." She unfurled a cloth napkin. "Honestly, T.K.,
I don't need a crazy FBI agent bird-dogging me."

"Sure you're not following me?"

"Yes. Positive. I need to get better at spotting a tail."

"A good skill to have. What's with the T.K.?"

"We're in a foreign country. I figure it's okay to be informal.
Don't your friends call you T.K.?"

"No."

Probably true. Kavanagh wasn't wearing a suit this morning,
but he had a buttoned-down, perpetually suspicious look about
him that she had come to know working with him in Afghanistan. She hadn't expected to see him again after she left the State
Department as an intelligence analyst, and then—*poof*—there
he was in London.

Except there was no *poof* about it. Ted Kavanagh was a deliberate, calculating, experienced federal agent.

That didn't mean he wasn't crazy.

Naomi pulled off her jacket and hung it on the back of her
chair. Kavanagh was a decade older than she was, and he had
been married when she knew him in Kabul. Since he wasn't
wearing a wedding ring, she guessed he wasn't married any longer. She supposed he could have developed an allergy to metals.
She didn't plan to ask.

"In a perfect world, T.K.," she said, "it would be spring, and

I'd be having breakfast outside with the chickens and the scent of wisteria."

"Wisteria's a flower, right?"

"It's a climbing flowering shrub. It's all over the Cotswolds but it's not in bloom this time of year. The flowers are typically purple."

"I guess that's good. People like purple."

"You don't care about wisteria. Did you stay here last night?"

He pointed at the ceiling. "Room above the pub. I rented a car and drove in from London."

"Not me. I hired a car. Driving in London is a nightmare. A shame I didn't know you were following me here. I could have bummed a ride off you and saved myself the money."

"Traffic was terrible. I'll never get used to driving on the left." He didn't sound as if he expected her to believe him. "You're staying in the building across the courtyard. What is it, an old pigsty?"

"I don't know. It's charming. I wish I could stay longer." She gave a slightly fake yawn. "I'm not a good conversationalist before coffee. What are my choices for breakfast?"

"Cold buffet and a choice of hot breakfast. English, grilled kippers, porridge."

"As many times as I've been to England, I still don't know what a kipper is."

"Fish."

"I know that much. Have you ever tried kippers?"

"Yes. They're good grilled. Not the most attractive food."

He was clearly not there to talk about kippers, either. The waiter returned with her coffee press. Naomi settled on porridge for her hot breakfast, and he again withdrew, giving no indication he sensed she wasn't that happy with her breakfast mate.

She poured coffee into the mug already on the table and added cream from a small pitcher. Kavanagh eyed her without comment. He didn't look tired or distracted or as if he'd had nightmares. He looked alert and impatient, a know-it-all who figured he could tell what she was thinking before she thought it. A good FBI agent, maybe, but not her favorite. She had tolerated him in Afghanistan because she'd had no choice.

Without comment, she got up and helped herself to the buffet. She filled a bowl with natural yogurt and added a couple of scoops of chopped fresh fruit, then put a croissant, still warm from the oven, on a small plate.

"I'm disappointed," she said as she returned to her seat. "I wanted scones."

Kavanagh frowned at her. "A croissant and porridge? That's a lot of carbs, Naomi."

"I'm flying later today." She figured he already knew that. "Carbs will help me sleep. I have to tell you, T.K., it creeps me out that you're here."

He poured the last few drops of his tea. It was the color of coffee by now. "You should feel well protected."

Naomi dipped a spoon into her yogurt and fruit. "Why is it that I don't?"

"Because you have a habit of placing your trust in the wrong people."

"If that were true, I'd be dead by now." She leveled her gaze at him. "So would you."

"Maybe so."

There was no *maybe* about it, but Naomi didn't argue with him. Kavanagh *wanted* her to have a habit of trusting the wrong people because it would help him somehow, if only to throw her off balance and get in her head.

He glanced at a row of framed botanical prints on the side wall. Local grasses, wildflowers and herbs. "What are you up to, Naomi?" he asked, shifting back to her.

She tried the yogurt. It was smooth and creamy, made without added pectin. With the fruit, it was perfection. "Are you following me because you think I'm up to something? As I told

you in London, you're wasting your time. I'm a crisis management consultant who met with a group of medical volunteers
who are planning their deployment to a hot spot in Africa. I'm
helping them assess their security needs and then take appropriate steps to meet them. That's all I'm up to."

Kavanagh smirked at her. "It's not all."

"I'm not arguing with you, T.K."

"Why this particular twee English village?"

Naomi ate more of her yogurt and drank some of her coffee.
What she wanted to do was to eat six croissants and go back to
bed. She made herself smile at the FBI agent across from her.
"*Twee*. I love that word. I've wanted to visit the Cotswolds but
never could find the time. Now I have, if only for one night."

"That doesn't explain why you chose this village," Kavanagh said.

"This place comes highly recommended by an internet travel
site I trust." It was true, as far as it went. "What about you? Did
you follow my car, or did you overhear me when I told the bellman where I was going? It wasn't a secret, but the only person
I actually told is my mother."

"How is your mother, Naomi?"

"Great. Sewing up a storm. Think where I could be now if
I'd paid attention and let her teach me how to sew drapes and
beauty-pageant dresses."

"Or if your father hadn't been killed by an IED when you
were a freshman at Vanderbilt," Kavanagh said quietly.

Naomi finished the last of her yogurt. "Yes, that, too." She
refused to let him distract her, even if she had given him the
opening. "This is a good place, don't you think? I'd love to relax
here for a few nights."

Kavanagh leaned forward, his pale green eyes narrowed on
her. "You're giving me careful answers, Naomi."

"Why wouldn't I, seeing how you're an FBI agent?"

Her porridge arrived. The waiter didn't linger. Naomi didn't blame him. Kavanagh wasn't in full-blown FBI interrogation mode, but it was close enough.

She decided to lighten her tone and change the subject. "Did the rooster wake you up this morning? He did me."

"I didn't notice a rooster. I sleep soundly."

She broke off a piece of croissant and popped it in her mouth as she noticed a drizzle of the promised blackberry compote in her porridge. Breakfast was delightful, she decided, refusing to let her companion spoil the moment. "Do you know what kind of rooster has white-spotted black feathers?"

"I'm not here to talk about roosters. Neither are you."

She picked up the fresh spoon that came with her porridge. It was a lot of porridge. "I'll look it up. I'm dying to know."

"You're playing with fire, Naomi. You know that, don't you?"

"By having yogurt and porridge with you, you mean?"

Kavanagh's eyes flared with anger, but he quickly got himself under control. All that FBI discipline and training, she supposed.

Assuming he still *was* an FBI agent.

She thought about asking to see his credentials to check if they were current, but she wouldn't be able to identify a good forgery—and Ted Kavanagh would only have a good forgery.

"You know how to get on people's nerves when it suits you," he said.

"Sometimes it just works out that way."

"It's not on purpose, you mean?"

She didn't respond. She started on her porridge. It was the chewy pinhead kind, and the trickle of warm blackberry compote turned out to be a sweet, delicious pool. In another life, she would do things like make compotes. In this life—her life now, at this moment—she did things like get through surprise breakfasts with FBI agents she didn't trust and who didn't trust her.

"I appreciate that it's your business to find out things," he said. "It's how you make your living. It's also who you are, though, isn't it? It's a control issue. This need to know things."

"Psychoanalyzing me? It won't get you far." She held up her spoon. "This porridge is incredible, T.K. I never would have thought to add blackberry compote, but it's a stroke of genius. I'm happy I chose the porridge instead of a full English breakfast, since I don't like black pudding and have trouble with the idea of baked beans before noon. There's not much you can do to a blackberry that I wouldn't like. Without the compote, I can't imagine how annoyed I'd be with you right now. You can't just make up stuff about me."

"I'm not making up anything, and I don't care if you're annoyed."

"I'm getting that picture."

He fingered a bit of loose-leaf tea that had fallen on the table next to his mug. "I need you to be straight with me, Naomi."

"That's a two-way street."

He shook his head. "No, it isn't."

"Now I remember. You never did have a sense of humor. I'm here enjoying a decadent breakfast before my long flight across the Atlantic. I'll take a good walk, too. I don't care if it's cold and rainy."

"Rain's ending. Where will you walk?"

"Not sure yet." It wasn't a flat-out lie but it was close. She knew where she was going. She just hadn't figured out the route. "What about you? What are your plans for the day, T.K.?"

"Leaving you to your own devices if you won't talk to me."

"Good."

He sucked in a breath and tapped the table with his fingertips, as though he wanted to let her know he was practicing self-restraint. He clearly wanted to throw the table aside and throttle her. "You know you can get into trouble lying to a federal agent, don't you?"

"I'm not lying. I do think it's good for you to leave me to my own devices. I don't want an FBI agent to waste his time on my account." Naomi set her spoon next to her porridge bowl. "Anything else I can do for you, Agent Kavanagh?"

"Why do you have doubts about me, Naomi?"

She glanced past him at the windows above the buffet table. Sunlight broke through the gray, at least for the moment, shining on puddles and brown, dripping vines. She hadn't mentioned—and wouldn't—that before she ventured into St. James's Park she'd visited an art gallery to have a look at a show by Aoife O'Byrne, an Irish artist. She knew damn well Kavanagh had followed her there and then into the park. Let him admit it.

She did know how to spot tails, but she hadn't been thinking about having one when she'd walked from her hotel to the gallery—and she wasn't sure she'd have spotted an FBI tail. Ted Kavanagh might be on her nerves right now, but he was good.

The sun seemed to be fading already. Naomi turned back to the FBI agent. "Well, T.K., for one thing, you were in London on your own and now you're here on your own. Most FBI agents work in pairs. Where's your partner?"

He settled back against the cushioned bench. "Feel free to call any FBI office if you want to check up on me."

"No, thanks. If you're on the level, I'd only heap scrutiny on myself. Not that I have anything to hide, but who needs the aggravation? And if you've gone rogue, you are most definitely not my problem."

"You're right. I'm not your problem."

"If you really are still an FBI agent, you're breaking a lot of rules. That sweater for one. Gad, T.K. That is not your shade of brown."

"My ex-wife gave it to me for my birthday."

"Mmm. Last birthday you were together?"

"As a matter of fact, yes."

Naomi broke off another piece of croissant. "Not surprised."

He grinned. "I should have known. She has passive-aggressive behavior down to an art form. Oh, well. At least it's a warm

sweater. I'll appreciate it today, even if it's a bad shade of brown."
He got to his feet, eyeing Naomi a moment before he spoke.
"It's good to see you. Enjoy your day in the Cotswolds."

"I will, thanks. You, too."

"I have a flight to catch myself. Do you ever worry about
your safety, Naomi? You're a one-woman show. Who's your
backup? Who helps you when things get scary? Who picks you
up when you fall?"

"I can always call 911."

"When you're at home. Out here…" He shrugged. "You can
call 999, I guess. If you realize you're over your head and need
help, you know how to reach me. Don't hesitate, okay?"

His comment caught her off guard. The knowledge behind it,
the absence of any hint of cockiness, frustration and impatience,
the softness of his voice, as if he could see into her heart—cared
about her feelings. Her safety.

A ploy.

Ted Kavanagh didn't *not* care about her, but if he was still a
legit FBI agent, he had a job to do.

Whatever he was up to, she would let the FBI figure him out.

"Thanks," she said, trying to sound matter-of-fact.

She expected him to walk away, but he didn't. "Be careful,
Naomi. You have a risk-taking streak that borders on reckless."

He turned abruptly and left the breakfast room.

Once he was out of sight, Naomi exhaled, then poured herself more coffee. She wondered if Ted Kavanagh ever fanta-
sized about taking a break for a few days and playing tourist.
He looked as if he could use a break.

But she found herself fighting off another touch of melancholy.
She drank her coffee as the waiter led a middle-aged couple to
a table. They spoke English to him—they asked for tea—and
German to each other. Naomi understood German and could
speak enough to get through a dinner, but it wasn't one of her
better languages. The couple was discussing their plans for the

day, which centered on celebrating their wedding anniversary with a long winter walk in the countryside.

The quaint English breakfast room fell away, thrusting Naomi back to a dusty night in Afghanistan. Federal agents, soldiers and civilian intelligence officers were often an uneasy combination at the best of times, and that hadn't been the best of times.

It certainly hadn't been a good time to fall in love.

But when *was* a good time to fall in love with Mike Donovan?

She set her mug on the table. No wonder she'd had nightmares about him.

She silently congratulated the German couple and wished them well, then frowned at the rest of her croissant. There was a small jar of gooseberry jam and a dish of butter on her table.

Well, why not?

She noted the jam was from the nearby farm owned by Oliver York, a wealthy Brit and, very possibly, an incomparable art thief.

Not coincidentally, he knew the Irish painter Aoife O'Byrne, whose uncle had been a victim of an art thief, and he also owned an apartment on St. James's Park in London.

What did Ted Kavanagh want with York?

The York farm was at least a brisk twenty-minute walk from the inn. Naomi figured she could burn off her breakfast and, at the same time, consider what Kavanagh's interest was in both her and Oliver York. She had her suspicions, but she put them aside as she opened the jar of the York farm's gooseberry jam.

5

The few rays of sunshine at breakfast seemed to be it for the day. Naomi didn't mind. She set off through the village, past a row of attached houses, a post office, a small school and a few cottages, then onto a lane that wound through well-marked fields, patches of woods and farmhouses. The York farm should be out the lane to her left, with Stow-on-the-Wold to the northwest, Chipping Norton to the northeast and Burford to the south. Cotswolds villages had sprung up during the Middle Ages, when the area had prospered around the sheep industry. With its proximity to London, the graceful landscape of rolling hills, pastures and quaint honey-colored stone houses drew tourists and wealthy second-home owners alike. The ubiquitous yellow limestone—Oolitic Jurassic limestone, technically—occurred naturally in the region and had been quarried there for centuries.

Naomi smiled, remembering when she thought something built in 1900 was old. Other than wishing she had brought a hat and gloves, she enjoyed the walk and tried to take in her surroundings without letting her thoughts intrude.

She crossed a bridge over a shallow stream, feeling the cold of the water below her, its trickle the only sound in the still, gray late morning. On the other side of the bridge, a sloping, tree-dotted lawn rose to an elegant house. The scene reminded her of a Jane Austen novel. According to her research, however, this was the York farm. Its owner would make an interesting Regency hero. Naomi couldn't picture the heroine for him. A prideful Elizabeth Bennett, or a trustworthy Anne Elliot?

A low stone wall hugged a curve. She followed it about thirty yards to an open gate on a dirt track. She noticed tire marks, footprints, horseshoe prints and a small sign indicating the track was public, although not part of the Oxfordshire Way. If her map and the guest information in her room were correct, the track would take her along the southern edge of the York property to an historic dovecote.

It would also take her through mud, she noted with a grimace. She would have to clean her boots before she ventured to Heathrow, given the rules about trekking through farms before boarding flights. Or she could just toss them in the trash. They weren't expensive. She could wear her flats on the flight.

She didn't want to think about the long flight later today.

She went through the gate. Within a few yards, she saw the dovecote up ahead, on the left side of the track. Pleased with herself, she picked up her pace. What a change the Cotswolds were from London, she thought. Despite her misgivings about her reasons for being here, it was a welcome break from the intensity of the past week.

Flat stones set into a dirt path created a rudimentary walkway to the dovecote entrance. Naomi stepped onto the path for a closer look. She supposed leaving the track meant she was trespassing, but no one seemed to be around. A quick peek and she would be off. From her cursory research, she had learned that dovecotes were once widespread throughout the area, typically on wealthy manor or ecclesiastic properties. As their name suggested, they housed pigeons, in past times considered a delicacy.

Only a fraction of the thousands of dovecotes built between the Middle Ages and the eighteenth century, when they fell out of favor, remained.

Naomi could see holes just below the steeply gabled roof that the pigeons must have used.

"Quaint."

Clay and ceramic pots were stacked by the entrance, as if awaiting spring and plantings. An ancient—by her standards—wheelbarrow was leaned up against the stone front of the building. She stepped into the soft ground in front of a window and peered inside. Two clay pots that looked as if they were planted with some kind of large bulb sat atop a thick wood worktable. Tools were lined up on hooks and nails on the wall above it. Shears, clippers, diggers, scratchers. She had never been much of a gardener but could guess the dovecote was now a potting shed.

At least the front half. At the far end of the workbench was an interior door.

Padlocked.

Wouldn't one padlock the main entrance and not bother with an interior door?

Naomi continued from the window along the soft ground—a mix of wet grass, sodden moss and dead leaves—to the back of the dovecote. She could hear water babbling in the stream down a tree-covered hillside.

There were no windows on the back of the dovecote. Too bad, she thought, ready to turn back and resume her walk on the track. She didn't know if Oliver York was at the farm. What if he caught her snooping? Nothing in what she'd learned about him so far indicated he was violent. Weird, maybe. Troubled. Haunted. Smart. All that, yes—and ultra-fit. He had to be to pull off at least a half-dozen brazen art heists over the past decade.

She heard a sound behind her and nearly jumped out of her damn skin. Her knees buckled under her, and she clutched her jacket at her chest, even as she scanned the hillside, saw nothing amiss and told herself to calm down.

Woods, a stream, a farm. There would be animals about. Farmers had dogs, didn't they?

She liked dogs.

She couldn't let her imagination get carried away.

Perspiration sprang up at the back of her neck, never mind the chilly air. She lowered her hand from her chest. Small white flowers spread across the ground below a gnarled oak tree right out of Tolkien. She smiled, her heart rate slowing.

She wondered if she would ever not startle easily.

She did a few deep, calming breaths. She promised herself she would come back here one day in the spring. Maybe not to the York farm. The Cotswolds, though.

A groan came from the woods down toward the stream.

Distinct. Human. Probably male.

This time Naomi wasn't startled. Someone was in clear distress.

"Bloody hell."

The voice was definitely male, and almost certainly British.

She stood by a thin tree and looked down the hill. About ten yards below her, a gray-haired man was on all fours, struggling to get to his feet. He reached for a tree trunk, missed, fell and cursed again.

"Are you all right?" Naomi called to him. "Do you need help?"

He looked up at her, squinted as if he couldn't focus or wasn't sure if he had conjured her up. He started to speak, then slumped facedown into the ground.

Naomi ran down the hill, deceptively steep. She slipped in the wet leaves and grass but managed not to fall. When she reached the man, she squatted next to him but didn't touch him. He was already pushing himself back up onto his hands and knees, grunting, clearly disoriented and in pain.

"Let me help you," she said.

"I just need to get on my feet."

It wasn't a clear yes or no, but he didn't protest when she hooked an arm around his middle. He was at least in his sixties, with only a bit of extra weight on him. He was a few inches taller than she was—nothing she wasn't used to—and cold and muddy, shivering and shuddering as she anchored herself and helped him to his feet. He slung one arm over her shoulder, then with his other hand grabbed onto the tree trunk he had missed on the first try. He was able to hold on this time.

"Thank you," he said, lowering his arm from her shoulders.

Naomi stood back, noticing he had on a Barbour jacket, too. From the looks of him, he had been out in the elements awhile. The jacket probably had helped save him from exposure. "Shall I call an ambulance?" she asked him.

"No, no. I'm all right. I took a nasty tumble."

"When?"

He blinked at her. "When?" he repeated.

"It's Thursday morning," she said. "Do you remember when you fell? Did you lose consciousness?"

"I was out overnight." He swallowed, licked his lips. "Thank you for your help."

His tone was formal, almost embarrassed. He started up the hill, his gait practiced if not steady. Naomi spotted him from behind but had no idea what she would do if he fell back against her. They would probably both end up plunging into the stream.

He didn't move fast, but he did make it to the top of the hill and the strip of grass behind the dovecote. He placed a hand at his right temple, his face ashen.

"Headache?" Naomi asked.

"Blistering."

Only then did she see the blood caked on his neck. "You're hurt," she said.

"I must have hit my head on a rock or a tree root when I fell."

"You've been bleeding. Do you want me to take a look?"

"I tore a chunk out of the back of my neck. Blood dribbled down my front. I landed facedown when I fell." He grimaced, sinking against the dovecote. "Sorry to be such trouble."

"You're no trouble at all. Is there someone I can call?"

He stood straight, looking steadier, then motioned toward the front of the dovecote. He started walking, stiffly and unsteadily. Naomi fell in next to him, but she couldn't tell how badly he was hurt. He could be acting out of stubbornness, disorientation, pain or, for all she knew, fear. How did she know his fall was an accident?

She also was guessing—was almost certain—the injured man was Martin Hambly, Oliver York's longtime personal assistant.

He stumbled once but shook off her help and instead balanced himself with a hand on the exterior of the dovecote. When he reached the entrance, he pushed open the door and collapsed onto a wood chair against the wall by the worktable. He looked as if he was about to pass out, or maybe vomit—or both. Although obviously cold, he didn't seem to be suffering from hypothermia. At the very least he had to be dehydrated if he had been out all night.

Naomi grabbed a bottle of water off the worktable, opened it and handed it to him.

He took a long drink and seemed to rally. "Thank you," he said. "You're American?"

"Mmm. Out for a walk." She tried to get a look at his head injury, but it was difficult to see with his coat collar. "I can hail someone."

"I'll do it."

He pointed at a cell phone on the worktable. She handed it to him, and he held it in his palm, trembling. He took in an audible breath, then managed to hit a few numbers.

"It's Hambly," he said when someone picked up on the other end. "I'm at the dovecote. I took a fall and need assistance. Not an ambulance. Thank you." He slipped the phone into his jacket pocket. "I feel better already getting off that wet ground."

"What happened?"

He seemed confused. "What do you mean, what happened?"

"How did you fall?"

"There are a thousand ways to fall in these conditions. I appreciate your coming to my aid, but you mustn't let me keep you from your walk. I'm fine, honestly."

"Head injuries can be dangerous, Mr. Hambly. If you lost consciousness—"

"I'll check with my doctor. Thank you again."

Naomi had no more desire to deal with the authorities than he did. Once she gave them her name, her situation could unravel fast from there. She wouldn't even have to mention the FBI agent who had joined her for breakfast a twenty-minute walk away. Then if Kavanagh found out what she had been up to that morning…

An elderly farmworker arrived, identifying himself merely as Johnny as he took over Martin Hambly's care.

Relieved and reassured, Naomi left them and headed to the track, turning back toward the village. She had resisted glancing at the locked door inside the dovecote, but she didn't want to make too much of it. Oliver York was a wealthy man. If he was in fact an art thief, he had plenty of places to conceal his misdeeds.

Naomi wasted no time on enjoying the bucolic scenery on her walk back to the pub. She ducked through the courtyard— not a chicken in sight now—into her room. Her wet, muddy pants and socks were definitely *not* appropriate for Heathrow. She peeled them off and dumped the pants and socks in the trash. She didn't have time to rinse them off and find a plastic bag to stuff them in for her flight. She cleaned the mud splatters off her jacket and boots as best she could. She had planned to wear her jacket on the plane but decided to pack it instead. She didn't want to risk *anything* interfering with her getting home to Nashville tonight.

She wished she had time for another shower but washed up at the sink, making sure there wasn't so much as a speck of mud on her. She didn't know if the dovecote counted as being on a farm—a definite red flag at customs—but better safe than having to explain.

Did Hambly really not remember what had happened to him? *Should* she have rung the police?

Her reaction had been normal, nothing any other tourist out for a walk wouldn't have done. Probably countless people had a peek at the dovecote. Nothing provocative in doing that, and, in any case, the injured Hambly might think she'd ventured off the public track because she'd heard him.

Her new clothes weren't as comfortable as the ones heaped in the trash, but they would do. She zipped up her suitcase, scanned the room for anything she might have missed and headed out, shutting the door behind her.

She debated mentioning her encounter at the York farm at checkout but only for a fleeting moment. It was madness, really, to say a word about it.

She was fast coming to regret her detour to the Cotswolds.

When she emerged from the pub and saw Reed Cooper leaning against the hood of a sleek, dove-gray car, there was no question anymore. Kavanagh, Hambly and now Cooper?

She should have stayed in London.

"Hello, Naomi," Reed said, his middle Tennessee accent not as pronounced as hers. "I'm your ride to Heathrow."

"You canceled my car?"

"I didn't think you'd mind."

That was Reed. "You're presumptuous," she said.

He stood straight, wearing an expensive suit with no overcoat despite the cool temperature. "Hop in or you'll miss your flight."

He went around to the passenger side of the car and opened the door. Naomi eased past him. He took her suitcase, and she slid into the car. What other choice did she have? The bus? Hitchhiking?

Reed shoved the suitcase into the backseat. She watched him circle around to the driver's side. She had bonded with him in Afghanistan because they were both Tennesseans and Vanderbilt graduates. He was from a prominent old-money Nashville family who had expected him to go into business, and she was from a small town east of Nashville, the older daughter of an army reservist killed in Iraq her freshman year in college and a seamstress who had loved and hated him and still missed him terribly. Reed was seven years older than Naomi—he had graduated by the time she stepped onto the beautiful Vanderbilt campus, dreaming of a life very different from the one she was leading.

She wondered what Reed's hopes and dreams had been as a college freshman, but she had never asked. He had risen to captain in the army and now was launching his own small team of private operators to provide security for people like her volunteer medical professionals.

On paper, maybe, she and Reed should have been romantically involved, but they never had been—despite Mike Donovan's suspicions. Mike wasn't jealous and possessive. To the contrary. He'd just drawn the same erroneous conclusions about her and Reed that others had.

She needed to put *that* out of her mind.

"You're still presumptuous," she told Reed.

"You left a trail."

"I haven't been trying to cover my tracks."

"That's good. Relax, Naomi. I'm saving you money."

"You're not here to save me money."

"That's true." Reed leveled his gray eyes on her. "We need to talk."

"About what? English chickens?"

He didn't look amused. "About your plans for the weekend."

"Barbecue and bourbon at my favorite Nashville bar. Beyond that, I don't know yet. It's been a busy couple weeks."

"How would you like to come to Maine?"

She wasn't as taken aback as she could have been. "Maine is Donovan country," she said, as if he didn't know.

Reed smiled now. "So it is," he said, starting the car.

6

Colin Donovan hated meetings, but a meeting at FBI headquarters first thing in the morning with his immediate boss and the director was its own special hell. He knew Matt Yankowski well, but he was just getting to know Mina Van Buren, newly confirmed and not necessarily a fan. Van Buren and Yank had a history. Not a good one, from what Colin had been able to gather.

He was in a suit—his Washington suit, he called it. Dark gray wool, white shirt, red tie. The small meeting room was devoid of anything that would remind him he was in Washington. He could have been anywhere, except for the company he was keeping. He sat between Yank at one end of the table and Van Buren at the other. They both had just gotten in and looked cold, although by Colin's standards, it was a mild morning.

Last night's call from Emma and this morning's call from Mike were on his mind. His fiancée and his older brother. FBI agent. Former Special Forces soldier. Emma had an art thief·

worried about an unauthorized FBI tail in London. Mike had guys he knew in the military coming in from London.

It didn't help that Oliver York was inviting Finian Bracken, Colin's Irish priest friend, out to the Cotswolds.

What the hell was Finian doing in England, anyway?

Not calls Colin had needed before talking about a deep-cover mission with his superiors.

He grinned at the two of them. "Washington's supposed to get a couple inches of snow this weekend. Would you like some tips on snowshoeing?"

"I don't want to know how to snowshoe," Yank said, with barely a trace of a smile.

"I already know how, but I don't like cold weather," Van Buren said. "I tolerate snow only when I have no other choice."

Yank looked like central casting's stereotypical pick for a senior FBI agent—tall, gray-streaked dark hair, handsome, born in a well-pressed coat and tie. He had flown down to Washington yesterday and was staying at his house in the Virginia suburbs, now, finally, up for sale.

Van Buren looked like Judy Dench, if a younger version. She was in her late fifties, a former federal prosecutor who made no secret she had differences with her predecessor as FBI director. So far, she wasn't shutting down HIT, Yank's special unit, and she wasn't relegating Colin to former undercover agent. From what he had seen so far, she was an efficient, no-nonsense type who did what she had to do to get the job done, whether it was testifying before Congress or hauling him and Yank to Washington to discuss a possible future undercover mission.

"Snowshoeing," Van Buren added, shaking her head. "I discovered a number of surprises when I came on board here. You're one of them, Agent Donovan. I expected surprises. I didn't expect you."

"Agent Donovan was necessary," Yank said.

Colin sat forward. "Was? You planning to feed me to the seagulls?"

Another thin smile from Yank. Van Buren snorted. "It's too damn cold to feed you to the seagulls."

"Pretty, though, isn't it? The Washington skyline outlined against the clear blue sky. The cold sharpens things."

Van Buren eyed him as if trying to decide if he was being serious or sarcastic.

Yank opened a folder on the table in front of him. "Donovan's a wiseass, but he's one of the best deep-cover agents you have."

"Perhaps the cold also sharpens people's sense of humor." Van Buren settled back in her chair, as if she were about to take a nap, but her eyes were intense, focused on Colin. "How are your wedding plans coming along, Agent Donovan?"

Her question caught him by surprise, but he kept any reaction under wraps. Look scared, nervous, irritated or eager beaver, and these two would eat him alive. "Fine."

"Have you settled on a date?"

"First Saturday in June."

"A lovely time to get married. Agent Yankowski mentioned that the ceremony will be at the convent of the Sisters of the Joyful Heart. I understand they have beautiful gardens. The foundress, Mother Linden, was friends with Agent Sharpe's grandfather."

"So I'm told," Colin said. He didn't like the direction of this conversation.

"And your Irish priest friend is performing the ceremony? Father Bracken?"

Van Buren was asking him questions to which she already knew the answers, but Colin decided not to point that out to her. Being an experienced prosecutor, she would know exactly what she was doing. "That's the plan," he said.

"How nice. The priest he's replacing for a year will return in June, won't he?"

"Father Callaghan. Also the plan."

"Presumably Father Bracken will return to Ireland once Father Callaghan resumes his post." Van Buren sounded hopeful. "The whiskey distillery he owns with his twin brother, Declan, is doing well. My husband and I tried a Bracken whiskey over the holidays. Excellent."

"Fin would be pleased to know you liked it."

"He's your family's priest," Van Buren said. "That means he's your priest, too."

"He's my friend," Colin said.

"Have you confided in him?"

"Confided what?"

"Anything."

"I've been burdened by this time in sixth grade—"

Van Buren waved a hand. "I withdraw the question."

"Why are we talking about Father Bracken?" Colin asked.

"Small talk." She smiled. "I've never been good at it."

It wasn't small talk but Colin didn't argue.

The FBI director folded her hands on top of the folder open in front of her. "An independent thinker is critical for undercover work, in my judgment, but it can have its downside. You don't really know for sure how you will react until you're under, do you? On a real assignment, with real people who would harm you. It can take a toll. That's why we have rules—rules the independent-minded can sometimes chafe at in their desire to do the work."

She waited but Colin didn't fill the silence with commentary. What was there to say? He had done difficult assignments in the past four years. He'd come out alive. He hadn't compromised investigations or prosecutions. The bad guys were in prison or on the way there.

Van Buren unfolded her hands and sat back in her chair, her gaze on him. "I'm told you're the best, and I've read your file."

But she hadn't seen him in action, Colin thought. She didn't know if the file was padded—if she could trust her predecessor's last days at the desk she now occupied. Colin trusted his instincts, and his instincts told him if Mina Van Buren wasn't sure about Yank, she sure as hell wasn't sure about him.

"Your life is more complicated than it used to be, isn't it, Agent Donovan?"

"Yours, too, Director."

She cracked a smile. Colin was positive. It didn't last, but it gave him hope. In his world, a serious mission required a judicious sense of humor, moments of levity that made everything else not just easier but possible.

Federal prosecutors and another agent or two would be joining them. The meeting was in relation to a new undercover mission, one that had arisen out of his previous mission—a dangerous, months-long investigation that had succeeded but also had created a vacuum in the world of illegal arms trafficking.

It wasn't an unforeseen consequence.

Jokes and talk of weddings, priests and snowshoeing ended as the conference table filled up. Colin wondered if any of the people who had joined the meeting had sent an agent to London to check on Oliver York. Because of him. Because they wanted to know if his life was becoming too complicated to put him undercover again.

Seventy minutes later, Colin told Yank about the calls from Emma and Mike. Yank had joined him on the walk from FBI headquarters to the inexpensive hotel where he had spent far too many nights over the past few weeks.

The senior FBI agent visibly gritted his teeth as Colin finished relaying the latest Sharpe and Donovan goings-on. "The Plum Tree? I'm supposed to get worked up about Mike's old army buddies showing up at a Maine country inn called the Plum Tree?"

"It has its own plum orchard," Colin said.

"Of course it does." Yank turned up the collar on his overcoat. "Think this Cooper sent his man to Rock Point to snoop on your family?"

"To get the lay of the land, anyway."

"They left it to your mother to tell Mike. That would piss me off."

"Mike wasn't happy about it," Colin said.

"Imagine that."

Colin wasn't happy about it, either. "Do you know Ted Kavanagh?"

Yank shook his head. "Not personally, no. Nothing says he can't meet with these guys on his own time. Why, what else is going on?"

Colin slowed at a wide intersection. He hadn't told Yank about Emma's call. He did now, keeping his recap as succinct as he could. "I'm wondering if this guy York saw could be Kavanagh. York didn't give much of a description."

"He's bound to be paranoid."

"He strikes me as very observant. He'd have to be to get away with stealing art and taunting Wendell Sharpe for a decade."

"Ten to one the guy he saw in the park is a London stockbroker. Even if we show him a photo of Kavanagh, there's no guarantee he won't say it's his guy just to spin us in circles."

"York says the guy he saw argued with a woman."

"Naomi MacBride?" Yank was silent as they approached Colin's hotel. "We have coincidences and conjecture. Not my two favorite things."

They entered the hotel and sat in a quiet nook by a gaslit fire. Colin watched a blue flame. He preferred wood fires, but this wasn't bad. "It occurred to me the director could have put someone on York without telling us."

"We wouldn't be here if she felt that was necessary. Either one of us."

It was a fair point. "You didn't do it, did you?"

"No. Same reasoning. You wouldn't be here if I felt that was necessary." Yank settled back in his chair. "While we're in the world of coincidence and conjecture, what if this Reed Cooper asked Kavanagh to look into what Mike's been up to since leaving the army? If Cooper wants to recruit him, it makes sense he would want to know about any issues that could blow back on his company. Figure out if Mike has any baggage that needs to get sorted."

"Never thought of myself as baggage."

"Never? Seriously?"

Colin appreciated the moment of levity, but it was short-lived. "Why would Oliver York turn up on a background check on Mike—even if it includes me? I know my name would pop up because of the murder in Boston in November, but it's not widely known that the British mythologist Oliver Fairbairn who was caught up in the investigation is also Oliver York."

"These are security types," Yank said. "They could find out. Even if they did, it doesn't mean they've figured out York is an international art thief. Being in the middle of a high-profile murder investigation that involved you and Emma could be enough to raise a red flag about Mike and get them digging a bit more."

"What's Kavanagh's role, then?"

"He doesn't have to be currying favor with Cooper over a future job. He could just be helping out an old friend."

Colin loosened his tie. "I like the stockbroker idea better."

"I don't blame you. What about Finian Bracken? Think he accepted York's invitation to visit his farm?"

"Knowing Fin? Yes. Without question."

"I don't like the idea of him and York getting together, even if it's for a fox hunt in the English countryside."

"I don't see Fin on a fox hunt."

"Drinking whiskey and checking out old tombstones, then. Are you going to get in touch with him? He's your friend."

"And do what—tell him to go back to Ireland?"

"It's a start."

Colin didn't disagree. He'd considered his options after learning about York's plan last night. He, too, would prefer his Irish priest friend and the British art thief keep their distance.

"I need to check out of my room," he said. "I'm flying back to Boston this afternoon."

"Emma's leaving this afternoon for her long weekend in Maine," Yank said, not as casually as he might have meant to. "Are you meeting her?"

"That's not the plan."

"What's she doing in Maine? Wedding things?"

"She's having lunch with my mother on Saturday."

"That could be interesting," Yank said, without elaboration.

Colin watched the fake burning logs. He had assumed Emma had told Yank about her plans for the weekend. But assuming anything with Emma was dangerous. "She's staying at the convent tonight and tomorrow night," he said, keeping his tone neutral.

Yank was clearly surprised. "For old times' sake?"

"I guess."

"Kind of like sleeping with an old boyfriend, isn't it? Never mind." Yank waved a hand. "Forget I said that. I should get moving, too."

"You done for the day? Off to plaster nail holes?"

"One more meeting. Then I plaster nail holes. I'm looking forward to unloading this house." Yank stood but made no move to head back to the revolving doors. "You hold your own with Van Buren. She'll do right by you. She knows you're not her private police force."

"I have always adhered to the principles and procedures of the FBI," Colin said. "I read the handbook cover-to-cover the other day."

Yank's eyes were flinty. "I'm serious, Donovan."

"Me, too."

"You're on my team because I shoehorned you in to keep an eye on you while you got your head screwed on straight. My opinion, you did the bidding of the previous director without enough oversight."

"Excuse me, I was a deep-cover operative on a sensitive mission to break up a network of dangerous international arms traffickers. I wasn't doing anyone's *bidding*. I'm an independent thinker. It comes in handy when you're being chased by alligators."

Yank sighed. "There were no alligators."

"It was South Florida. I was in the water. There were alligators as well as guys who wanted to kill me."

"Are we done here?"

Colin was half-serious. Maybe not even half. He got to his feet. "We're done. Good luck with the house. Will you miss it?"

"More than I will miss my old apartment. It was a daily battle with the roaches." Yank gave an exaggerated shudder. "Some of those bastards were the size of rats."

Colin kept his mouth shut. Yank had no sense of humor where roaches were concerned. He hadn't counted on his wife balking about moving to Boston. Lucy Yankowski's reluctance to leave her home in northern Virginia had thrown their marriage into turmoil as well as kept her husband in his roach-infested apartment longer than he had planned. Colin had watched Yank slowly come to realize he had made assumptions that could cost him the woman he loved. Whatever he had done to win Lucy back, she was in Boston, getting the keys to their new Back Bay apartment.

"Lucy's serious about opening a knitting shop," Yank said.

"Knitting as therapy, maybe."

"Whatever makes her happy. We don't have kids. We can afford to live in Back Bay and for her to explore a career change."

"Glad things worked out," Colin said.

"Yeah. Any worries about Emma returning to the convent?"

"She's sleeping in the quarters used for retreats, not in the novitiate."

"I guess that's something." Yank waved a hand. "Never mind. It's none of my business. Emma was a novice when I recruited her. It's not news to me."

"That's right." Colin started out of the nook, away from the fire. "You saw her in her sensible nun shoes."

"I did." Yank's mood visibly lightened as they continued across the lobby. "I'll see you back in Boston on Monday."

"Good luck with your meeting. This morning's meeting was fifty-seven minutes too long."

"It was an hour," Yank said.

"First three minutes we stirred our coffees."

Yank made no comment and headed out through a revolving door. He was better at navigating the treacherous waters of Washington, but he had decided to base his new HIT team in Boston. Colin had never heard him explain why and doubted he ever would.

When Colin reached his room, he packed and texted Mike: Where are you?

The response wasn't instant. Hurley's.

A favorite Rock Point restaurant on the harbor. It meant Mike had left the Bold Coast early. Should I be worried about you?

No.

That was Mike. A man of few words. Kavanagh?

FBI.

Meaning, he was Colin's headache. Reed Cooper?

My problem.

No argument from Colin. Not yet, anyway. Stay in touch.

This time, there was no response. He hadn't expected one. Mike had always been taciturn but was more so since leaving the army and moving out to the Bold Coast.

Colin stared out his window at a gloomy alley. Emma would be at the HIT offices at least through lunch. He wouldn't be interrupting her long weekend on her own if he called.

She answered on the first ring. "Hey, what have you been up to?"

"Just got out of another meeting."

"Ah."

He wasn't sure she believed him. He told her about Mike's call about the gathering at the Plum Tree. "He's in Rock Point," Colin added.

"If the man Oliver spotted in London was Ted Kavanagh, he has his own agenda. We can't have him spooking Oliver if we want those two Dutch landscapes returned."

"They're his last leverage."

"Exactly. He'll hold on to them until he knows what's next. He wants to keep Scotland Yard off his doorstep."

"He's never threatened to dump them in the Thames."

"That's a plus," Emma said. "I don't think he's worried about getting arrested at this point. It's more like MI5."

"Our friends in the British Secret Service." Colin knew a number of British agents, although not well enough to mention Oliver York. "With Oliver's contacts and skills, he can maneuver in a wide variety of worlds. Think of the bad guys he could stop. Has MI5 been in touch with you?"

Emma didn't answer right away. "Sort of."

"I can see York as James Bond."

"What are you doing now?"

"Packing. I'll be back in Boston tonight. You?"

"Leaving for Maine as soon as I can get out of here.

"Say hi to the sisters for me."

"I will."

He heard a brightness in her voice—an eagerness to be at the convent again. Many of the current crop of religious sisters had been there when Emma had been Sister Brigid, young, eager, not so much confused as figuring things out. Specifically what *things* Colin didn't know. At nineteen, he'd been figuring out how to keep himself in cash and women while he got through college. He'd majored in criminal justice, but he'd never been a deep thinker. He swore Emma had been born thinking deep thoughts.

As he disconnected, he noticed pigeons huddling on a trash can. They looked cold.

What would his life be like if he'd stayed in the Maine marine patrol, or if he had never volunteered for undercover work? Would he and Emma have ever met? They'd grown up a few miles apart from each other but hadn't met until last September, despite both being with the FBI.

It didn't matter, he thought. If he'd been a lobsterman, a Maine cop or a bartender at Hurley's, somehow he and Emma would have met. He knew it in his gut.

They were meant to be together.

He would arrive in Boston after she'd left for Maine, probably while she was singing vespers with the sisters.

He wanted her to enjoy her time at the convent.

He finished packing and headed to the lobby. He had time for lunch, then he would take a cab to the airport and catch his flight.

7

Near Stow-on-the-Wold, the Cotswolds, England
Thursday, 4:00 p.m., BST

For the first time in hours, Martin felt warm again. Now all he had to do was get rid of Ruthie Burns, the housekeeper. She liked to fuss. She had insisted on lighting a fire for him in his cottage on the York farm, up from the dovecote and down from the main house. The cottage was constructed of stone and timber, small and cozy, perfect for his needs. He had sent Johnny, the farmworker who had come to his aid, back to work with a stern admonition not to call an ambulance.

"I'll be right as rain in no time," he told Ruthie.

"I'll finish preparations for Mr. York's arrival," she said, ever eager to be of greater assistance. She was a stout woman, a widow with two grown sons and four grandchildren. "I'd just started to look for you this morning when Johnny told me about your tumble. It's a stroke of luck this woman found you, but we wouldn't have left you out there."

"Thank you, Ruthie. I'd have managed whether or not anyone found me. I fell late in the afternoon. It's no wonder I wasn't missed until today. No worries."

"Are you sure you don't need to see a doctor?"

"Positive," he said, coaxing her out the door.

He managed to stay on his feet until she withdrew, clearly unconvinced. Knowing her as well as he did—she had worked for the Yorks for nearly as long as he had—he waited, one hand on the entry table to keep himself upright.

Sure enough, within thirty seconds she knocked on the door again, then pushed it open, obviously expecting to catch him dead on the floor. "I forgot to tell you the courier service picked up the package at the dovecote yesterday. It must have been after your tumble. The driver rang the house to let me know, since you weren't there. It didn't occur to either of us you were lying outside in the wet and the cold."

"No reason it should have."

"Reason enough, as it turned out." She eyed him warily. "Promise me you won't keel over when I shut the door."

"If I do, best you not witness my demise."

"You're not a bit funny."

Martin reassured her of his well-being and once again sent her on her way. When the door shut behind her, he frowned, wobbly and uncertain.

Package? What bloody package?

A sharp pain pierced from the back of his head straight through his nose. The stress of trying to remember seemed to worsen the pain. Medical attention was undoubtedly a sound idea, but he didn't want to risk the scrutiny, especially when his memory was so uncertain. Ruthie's hovering was bad enough. Johnny had been more matter-of-fact. Falls in wet, slippery conditions weren't unheard-of.

Martin gave a small groan. He couldn't remember a damn thing about his fall. Ever since the American woman had discovered him, his mind had been wandering, unfocused, frustratingly ill-equipped to provide him the details of what had happened to him at the dovecote.

Nothing good, obviously.

A sheep? Had the bloody ram knocked him on his arse?

He remembered the cold ground, the sodden leaves, the dark night. Bits and pieces of it all, at least. That had to be a promising sign. He had vague memories of nausea and pain and shivering, the panicky sense that he would die if he didn't find a way to stay warm enough to ward off hypothermia.

He couldn't say how much of what he remembered was a dream, the fog of semiconsciousness—the tricks of the mind as the body fought hypothermia and coped with a head injury.

He settled into a chair by the fire and put his feet up on a cushioned stool his grandfather had made back before World War One. The Great War, he had called it. The war to end all wars. Would it had been such.

Martin lifted a bottle of Scotch on the table next to his chair and splashed a dram into his glass. He needed to remember what had happened to him at the dovecote, but patience and rest would help him more than force and frustration.

Should he know who the woman was who had come to his aid?

Hadn't there been another American?

A man...

His head ached.

He swallowed some Scotch, smoky and strong, and closed his eyes, glass in hand as he listened to the crackle of the fire and the spray of rain on the windows. A passing shower, darkening the afternoon.

Another sip of Scotch and he set the glass on the table.

He sank into the soft, worn cushions of his chair.

Best to relax now...sleep...right here by the fire, where he was warm...and safe.

8

London, England
Thursday, 4:30 p.m., BST

"Are you certain, Fin?" Declan Bracken asked.

Finian smiled at his brother with a confidence he didn't feel. They were in the lobby of Claridge's, not far from Oliver York's London Mayfair apartment. "Oliver is a curious fellow," Finian said. "It will be interesting to see his farm. I've never been to the Cotswolds."

Declan looked dubious. They were fraternal twins, always close. Dreamers, too naive to fully realize what they were getting into, they'd launched Bracken Distillers at twenty-two. Now, seventeen years later, it was a thriving whiskey business, earning a name for itself in that tough, competitive world. Until tragedy had torn Finian apart—leaving him without the woman he loved, the beautiful daughters she'd born—he had expected to work side by side with his brother. If Declan had ever felt abandoned, first by Finian's spiral into depression and alcohol, then by his call to the priesthood, he had never said so. Finian, still a co-owner in Bracken Distillers, had joined Declan on visits to various London whiskey clients. Declan didn't need his brother's help these days, but Finian had welcomed dipping a toe back in his old life. He thought Declan had enjoyed it, too.

Oliver York frequented Claridge's bar and had joined them for whiskey last night. Scotch for the Brit, Irish for "the Bracken twins," as Oliver called them. They had argued the merits of adding water to whiskey—in Finian's view, there were no merits, but Declan was more open to the idea, particularly if it sold whiskey.

"A couple of nights in the English countryside, and then it's back to Maine," Finian said.

"All right, then. Stay in touch, Fin. It was good to have you home."

Finian understood what was left unsaid. Declan and the rest of the Brackens wanted Finian to return to Ireland after his one-year assignment in Maine. Whether he took a parish in Ireland or quit the priesthood and returned to Bracken Distillers wasn't as important to them as being back on their side of the Atlantic.

Declan was off to another appointment, then flying back to Ireland that evening. His wife and their three young children were meeting him for a weekend in Dublin. Not long ago, Finian would have figured out how old his daughters would be now and pictured them with their mother, greeting him for a Dublin break. Instead, he was aware of the urge but didn't let it take hold of him.

He waited for his brother to get into a cab, then headed out from the hotel on foot. London was clear and chilly, a change from yesterday's clouds and rain. He was clad in his priestly garb and a black overcoat, with no gloves or hat, but it was a short walk to the Mayfair gallery where Aoife O'Byrne's work was on display. He had investigated the gallery, briefly, yesterday. He'd had no reason to expect Aoife to be there. The opening cocktail party had passed, and Finian knew she hated such things. She resisted looking at art she'd completed. Solitary and driven, and quite beautiful, she preferred creating new art in her Dublin studio.

Aoife didn't need him turning up in her life again—or Oliver York, either, for that matter. Oliver was a thief who had begun his career stealing paintings from her uncle, and Finian was… well, he didn't know what he was to her.

Another self-delusion. Finian did know. He and Aoife had been lovers for one mad weekend a few months after the deaths of his wife and daughters, before his call to the priesthood. Aoife had convinced herself she was in love with him and he with her. The only cure was to keep his distance. Let time heal and prove she was wrong about him—that he did, indeed, belong in the priesthood, keeping his promise of celibacy.

Finian slipped into the gallery. He hadn't meant to return after yesterday's visit, but here he was. His heart jumped when he spotted Aoife in a far corner, alone. He knew he should leave, but he couldn't move. She glared at him, then spun away from him, her long, dark hair gleaming as she darted into a private back room.

Aoife O'Byrne didn't take well to being the jilted lover.

It wasn't Finian's view, but it did no good to explain to her that he hadn't jilted her. The truth was, he had been wounded, raging and drinking, blinded by indescribable pain, and she had provided solace and relief. Their stormy Irish weekend together had helped open the way for him to carry on, to turn from self-destruction and, eventually, to experience the call to a religious life.

Their mad, doomed attraction to each other hadn't been only about him. It had been about her, too. Aoife O'Byrne was a committed artist, absorbed by her work. Perhaps she needed to cling to an unattainable love to justify her own solitary life.

That he and Aoife had made love in the same run-down seaside house Oliver had burglarized a few years earlier wasn't lost on him.

Finian didn't want to cause Aoife further distress and left the gallery immediately.

He returned to Claridge's, regretting his impulse to visit the gallery again today. On yesterday's visit, he'd been struck by another woman—an American with dark curly hair and high energy. He'd overheard her pepper a gallery worker with questions about Aoife. Was Aoife in London? Had anyone sponsored the show? Then she'd looked straight at Finian, took in a breath and exited the gallery. He'd been wearing his priestly garb and occasionally encountered strong reactions, but this was different. It was as if she'd known exactly who he was.

Oliver had been at the gallery, too. That evening, he'd joined Finian and Declan for drinks and extended the invitation to visit his farm.

When Finian arrived back at Claridge's, the car and driver Oliver had hired for him were waiting. Already checked out of the iconic Mayfair hotel, Finian retrieved his bag from the bellman. He climbed into the back of the Rolls, thinking that London had been a bad idea. He hoped this side trip to the Cotswolds wouldn't be a worse idea. He had accepted Oliver's invitation out of curiosity, plain and simple. He could try to dress it up and credit priestly duty and friendship, but he would be fooling himself, if not outright lying to himself.

About two hours later, the Rolls came to a stop under a portico at the side entrance to the stately York country home. Finian got out before the uniformed driver could come around and open the door for him. He let the poor fellow collect his bag but then took it from him, obviously another disconcerting surprise. Finian saw no problem. He packed light. The bag wasn't heavy. Even during his heyday as a whiskey distillery executive, he had rarely hired his own driver. Now, as a rural parish priest on the

New England coast, he seldom had reason even for a taxi. He drove himself everywhere—although he did drive a BMW, an indulgence he especially appreciated with the onslaught of the harsh Maine winter.

Oliver York opened the solid wood door to his farmhouse. "Welcome, my friend," the Englishman said. "That's your only bag? For some reason, I expected a priest would need more. You know, with your collars and vestments and such. Not that I have any idea. Come in, come in."

They went down a stone-tiled hall to a spacious living room where a wood fire crackled in a stone fireplace under a beamed ceiling. Two dark brown leather sofas faced each other perpendicular to the fire, an ottoman covered in red-and-brown plaid between them. A large oil painting above the mantel depicted a lazy, bucolic scene of hounds on a tree-lined lane, probably on the York property. Shelves, tables, lamps and side chairs all had an inviting, contemporary feel.

Oliver smiled as Finian set his bag on the threshold. "You were expecting chintz, weren't you? I had the place redecorated a few years ago. I hired a decorator and left for the winter. When I came back, it was done." He entered the room and nodded to the painting above the mantel. "My grandparents' dogs. They used to follow me everywhere. They knew what happened to me—to my family, Father Bracken. They knew."

"I've no doubt." Feeling distinctly out of place, Finian followed Oliver to the fireplace. Neither sat down. "Please, call me Finian."

"I will, then, thank you. Make yourself at home. Martin is recuperating from a nasty fall yesterday on the farm. He spent the night outside on a stream bank. A miracle he didn't die of hypothermia. I wasn't here. If I had been, I suppose I would have wondered what he was up to and gone looking for him. I stopped by his cottage after I arrived earlier today and learned of his ordeal. He says he'll be right as rain in the morning. I believe it'll be a few days."

"What kind of injuries did he sustain?" Finian asked.

"Bumps, bruises, scratches and a laceration on the back of his head. He refuses to see a doctor." Oliver sounded more miffed than concerned. "He doesn't remember if he lost consciousness. What does that tell you?"

"Head injuries can be dangerous, Oliver."

He waved a hand. "I told Martin that, and he told me he had hit his head before and knew what to watch for. He spouted some rubbish his mother told him about bleeding relieving pressure and preventing infection. There might be truth in it for all I know, but I remember his mother. She looked like Queen Victoria. I'm sure she still believed in leeching."

Finian had no idea if Oliver was serious. He had first encountered the Englishman in Boston last fall, under his alter ego of Oliver Fairbairn. He'd yet to meet Martin Hambly.

"Martin looks like hell," Oliver added. "He reminded me this is a farm and accidents happen. He made it through last night in the open without dying, so I suppose that's something. He lives in a cottage on the property. He ran me out. He was sitting by the fire with an ice pack and a pot of tea and planned to be there all night. A farmworker helped him get settled."

"I'm sorry he's in pain. Let me know if there's anything I can do."

"You, my friend, can relax and enjoy your visit."

Wind buffeted the windows, and Finian could hear a rush of rain in the evening gray. His reservations about accepting Oliver's invitation eased, then dissipated altogether when Ruthie Burns, the housekeeper, who also looked like Queen Victoria, entered the room with a tray of tea, scones, cream and jam that she set on the ottoman. She poured tea, handing Oliver and Finian each a cup and saucer, then arranged two small plates with scones, jam and cream, placing Finian's on a small table next to him, along with a knife and napkin. She did the same for Oliver. Finian thanked her. She smiled at him and made off with his bag before he realized what she was up to.

"It wouldn't surprise me if Ruthie gave Martin a little shove down the stream bank," Oliver said. "Those two have been in a turf battle here for forty years. They don't think I notice."

Oliver, Finian had discovered, noticed everything. One reason he had eluded capture as a thief for so long, no doubt. "The farm looks delightful, Oliver. Thank you for inviting me."

"We'll have whiskey while you're here," he said, settling back with his tea. "I managed to secure a bottle of single malt Bracken 15 Year Old. No peat. I wasn't able to get the peated expression."

"It's almost gone," Finian said. "It was a bit of fun for Declan and me."

"Life was different for both of us when it went into the cask, wasn't it, Finian?"

Back then, Oliver had been an orphan but not yet a thief. Finian had been an ambitious young man with plans. He and Declan had taken over an abandoned distillery near Killarney and dived in, learning as they went.

"Yes, life was different," Finian said quietly.

"If only we could go back in time. You could save your wife and daughters. You could stop them from getting on that boat. Or do you believe no matter what you did, their fate was already cast—if you'd saved them from drowning, they'd have died that summer some other way?"

"I don't ask myself such questions."

"You're a smarter man than I am. I'm sorry to be so blunt. I don't mean to dredge up the past. It's always close to me, in part because of what I endured but also because of my work in mythology. You chose the priesthood after your loss. I chose a dual life of scholarship and playing the dashing English aristocrat. Oliver Fairbairn and Oliver York." He drank some of his tea and watched the fire. "I've had women, Finian. Women I've loved. Not many, but enough to know what I'm missing."

"You're still a young man. There's time, if that's what you want."

He smiled. "Aoife kicked me out of the gallery."

"She wouldn't speak with me. Aoife O'Byrne is…"

"Out of reach, and angry at both of us. What do you think, Finian, is she angry at you more because you became a priest or because you've stayed a priest?" Oliver inhaled, pausing as he studied his guest, then pointed his cup at Finian. "Because you stayed. She could understand becoming a priest, even after she fell in love with you, because you were still in pain. She could rationalize seminary as part of your grief process."

"Maybe so," Finian said, not caring to explain. He was no longer surprised at how much Oliver knew—or guessed—about his past, including his relationship with Aoife.

"Staying in the priesthood, though. Now that *really* angered her, my friend. Especially after she saw you in Boston in November."

"Aoife's a friend."

Oliver snorted. "And that's all there is to it?"

"As far as I'm concerned."

"Sometimes you can remain friends with a woman you slept with and ditched. Sometimes you can't. In any case, our Aoife is a beautiful, talented, successful artist, and we both hurt her, each in our own way."

"Is that why you invited me here, Oliver? To talk to me about how you hurt Aoife?" Finian tried some of his scone. It was light and simply made, good after the drive from London. He hadn't expected Oliver to dive straight into such deeply personal matters. "Or did you invite me here so you can reassure yourself that I plan to stay a priest and the way is clear for you to pursue her?"

Oliver laughed, his eyes crinkling with good humor. "Aoife knows far too much about me to allow me into her life. No,

Father Bracken, I invited you here to see the farm. I have many acquaintances, but I don't have many friends. I'm…" He stood abruptly, took in an awkward breath. "I'm trying to change that."

Finian thought he understood. "Change begins with one step."

"In my experience, one step can lead you off a cliff. Come. Ruthie will show you to your room. She'll bring your tea and scones. You can get settled."

"Who was your last guest, Oliver? Dare I ask?"

He grinned, setting his teacup on a side table. "Wendell Sharpe."

Finian wasn't surprised. He had met the octogenarian private art detective, the determined, dedicated founder of Sharpe Fine Art Recovery. For a decade, Oliver had been the thief that world-renowned Wendell Sharpe couldn't catch. Finian didn't have all the details—nor did he want them—but he doubted Oliver would ever be publicly identified or prosecuted as a serial art thief.

"Did you invite Wendell or did he invite himself?" Finian asked.

"A bit of both. Better to invite Wendell than find him sneaking around in the shrubbery. It's hard to tear a Sharpe off a theory. I arranged for him to do a talk at Oxford and had him stay here."

"The talk went well?"

"He was brilliant. He didn't tell Emma about the visit."

Finian very much doubted he had, either. "He keeps saying he's retiring."

Oliver scoffed. "That will never happen. No Oxford seminar for you, I'm afraid," he added.

Finian laughed. "Thank goodness."

"You might want a walk in the countryside while you're here. There are maps in your room. You don't suppose you can lay hands on Martin and cure his headache? Pass some sort of miracle? I need him."

Finian smiled, getting to his feet as he polished off the last of his scone. Oliver clearly knew the liberties he was taking, but he also clearly didn't care whether he was being offensive, never mind wrong. "I recommend that he see a physician."

"I *did* recommend it, but he's stubborn. You'll see."

Ruthie appeared with a small tray and loaded up Finian's tea and remaining scone. After breakfast with Declan and then a business lunch, Finian wasn't particularly hungry, but good scones were impossible to resist. He kept silent and followed the housekeeper down another hall. The door was open to a guest suite, in its own small wing at the back of the house. It consisted of a small living room, bedroom and private bath, done in soothing neutral colors that invited relaxation. Someone—Ruthie, presumably—had drawn the drapes, filled a water pitcher and small fruit bowl and laid out a bathrobe and slippers.

"Is there anything else you need?" she asked him.

"I can't think of a thing, thank you."

After she retreated, shutting the door behind her, Finian went to a window and drew back a heavy drape. It was dark now, and as he looked out at a small stone terrace, contemplating his sanity, he noticed a light from the house shining on a puddle. Having never been to this part of England, he had paid close attention to the scenery on the drive from London. Even in February, the rolling hills and honey-stone villages possessed a beauty and charm that were easy to appreciate.

He felt a pang of nostalgia for South Kerry and its brightly colored villages and stunning natural scenery. Before leaving for London, he and Declan had walked the old road, now part of the Kerry Way walking route, from Killarney to Kenmare, talking about family and whiskey, never mentioning Maine, Finian's FBI agent friends or Aoife O'Byrne. Most of all, they had steered clear of talk of the priesthood and what Finian would do when Father Callaghan, now on sabbatical, returned to his post in Rock Point.

Sally and the girls had come into the conversation a few times, naturally, with smiles and even laughter at memories of their antics. In years past, Declan would blanch when accidentally speaking their names, as if to do so were a breach of etiquette, if not forbidden then at least an unwelcome reminder of pain and loss.

His dear Sally would have loved this place, Finian thought with a smile.

He pushed opened a glass door and stepped out onto the terrace, welcoming the brisk air and clear evening sky. He could smell the damp ground, the garden dormant now in winter. The York farm struck him as being as contradictory and unpredictable as its owner.

He went back inside, pulling the drapes again. He noticed the painting above the bed, featuring more dogs in a scene of rural nineteenth-century English prosperity. The house—*this* house, Finian thought—was featured in the background. During the time of the painting, his own family in southwest Ireland had struggled to survive famine and eke out a subsistence living.

He poured more tea. Although not yet convinced, he was hopeful this trip to the Cotswolds hadn't been a bad idea after all.

9

Emma managed to get out of Boston by midafternoon. In less than two hours, she was in southern Maine. She had anticipated that by now she would be putting work aside and focusing on her mini retreat at the Sisters of the Joyful Heart, but instead she found herself at the small shop and art studio they ran on a side street in her hometown of Heron's Cove. In summer, it would be difficult to find a parking space, but not on a late-February Thursday afternoon.

Sister Cecilia Catherine Rousseau emerged from the studio and greeted Emma in the shop. "Emma!" she said, smiling. She wore a wide white headband, on slightly crooked over her wispy blunt-cut brown hair, and a dove-gray tunic and skirt with dark tights and walking shoes. "I didn't expect to see you until this evening at the convent."

"How are you, Sister?"

"I just finished teaching a wild after-school pottery class for fifth and sixth graders. I broke up several clay fights. It must be cabin fever." She spoke cheerfully, her passion for art education evident. "Did you just get in?"

Emma nodded, fingering a beautiful pottery bowl for sale. She'd never had a knack for pottery, although she'd tried it a few times. Her expertise as a novice had been in the convent's work in art preservation and conservation. "I'm not staying at the convent tonight," she said. "I'll call Mother Superior, but I wanted to let you know myself."

"Has anything happened? You're all right, Emma?"

"Nothing's happened. I'm fine. I'm heading to Colin's house in Rock Point."

"And that's where you need to be right now," Sister Cecilia said.

Emma touched the ring on her finger. There were times it still felt new, not quite real. "I guess that sums it up. I don't belong at the convent. I haven't in a long time. Planning the retreat helped me see that."

"Mother Superior will understand."

"I hope canceling won't cause any trouble."

"Of course not," Sister Cecilia said with confidence. "The whole point was *not* to plan anything special, wasn't it?"

Emma nodded. She'd wanted to experience the life she'd left behind—but driving to Maine, getting closer and closer to walking through the convent gates for her retreat, she had realized that she wouldn't stay. Not tonight, not ever again. It wasn't a question of bad timing given Oliver York's latest news. She always had cases, developments, unfinished work.

"Are we still on for your painting lesson tomorrow?" Sister Cecilia asked.

"Absolutely. I look forward to it." Emma smiled. She would never be much of a painter, and both she and Sister Cecilia knew it. That wasn't the point of the ongoing, if erratically scheduled, lessons.

Sister Cecilia clapped her hands together. "Excellent. I'll see you then. Enjoy your evening in Rock Point. Will Colin be joining you?"

"He's on his way back to Boston from Washington. I haven't told him I've canceled my retreat yet."

"I'm going to make a bold guess that he will be pleased you did," the young sister said, her eyes twinkling.

Relieved to have the decision about the retreat made and dealt with, Emma left Sister Cecilia to closing up the shop. They had become friends last fall, after the murder of a longtime nun with the Sisters of the Joyful Heart and Sister Cecilia's own close call with the killer.

Emma drove back through Heron's Cove, a pretty southern Maine village known for its quaint shops and restaurants and sprawling summer "cottages." She continued on to Ocean Avenue, along the tidal river and out to the ocean. Just past a marina, at the mouth of the river, she parked in front of the small, gray-shingled Victorian house where, sixty years ago, Wendell Sharpe, a museum security guard, had launched his fine art recovery business in the front room. Fifteen years ago, he had opened an office in Dublin, the city of his birth. No one had expected him to stay. His wife had died too young, too soon, and he needed a break. He would be back.

Her grandfather was still in Dublin, and Emma doubted he would ever return to Heron's Cove to live.

At first, her father had run the Maine offices of Sharpe Fine Art Recovery, but his chronic, debilitating pain had forced Emma's older brother, Lucas, to step in far sooner—and far more alone—than he had planned. She'd worked for her father and grandfather in high school and always expected to join the family business. Then came college and a calling—or whatever it had been—to a religious life, or, more specifically, to the Sisters of the Joyful Heart and their romantic coastal convent and work in art preservation, conservation and education.

Even before Matt Yankowski had visited her as Sister Brigid, Emma had known she would never profess her final vows. The process of discernment she'd gone through as a postulant and a novice had done its job, leading her to where she was now. She had left the Sisters of the Joyful Heart shortly after meeting Yank, then worked for her grandfather in Dublin for almost a year before heading to the FBI Academy.

Early on in her work in art crimes, she had discovered that the FBI had less than Wendell Sharpe did on a serial international art thief who had first struck in Ireland, in a tiny village on the south coast.

And her grandfather hadn't had much.

She climbed out of her car, welcoming the cold air. There was more snow in Heron's Cove than in Boston, but with no fresh storms in more than a week, the snowbanks were partially blackened and turning icy. The house backed up onto the mouth of the tidal river, between a marina and a popular inn and within sight of the ocean. The big houses that overlooked the ocean up the street were mostly empty now, in the off-season.

The front walk was neatly shoveled and sanded, but Emma knew no one was there. She stood at the base of the steps, noting the shiny black paint on the front door. Over the past six months, the house had been gutted and renovated to create modern offices for Sharpe Fine Art Recovery. She had managed to persuade her brother, who didn't have a sentimental cell in his body, to keep the back porch, but he had already included a small apartment in the plans. It wasn't a house anymore, but the apartment was available to their grandfather, should he finally decide to return to Maine.

Emma decided not to go inside. Lucas was in Dublin with their grandfather. Their parents were in London. The process of shutting down the temporary offices and moving everything back here would be getting under way and didn't need her input. There was talk of a grand opening party. She'd be invited, although she had no official role any longer with Sharpe Fine Art Recovery.

She returned to her car, looking forward to her evening in Rock Point. She took the coast road northeast to Rock Point and its working harbor and smattering of houses on narrow streets. Donovan country, Emma thought. She continued up to the Craftsman-style house Colin had bought as a refuge at the height of a long, difficult undercover mission. His independence, always an asset, had proved to have a dark side, isolating him, fraying his relationships with some of his FBI colleagues and even his family.

Not that he saw it that way.

Emma let herself into the house through the back door, but she didn't stay. She slipped back outside, hunching her shoulders against a cold gust of wind. Before leaving Boston, she had changed into casual leggings, an oversize sweater and her Frye boots, in anticipation of her convent retreat. She grabbed her hat and gloves out of her car. She would walk to St. Patrick's rectory to see if Oliver York's package had arrived. If it had, she would decide what to do once she saw the contents. Enjoy her long weekend in Maine, or delve back into the world of an accomplished art thief.

Clouds and fog moved in, adding dampness to the air, making it feel colder. Emma navigated an icy patch on the sidewalk that curved onto the quiet, narrow street where St. Patrick's was located. The rectory, a small Victorian, was next to the white-sided church, which had started life a hundred years ago as an American Baptist Church. Both church and rectory were dark now, with Finian Bracken in Ireland.

Actually, in England, Emma thought with a sigh of frustration. Finian was likely settling into a guest suite at Oliver York's Cotswolds farm.

She didn't run into any residents or passing cars, everyone either at work, running errands or inside their homes. She wasn't used to Rock Point on a weeknight in winter. She and Colin had been up a few times since Christmas, but always on a weekend.

She adjusted her scarf, covering more of her face against the breeze and damp air. The fog was thick and bone-chilling, tasting of salt. There was definitely no sign of spring tonight on the southern Maine coast.

If the package was too large to carry, she would have to go back for her car, but the walk and fresh air were doing her good after her drive, especially given her crowded mind. She needed to sift through everything simmering—her wedding, her canceled retreat, this latest with Oliver—and create some order. Walking, inevitably, helped.

She passed in front of the church and turned onto the walk that led to the front door of the rectory. Finian Bracken was a hit with parishioners with his good looks, Irish accent and approachability. His tragic past, while nothing anyone would wish upon him, seemed to help people identify with him. He and Colin were already friends when Emma had met them both in September. Finian had agreed to perform their wedding service before he returned to Ireland in June—if he did return, Emma thought. She had her doubts, whether or not Father Callaghan resumed his post in Rock Point.

She didn't need to tell Finian that Maine couldn't be an escape. Neither could the priesthood. That was one of the lessons she'd learned at the convent. He would have gone through a rigorous process of discernment before being admitted into seminary, but how had life in Maine affected him? His friendships with the Donovans—seeing Aoife O'Byrne in Boston in November?

None of her business, Emma reminded herself. She shook off her ruminating and headed down the walk to the rectory, built around the same time as the Sharpe house in Heron's Cove and as in need of an overhaul as it had been.

There was no package on the front steps. Oliver wasn't above sending her on a wild-goose chase, but his package might not have arrived yet, or the part-time church secretary or a volunteer could have picked it up. It was also possible delivery trucks would circle through the church parking lot and drop off packages on the rectory's side porch, easily accessible for the driver and out of view of passersby.

Emma took a narrow, icy walk to the enclosed side porch. If anything, the fog seemed denser, impenetrable. She wished she had thought to bring a flashlight with her. She mounted the porch steps, immediately noticing a large package in front of the kitchen door. She flipped on the porch light and checked the label.

It was Oliver's package.

What did he consider a surprise she would love? Short of the missing Dutch landscapes or a confession, she couldn't think of anything she would want to receive from him. Whatever he had sent, she would promptly report to Yank. She wasn't accepting gifts of any kind from Oliver York.

She turned off the porch light and, using both arms, lifted the package. It was bulky but not heavy. A sweater? A stuffed sheep? It was too big for a shipment of English scones and not heavy enough for jam or whiskey.

She was tempted to rip open the package there on the porch but resisted. She'd get back to Colin's house first. She debated whether to leave the package and fetch her car but decided she could manage carrying it.

While she'd been on the porch collecting the package, a car she didn't recognize had parked on the street in front of the rectory, its trunk open. She didn't see the driver or any passengers. Probably a parishioner dropping off something at the church, although there were no lights on yet in the building.

Slowing her pace, Emma adjusted the package in her arms.

She heard a sound behind her—a quick intake of breath, like

a warning of what was to come. She started to drop the package, but she knew she was too late.

A blanket thrown over her head...a choke hold...

Give in to it. Don't risk permanent injury or death.

Fight later.

She let her body go limp, felt the pressure on her carotid artery as unconsciousness overtook her.

Breathe...

Emma pushed back the instant panic as she regained consciousness, dizzy, unable to move, suffocating.

Not suffocating.

It was the blanket. She could smell the fleece, taste the fibers.

Her hands were bound behind her. Her ankles, too, were bound.

Her attacker would have had only seconds before she regained consciousness and must have been ready, must have waited for her and known exactly what to do.

An ambush.

She slowed her breathing. She had to stay calm.

I'm in the trunk of the car that was parked at the rectory.

She felt the movement, heard the engine.

Where are we going?

Her attacker hadn't killed her straightaway. That was something, even if the plan was to kill her outside the village and dump her body.

Colin.

Emma closed her eyes and imagined him, felt him close to her, heard his laughter.

"Emma Sharpe, I'm madly in love with you, and I want to be with you forever."

His words to her on that rainy November night in Dublin when he'd asked her to marry him, and she'd said yes.

She brought herself back to the present, the effects of the

choke hold easing. She risked a deeper breath, inhaling to the count of four, holding for four, exhaling for eight...

First things first, she told herself.

Right now, her job was to stay alive.

10

Colin took a cab from the airport straight to the HIT offices in an unobtrusive brick building on the Boston waterfront. He wasn't surprised to find Sam Padgett in the open-layout area in the center of the main floor, outside the individual offices. He had a laptop and two monitors arranged on U-shaped tables, with his scuffed boots up on one of the tables. He was HIT's newest member, in his midthirties, dark, an ultra-fit type and a hard-ass with a sense of humor. He made no secret he preferred his native Texas. He'd started griping about New England winters at the first snowflake.

"Good flight?" he asked, not glancing up from his laptop.

"Uneventful," Colin said.

"Best kind. I heard our favorite art thief has been in touch. When are we going to nail his ass?"

"Probably never."

"Is Oliver York the wrong man or the right man for the thefts?"

"Right man."

"Then we could find a way to nail him if we wanted to. That means we don't want to."

Colin didn't disagree.

Padgett tilted back in his chair. "At least it's another chapter in the annals of Sharpe Fine Art Recovery closed."

"Closing, maybe."

"Old Wendell must be happy."

"He's happy the stolen art is being returned intact. We all are."

Padgett dropped his feet to the floor and shut his laptop. He was blunt and consistent about not getting Emma's role with HIT or the value of her expertise in art crimes. He never would have recruited her for the FBI in the first place, never mind hand-picked her for an elite team. Her family's work in art recovery and her grandfather's status as one of the foremost private art detectives in the world would have disqualified her if Padgett had been doing the disqualifying. And art crimes mystified him.

"What are you working on?" Colin asked.

"Numbers."

Padgett was as good with numbers as he was with firearms. Colin had seen him take enormous pleasure in catching people in their own stereotypes since he didn't look like the classic numbers guy.

"Give me two minutes," he said. "I've got some info for you on your brother's friends."

He snapped up straight in his chair, reopened his laptop and tapped a few keys on his keyboard, back into his work.

Colin entered an empty conference room. Before he'd boarded his flight, he had given Padgett the names he had from Mike. He felt only mildly guilty that he hadn't asked his brother for more information, but Oliver York's call to Emma mentioning the possible sighting of an FBI agent on his tail was too coincidental for Colin not to take a closer look. Best-case scenario still was a London stockbroker.

Boston Harbor was glasslike, reflecting the city lights. He'd texted Emma when he'd landed at Logan, but she hadn't responded. He didn't know what the sisters' rituals were in the evening. Dinner, cleanup, reading, games, vespers. He'd been to the convent and could picture its stone buildings, a renovated nineteenth-century estate on its own small peninsula overlooking the Atlantic. Mother Linden, who had been friends with Wendell Sharpe in his younger years, had transformed the run-down property when she'd founded the Sisters of the Joyful Heart decades ago.

Padgett entered the conference room without notes or a laptop. "Let's start with Ted Kavanagh," he said. "He's an active agent. He's forty-four, divorced, two kids in college, and he's supposed to be in a hammock on a beach."

"He's on vacation?"

"He's supposed to be taking an overdue break to decompress after wrapping up a difficult investigation into money launderers—guys he started chasing when he was assigned to Afghanistan a few years ago. They hooked up with local drug lords. One of those tangled webs. You can identify."

Colin nodded without comment.

"Kavanagh should have taken a break two months ago, but he stuck around, pissed people off and finally got told to take a break."

"I can identify with that, too," Colin said.

"He packed his suitcase and said he was going to the beach. I'd have assumed he meant sand and eighty degrees, not ice and—what was it this morning in Maine? Two?"

"A balmy twenty degrees."

"I'll have to get out my swim trunks." Padgett stood at the window and glanced at the glittering harbor. "Reed Cooper is an army captain turned private contractor. He worked with one of the big outfits until going out on his own in October. Cooper Global Security is still a fledgling company. He's taking his time pulling the right people together. He has family money. He has a solid reputation and a breadth of operational and logistical experience."

"No alarms yet," Colin said. "What else?"

"Cooper, Naomi MacBride and Buddy Whidmore are all Tennesseans. Cooper is from Belle Meade, MacBride from a small town east of Nashville, Whidmore from Memphis. Cooper and MacBride are Vanderbilt grads. Buddy dropped out his sophomore year—one of those guys too smart for college. They were all there at different times. MacBride is a security and crisis management consultant who used to be an intelligence analyst for the State Department. She's based in Nashville. Whidmore is a freelance tech guy. He's based twenty miles southwest of Nashville. Nashville—not coincidentally, I'm sure—is where Cooper decided to open his offices for Cooper Global Security."

And now, Colin thought, they all were on their way to see Mike in Maine.

"I can do more digging," Padgett said, "but it looks to me as if these are key relationships formed at a tough, dangerous time. As far as I can see, this thing at the Plum Tree is a big old spook and soldier reunion in the wilds of Maine. With Cooper's new outfit, he'll want to do some networking and recruiting with people he knows and trusts."

"I won't try to explain that the Plum Tree Inn isn't in the wilds," Colin said.

Padgett grinned. "I'll have to get up to Maine when the weather warms up, if it ever does."

"Depends on how you define *warm*." Colin nodded toward the door. "Come on. Let's get out of here. I'll buy you a beer and listen to you bitch about the cold weather."

"Done."

While Padgett put away his laptop and monitors, Colin

checked his phone again. Still no response from Emma. He hadn't expected one, and the last thing he wanted was to bug her while she was on her retreat. He debated texting her that he wouldn't text her again, but it would be another interruption—assuming she even had her phone turned on.

Forget it.

Let her enjoy her time with the sisters.

Colin and Padgett walked to a waterfront restaurant crowded with people who weren't in law enforcement. Padgett refused to sit by a table overlooking the harbor. "Too damn cold," he said, agreeing instead to a table by a gaslit fire. He grinned at Colin as they sat down. "I'm not warming up to the frozen north, in case you haven't noticed."

"Helps to be on Yank's team."

"So far it's been interesting, I'll say that."

They had burgers and beer and watched some of a Bruins game on the television above the bar. Padgett was clearly preoccupied with whatever numbers rabbit trail he had been following. Colin left him to coffee and headed out for the short walk to Emma's waterfront apartment. It was small for the two of them but at least reasonably roach-free. She had rented it last March when she arrived in Boston to join Yank's team. Colin had been posing as an arms buyer then, deep inside the network of a Russian now in prison in California.

He pictured Emma when they'd met in September on the grounds of her former convent.

She'd been all set to shoot him.

He smiled, trying to picture her now, in the convent where she had once expected to live out her life. Sometimes he had no trouble imagining her as Sister Brigid. Other times he couldn't imagine it at all.

Tonight would be one of those other times.

The wind kicked up, and he was cold when he arrived at the

apartment. He had never stayed there without Emma. It still felt like her space, not their space, but that was fine with him. He tossed aside his jacket and got a beer out of the refrigerator—his six-pack one of the signs that he did, in fact, also live here.

He debated getting in touch with Mike. Was his brother still in Rock Point or had he gone to the Plum Tree? Or had he decided not to bother with his old friends and gone back up to the Bold Coast?

Colin remembered the day Mike had given him the keys to his cabin. *If I get eaten by a whale on the high seas, I need someone to burn down my cabin. You're it, Colin.*

He hadn't known if Mike had meant literally he wanted his brother to burn his cabin in the event of his demise, and he hadn't asked.

Mike lived simply and worked hard. He would be taking advantage of winter to get things done that he couldn't during summer. Refurbishing gear, painting, fixing, oiling. It was a life Colin knew, if not to the degree Mike did, but hadn't chosen for himself.

In some ways, he wasn't sure Mike had chosen his life as a guide and outfitter, either. It was more as if he had fallen into it after the army because he hadn't known what else to do, and because it allowed him to be something of a loner and keep family and friends at a distance.

Colin understood the drive toward solitude and isolation. Mike had never talked much about his years in the army, but they had to have taken a toll. It had taken Colin some time to recognize that his work as a deep-cover agent had taken its own kind of toll.

Maybe, he thought, Emma's decision to spend this time at her old convent was driven in part by her own need for solitude and isolation. Maybe the recent months of change and violence in her life had taken a toll that she was only now beginning to recognize and deal with.

Would it occur to her to talk to him about it?

It hadn't occurred to him to talk to her about the dangers he'd faced.

He sat on the couch with his beer. On his last visit with Mike on the Bold Coast a couple of summers ago, they had split a six-pack on the porch and watched kayakers in the cove. Mike hadn't said much. He seldom did. Colin had been on a short break in an undercover mission. His family had believed he worked at a desk at FBI headquarters in Washington.

Pretended to believe was more accurate, especially for Mike.

Colin's life had changed considerably since that last visit. For one thing, he was engaged to Emma. When he had been drinking beer with Mike, he hadn't even known she existed. Yet she had grown up in Heron's Cove, a few miles south of Rock Point, and was a Sharpe, a family of art detectives not unknown to the Donovans.

Although he had met her over the murder of a nun, he hadn't guessed she was herself a former novice with the Sisters of the Joyful Heart.

He hadn't planned to be in Rock Point this weekend, but he would head up there in the morning and satisfy himself that Mike's friends weren't going to be a problem.

He didn't finish his beer. The apartment wasn't as nunlike as when he'd first slept there, pillows lined up between them on the bed to create a barrier.

No barriers now, he thought, entering the tiny bedroom.

11

The scraggly fishing village of Rock Point, Maine, was just as Naomi imagined it would be. Fog, lobster boats and Donovans. Darkness had settled over New England but the stubborn fog that gripped the coast had turned everything gray. Even the white snow was streaked with gray shadows.

Freaking bleak was what it was.

Her driver pulled in front of a sprawling house out from the village center but still, technically, on the harbor. Made sense since the house—supposedly a former sea captain's house, complete with a widow's walk—was now the Rock Point Harbor Inn. According to its website, the innkeepers were Rosemary and Frank Donovan. There was no photo of the couple, so Naomi wasn't positive they were related to Mike. But what were the odds?

Booking a room in Rock Point had seemed like a good idea at Heathrow.

Flying to Boston and driving up to Maine instead of flying to Nashville and driving to her favorite bar for barbecue and bourbon hadn't seemed like such a great idea, but Reed had convinced her to join him at the Plum Tree tomorrow. They weren't prepared to receive guests tonight, and shaving off a flight had seemed pragmatic at midday British Standard Time.

The five-hour time difference between England and Maine was making for a very long day.

Of course, she could have booked a room at an airport hotel and driven up from Boston in the morning. Reed had offered to pay for changing her flight from Nashville, but she had declined. She hadn't been 100 percent certain that she would go to Maine until he was out of sight, dropping off his car and heading to his own flight. *You'll be there*, he had told her.

Annoying as that comment had been, he was right. She *would* be there.

Too late to change her mind now, she thought as she tipped her driver, grabbed her suitcase and headed up a shoveled, sanded but nonetheless treacherous-looking walk.

She'd hired a car only because she was too tired to make the almost two-hour drive herself. She wouldn't need a car once she was at the Plum Tree.

She managed to hit a small ice patch and almost fall. *Almost* being key because it meant she didn't fall. An image flashed of her holding her broken wrist, explaining to a Donovan or Donovan friend who she was as they waited for an ambulance to take her to the ER. She wasn't hiding her identity. She just didn't want to fall in front of these people.

She mounted the steps to a wraparound porch and took a moment to get her heartbeat back to normal after her almost-fall. She finished the bottle of water her driver had provided. It didn't eliminate jet lag and travel fatigue, but it helped. She didn't need to check her email. She had checked it a billion times at Heathrow, in Boston and in the car. She'd had the sense not to try to email Mike. She'd looked him up on the internet, though. He had a terse website for people who wanted to book his services as a Maine outfitter and wilderness guide. There was one photo of him standing next to a red canoe on a rocky beach.

He had always told her he would be going back to Maine after the army.

The porch light came on.

Someone must have noted her arrival. She slipped her empty water bottle into a sleeve on her compact, cleverly designed suitcase. It didn't have wheels and fit everything she needed for a typical business trip. She didn't quite know what this trip was. Business? Personal? Both?

Right now, she needed a warm bed and sleep. The driver had told her about his passion for downhill skiing. She hadn't had the heart to tell him she had been on a plane for hours and hours, after breakfast with a suspicious FBI agent, after helping an injured Brit who worked for a mysterious international art thief *and* after finding out she was supposed to go to Maine, where she would likely see an ex-soldier she had hoped never to see again—and who hoped never to see her again, either.

And now she was *in* Maine.

Not only in Maine, but in said ex-soldier's hometown, thanks to her bright idea as she had waited in the lounge at Heathrow.

Then he opened the door to the inn and she thought she was hallucinating. Seriously. Jet lag and sleep deprivation could do strange things to people.

So could being face-to-face with Mike Donovan.

"Hello, Naomi."

"Mike."

His blue eyes steadied on her. "I didn't expect you to show up here."

If anything, he was more hard-edged than she remembered. "I didn't expect it myself. It seemed like a good idea in England. You're catching me at a disadvantage. I'm on London time."

He stepped back from the door, allowing her to enter a cheer-ful, tidy entryway. He had his arms crossed on his chest, and the overhead light caught the angles of his face.

Naomi's step faltered, but she didn't berate herself.

No one took her breath away like Mike did.

"Why are you here?" he asked.

He knew why. She could see it in his eyes. "Reed's been in touch, hasn't he?"

"Yesterday."

"He didn't tell me about his plans until this morning."

"He was in England?"

She nodded. "Are you going to join him at the Plum Tree?"

"Maybe."

There was no *maybe* with Mike. He was black-and-white. Yes or no. Go or don't go. But Naomi didn't press him for an an-swer. She shivered, more for effect than because she was actu-ally shivering. "I swear there are icicles in the air."

"Ocean effect."

"I'm not home in Nashville, am I?"

"My folks own this place. They've turned in for the night. I'll get you settled. Leave your suitcase here for now." Again that steely-eyed gaze. "You can tell me what you've been up to since I saw you last."

Last being the helicopter ride after he had rescued her from some very nasty people on what had turned out to be her final day in Afghanistan. When the helicopter landed, Mike had looked at her in her stretcher. *Never again, Naomi,* he'd said, then hopped off the helicopter, leaving her to the paramedics and her fate.

"Did you come down from the Bold Coast today?" she asked, easing the thick strap off her shoulder and letting her suitcase drop onto the floor by the front door.

A nod as he started down the hall ahead of her.

She gathered she was to follow him. "It's a long drive here, isn't it? I looked it up on the internet." She went down the hall, wondering about her boots; but she saw he was wearing boots, too. Not city boots like hers. L.L.Bean, probably. "Did you come by boat? I get seasick. I used to go canoeing once in a while. I don't think I like the water."

Mike stopped in the doorway to a big country kitchen and turned to her. "I came by truck."

"Got it. I feel like I'm about to start babbling. Or is it too late? Am I already babbling?"

He didn't smile. Not a lot of a sense of humor there. He turned and entered the kitchen. She hesitated, but realized she had few choices. Middle of the night. Fog. Cold. Maine. A suspicious Mike Donovan.

"What prompted you to come here?" he asked.

"I told you, because Reed—"

"Rock Point."

She shrugged. "I thought I'd take a look. I couldn't see much on the drive in since it's dark and foggy. Maine is beautiful, isn't it? I'm looking forward to seeing the coast in daylight." She eased off her Barbour jacket. It provided some warmth, but a down parka would have been better. "I'm not here to cause trouble for you, Mike."

"That doesn't mean you won't."

It was the old dance between them. He didn't trust her not to cause trouble. He had come to believe it was the way she was wired. It didn't matter that she'd saved his damn life, discovering important details after he and his team had been deployed on a dangerous mission, alerting them—unwittingly putting herself at risk as a result.

That had held no water with Mike. He'd known her actions would come back to haunt her, and they had, two months later. He'd had to pluck her out of harm's way, and that was that. She'd become a magnet for trouble. Reckless. A bad-luck charm.

Two mad nights together in Washington in between the

screwed-up mission and her rescue hadn't affected his attitude toward her, at least not for the good. Falling into bed had addressed the simmering tension between them through sex instead of a shared six-pack, a game of darts or pistols at dawn, but it had resolved nothing.

Then no sooner had she arrived back in Afghanistan, she was snatched out of a restaurant and threatened with certain death. Mike had rescued her, but the incident had confirmed his suspicions about her.

It was hard to argue with him once he had his mind made up, and he had it made up about her.

That she'd saved his life didn't count for much when her actions—in his view—had endangered her own life.

As far as she was concerned, they were even. She'd saved him. He'd saved her.

Assuming they were keeping score.

"I'm not here to regain your trust," she told him now, in the Maine hometown he had missed so much.

He glanced at her. "That's good."

She reminded herself she was the one who had decided to come here.

His eyes were narrowed on her. She hadn't experienced such open suspicion and skepticism in a long time. "Hungry?" he asked.

Her breakfast in the Cotswolds seemed like a dream. How many hours ago had she sat across from Ted Kavanagh with her porridge, fruit, yogurt and croissant with York farm gooseberry jam? She'd only picked at her meal on the plane.

"I am hungry, actually, but don't go to any trouble."

"Too late." He gave her a quick wink, if only to take the edge off his words. "We've got fish chowder and pie. Would that suit you?"

"Sounds great. What kind of pie?"

"Wild blueberry."

"Did you pick the blueberries yourself?"

"My mother did."

A reminder that this was his home, his family. Naomi gri-maced inwardly, regretting her impulsive decision to come to Rock Point, but there was nothing to be done about it now. She didn't even have her own car. Did they have cabs in this little town? Where else would she go this late at night? She supposed she could show up at the Plum Tree and see if she could come early. But she was exhausted and she was here, about to have chowder and pie. Might as well get seeing Mike again out of the way, before the meetings with Reed and his crew.

"What's the difference between fish chowder and clam chow-der?" she asked, sitting at a square table with a vase of realistic-looking faux daffodils in the middle.

Mike pulled open the refrigerator. "One's made with fish and one's made with clams."

"Got it. I didn't know if *fish* covered everything that swims." She smiled. "Fish chowder and wild blueberry pie. Can't get much more Maine than that."

He made no comment as he withdrew a glass container. Even if she had a mind to, Naomi was too beat to offer to help, and Mike seemed comfortable and self-assured in the inn's kitchen. He scooped the chowder into a bowl and microwaved it while he got out the pie and sliced a piece onto a plate.

Drooping as she was with jet lag and fatigue, Naomi still man-aged to relish the chowder and pie, her first meal in Maine and perfect. She wished she could talk to Mike like an old friend. They could chat about Rock Point and his family, and what Ted Kavanagh and Reed Cooper were up to—and what it had to do with him, or, for that matter, with Oliver York and his farm in the Cotswolds. She thought of the man she had helped that morning—had it only been that morning?—and hoped he was all right. She hadn't thought of asking him for his contact information until she was well on her way to Heathrow with

Reed Cooper. She had no way to get in touch with the injured Englishman, particularly if she didn't want to draw attention to herself. Head injuries were notoriously deceptive. She hoped he had seen the wisdom of visiting a doctor.

"I remember you have three younger brothers," she said, dragging herself out of her wandering thoughts. "Do they all live in Rock Point?"

"More or less."

"One is an FBI agent, as I recall, right?"

"Uh-huh."

"He's not based in Maine, though, is he?"

Mike leaned back against the kitchen counter. "Are you asking because you don't know or because you don't want me to know you know?"

His suspicion irritated her, but she pushed it aside. "Just making conversation."

"Sure, Naomi."

"You mentioned your brothers when we knew each other in Afghanistan."

By *knew each other* she included *slept with each other*, which Mike obviously got. He looked at her. "I remember."

His tone, his deep blue eyes, his stance communicated where his mind was—on their nights together in Washington. It was three years ago but time seemed irrelevant. She could have been in his arms yesterday, or that morning. There was no explaining what she felt now.

"What are your plans for tomorrow?" he asked.

The pragmatic question broke through her fog of memory and feelings best forgotten. She pushed her pie plate to one side. "I don't have a car, obviously, so I'll have to figure out how to get to the Plum Tree. I wanted to swing through Heron's Cove on my way."

"Other direction."

"I know. I checked the map when I was waiting at Heathrow. Heron's Cove looks cute from photos I saw on the internet."

"Why were you looking up Heron's Cove on the internet?"

"Why shouldn't I?"

"You don't do anything by happenstance, Naomi."

She felt caught, as if she'd done something wrong. In a way, she had. She should have at least kept her mouth shut. On the other hand, what was she hiding? She got to her feet, scooping up her chowder bowl and pie plate. "I read about Sharpe Fine Art Recovery and Emma Sharpe," she said casually. "She and your brother Colin are engaged, aren't they?"

Mike drew away from the counter. "I know you're an intel type and you like to know everything, but why are you looking into Emma and my brother?"

"As you suggest, it's what I do." She set her dishes in the sink. She was twitchy and yet her eyelids were heavy with fatigue given her very long day. "The Sharpes sound fascinating. Do you approve of Emma?"

"As what?"

"A sister-in-law."

"Emma's cool." Mike seemed to debate whether to say more. "I wasn't sure about her at first. The Sharpes are high profile and Colin isn't. She's an expert in art crimes. Whole different world."

"Must be fun going to a museum with her."

"Did Ted Kavanagh ask you about Emma and Colin?"

The question took her somewhat by surprise. "Reed told you he invited Kavanagh to his Maine get-together? Interesting."

"Have you been in touch with Kavanagh?"

"I saw both him and Reed in England. This morning, in fact." She left it at that. "I can wash the dishes."

"I'll take care of them."

She realized suddenly how close he was. "I remember you telling me about Maine and how much I'd like it. Once I was here, you would say, I wouldn't think twice about the cold-weather months."

"Not true?"

She smiled. "Maybe if I had wool socks."

"You can borrow a pair of mine."

"Ha. That would be something. Me in Big Foot wool socks." But her humor—her attempt at lightheartedness—dissipated as fast as it had bubbled up, and she lifted her eyes to his. "Mike... I'm sorry I came here. I didn't realize the Frank and Rosemary Donovan who own this place were your parents."

Mike studied her a moment. "What else is going on, Naomi?"

She fought a yawn. She could have curled up on the floor in front of the sink and fallen asleep for the night. Instead she had Mike Donovan, a former Special Forces soldier, interrogating her. At least it seemed that way. Maybe with a night's sleep it would have seemed like a normal conversation. But she doubted it.

"Kavanagh's as closemouthed as ever. I don't know what his game is with Reed. He says he's still an FBI agent. I have no reason to doubt him. That's all."

"All you're saying. Not all you know."

"I don't answer to you, Mike."

"No, you don't."

She angled a look at him. "We're not off to a good start, are we?"

"About what I expected."

She sighed, less self-conscious than when he'd surprised her by answering the door. "You aren't the same Mike Donovan I knew in Afghanistan, are you? I thought you might have matured in the past few years. Since you came home."

"Matured?" He grinned. "What does that mean?"

"Gained perspective and objectivity, learned not to nurse grudges and hold people to impossible standards."

"Like what?"

"People make mistakes."

"Yes, they do."

His tone said that she had been one of his mistakes. She ran a hand through her hair, felt knots and tangles—a hopeless rat's nest after her travels. Mike, she noticed, wasn't giving much away about what he was thinking, certainly not what he was feeling. "You're not budging, are you?" She shook her head. "Honestly, Mike. I'm not an enemy invading your turf. I'm an old friend from a difficult time in both our lives."

"I'll budge when you tell me the truth about why you're here."

"I have told you the truth."

"Just not all of it. Nothing new, is it?" He stood straight. "Come on. I'll show you up to your room."

Her room was at the top of carpeted stairs and looked out on the harbor. The fog was clearing, a few stars appearing in the night sky. For a moment, Naomi thought she could hear the tide, then decided that was impossible given the distance and the shut-tight window. More likely it was the wind.

Mike had insisted on carrying her suitcase. He set it on a luggage rack.

She glanced around the attractive room, taking in the homey furnishings and cheerful seacoast colors. "Do you visit Rock Point often?" she asked.

"I help out here when I can."

"Must be fun to come down by boat, especially if you don't get seasick. Did you ever get seasick, or are you born with your sea legs as a Maine Donovan?"

"I don't think about it." He walked over to the windows, pulled the drapes.

"That's all it takes? What about fog, rain, cold weather, giant waves? Do you ever get scared out on the water?"

He frowned at her. "What are you talking about?"

"Being on a boat on the ocean."

"Naomi, Naomi." He moved from the window. "You never stop, do you? No, I don't get scared out on the water."

"Or seasick?"

He didn't answer. He opened the door to the adjoining bathroom, flipped on a light and took a quick look inside. Satisfied, he turned off the light and shut the door.

"You wish I'd spent the night in Boston," Naomi said.

"I wish you'd gone home altogether."

She rolled her eyes. "It's not like I'm an ax murderer."

Not so much as a hint of a smile. "Think of the people you know, Naomi. You live in a world of trouble. I don't want you to bring that world to my family."

"I'm not. I won't. I'm here because I wanted to see Rock Point and was on the other side of the Atlantic when I booked a room at this place—which also happens to be the only real inn in town. And I'm in Maine because of Reed, not because of you. That's all." She felt blood rush to her face. "Damn, Mike. The last time I saw you, I was half in love with you. Can't you allow a girl some emotional closure?"

"Nice try. You're not here for emotional closure."

"Must be nice to be perfect," she muttered, jet lag getting the better of her. High emotion wasn't the best way to handle herself with this man. She'd figured that out within two minutes of meeting him three years ago. That hadn't changed.

"Never said I was perfect," he said.

"Good, because you're not. You're an unforgiving SOB."

"Hold that thought."

Now there was a hint of a smile. It almost undid her. She nodded to a pottery pitcher on the dresser, decorated with what she guessed were hand-painted blueberries. "When do wild blueberries ripen in Maine?"

"August."

"Do you have wild blueberries on the Bold Coast?"

"There's a patch next to my cabin."

"I wonder what that must be like," Naomi said half to her-self. "Picking blueberries on the Maine coast under the August sun. I can picture it, and I haven't seen the coast yet in daylight."

"A lot of snow and ice right now."

"Always the skunk at the picnic, huh, Mike?"

He didn't answer. Instead he stood close to her and tucked a stray curl behind her ear. "Where were you last August, Naomi?"

His unexpected touch and the softness of his voice melted her knees. He stood back, and she sank onto the edge of the bed. "I was at home in Nashville the first half of August. On the road the second half. I attended a conference in Denver."

"You're always working, aren't you?"

"Making a living. I don't have a trust fund to fall back on." Reed Cooper did, which she and Mike both knew. "Business is good, though. No complaints. No regrets, either. I knew it was time to make a change when I left the State Department. I don't look back. Do you regret leaving the army when you did?"

"No," he said quietly, walking toward the door.

She fingered a fluffy comforter folded up at the foot of the bed. It would come in handy, given the modest heat in the room. She was on Mike's turf and couldn't let him get under her skin—annoy her, remind her how they had seduced each other three years ago. That was how she had decided to think of their brief, fiery love affair. She didn't know how he thought of it. She'd never asked and never would.

He had his hand on the doorknob as he turned back to her. "Are you happy, Naomi?"

She let go of the comforter and grinned at him, pretending he wasn't serious—that his question was another attempt to get under her skin. "You should see me on karaoke night at my fa-vorite Nashville bar. My pals and I have a great time. Singing, hooting, hollering. Happy. When I'm in town. That's not often these days."

"Do you ever think about settling down?"

"As in a husband, kids, a dog and a nine-to-five job?"

The barest smile. "Something like that."

"My sweet, crazy mama would welcome me into her sewing business." But Mike didn't laugh, and Naomi wondered if her flippancy was getting on his nerves. "What about you, Mike? Is living out on the Bold Coast as a wilderness guide your dream life?"

"Close enough."

"Why not Rock Point?"

He shrugged. "I moved into my grandfather's cabin when I got out of the army. I figured I'd fix it up and rent it out, and I ended up staying."

"This is all more awkward than I thought it would be. Being in your world."

"You're here because of Reed." Mike tugged open the door. "I'll give you a ride to the Plum Tree in the morning. You can figure out what to do after that."

"The two of us together—Reed will want an explanation."

She hadn't meant it seriously, but Mike steadied his gaze on her. "Figure out a story that suits you, then. That shouldn't be too hard. You're good at stories."

"Jackass."

He grinned. "You and my brothers are going to get along fine. They'll join us for breakfast. I'm down the hall if you need anything."

She smiled. "Lucky me."

He winked at her and was gone.

She didn't breathe again until the door shut behind him.

Weirdly restless, Naomi couldn't fall asleep. She had peeled off her travel clothes, washed her face, brushed her teeth and crawled into bed under the comforter. One minute she was on the plane, another minute she was eating porridge and black-

berry compote, walking in the bucolic Cotswolds, helping injured Martin Hambly into the dovecote.

She tossed and turned for a while longer, then turned on
the light, sat up in bed with her laptop and looked up chicken
breeds on the internet.

She decided the rooster who had awakened her at her Cotswolds pub that morning was a speckled Sussex.

Or not.

She checked the Maine weather for the weekend.

Cold. Chance of snow.

What else had she expected?

I didn't grow up in a Norman Rockwell painting, Mike had told
her. *Rock Point is a real place.*

It had to be to have produced him.

Ted Kavanagh was probably right and she was playing with
fire.

"What else is new?" she asked aloud, then shut her laptop and
set it on the nightstand. She switched off the light and crawled
back under the comforter.

This time, she was positive she could hear the steady, rhyth-
mic wash of the tide.

Reed Cooper hadn't told her everything on the drive to
Heathrow about his reasons for this get-together at the Plum
Tree. She had good instincts for when pieces were missing from
a story, even if she didn't know what they were. Reed was confident and smooth, but she'd noticed his tight grip on the wheel
earlier today, the hard set to his jaw.

Yeah. Something was up.

Naomi concentrated on the sounds of the ocean. A good
night's sleep, and she would be ready in the morning to deal
with ex-soldiers, rogue FBI agents and Maine wilderness guides.

12

Emma lay in the dark on a cold wide-board floor. She hadn't moved in what might have been hours but she suspected had been considerably less than that. But she'd been here for hours, in this room—bound at first, aching but relatively unharmed.

She was alone, at least in her makeshift prison cell.

She could hear the ocean and let the sounds wash over her, as if she were lying on a sandy beach on a hot summer night. After a few minutes, she sat up and leaned against a plaster wall, stretching her legs out in front of her. She listened to the waves, any thoughts and emotions flowing with the tide, never staying, never overtaking her.

She tucked her knees under her chin. She needed to stay warm. She was in an unheated barn or shed—some kind of outbuilding. Bound, barely able to breathe, she had survived the short drive to this place. Her attacker had dumped her in here. Out of the trunk, straight into the shed—like unloading a heavy sack of road sand in one swift motion.

That meant a driveway or road was close to the room's single door.

A long list of places she could be. But did it even matter?

Was there more than one attacker? She hadn't heard anyone else in the car, but someone could have been tucked up front, stayed silent—or she hadn't been able to hear a passenger from the trunk. She was fairly certain only one person had dumped her in the shed. No help.

Man? Woman?

She couldn't say for certain.

She'd managed to untangle herself from the blanket first, working deliberately, careful not to thrash and make her situation worse, knot herself inside the shroud of fleece. Once free, she had tackled the bounds on her hands and feet. Simple bungee cords, enough to restrain her temporarily but not for long. It hadn't been difficult to get them off. Her attacker must have known it wouldn't be.

Finally able to move and breathe freely, she had examined herself for any injuries, in case her mind was playing tricks on her or she had been drugged without realizing it. But there was nothing except for bruises on her right side from being tossed in the car and into the shed. No nausea, spinning head or other signs of having been drugged or incurred permanent damage from the choke hold.

She'd been locked up and was relatively unharmed. What did that mean? What did it say about her attacker's intentions?

It was too dark to know for certain but she doubted there was food or water in her makeshift prison cell. If she didn't find a way out...

Don't think about that now.

A ray of light took her by surprise. It came from above her. She looked up and saw the sliver of moon shining in the clearing night sky, through a window in the rafters. She hadn't noticed it with the fog. It was a normal-size window but installed on its side, as if it had been lying around and put to use. What did that tell her about where she was? The owner was practical, frugal—or had been. The window could have been installed decades ago. The building could be on property now owned by a wealthy summer resident.

Emma fixed her gaze on the moon. If she could climb up to the window, she could figure out where she was and whether her attacker was in the immediate vicinity and had allies. She could even get out through the window. But it was a good twelve feet up there, and she was wobbly. She needed to be smart about her tactics. Falling and breaking a leg wasn't an option.

She shivered but at least she had her coat. Her hat and gloves were gone, along with her cell phone. She wrapped the blanket over her head like a kerchief but shuddered at the memory of nearly suffocating.

Why not kill me outright?

Did her attacker plan to come back and question her? Was this part of a plan to get ransom? She was a member of an elite FBI unit, a Sharpe. She knew the identity of an international art thief who had stolen art worth millions.

Where is Oliver's package?

Was *that* what the attack was about? It felt, oddly, both impulsive and planned. Perhaps her attacker had arrived to collect the package about the same time she had and had been prepared to grab anyone in the way.

None of that mattered now. She had to focus her energy on getting out of here.

She shut her eyes. She couldn't hear any vehicles, boats or people, but on a cold New England night in February, that didn't tell her much. Shivering, she tucked her hands into her coat pockets. She felt something, then smiled—her first smile in hours—as she discovered a small bag of dried fruit and nuts in her left coat pocket.

Fill us at daybreak with your love, that all our days we sing for joy.

The motto of the Sisters of the Joyful Heart burst into her mind. The words were from Psalm 90. She could see the sisters working in the convent gardens, going about their daily chores, teaching, assessing damaged art. They were real women with real lives, and she appreciated her time with them. But she was no longer Sister Brigid, no longer a part of that world.

She could feel Colin close to her, hear him breathing as if he were with her here in the dark and the cold. This was her life now. She was an FBI agent, and she was engaged to a man she loved with all her heart.

Had he managed to get back to Boston tonight? Had he and Sam Padgett gone out for a beer together?

Was Colin home now, in their bed, thinking of her?

He wouldn't know she had canceled her convent retreat. She hadn't had a chance to tell him.

She shut her eyes, listening again to the ocean. When Colin figured out she was missing, he would be angry, but he would also be focused and determined.

And he would find her.

13

Finian had breakfast in his room. Ruthie Burns set a tray on a small round table in front of the windows. "A lovely morning, isn't it? Spring's in the air, I can tell you." She stood back from the steaming food. "Here you go now, Father. Boiled eggs, toast, grilled tomatoes and mushrooms and a nice pot of tea. That will do you for whatever adventures Mr. York has in mind, don't you think?"

"I do indeed."

"Can I get you anything else?"

"This is perfect, thank you."

"It's almost warm enough to open windows. I'm ready for spring. The hillsides soon will be covered in daffodils."

"What a sight that must be." Finian helped himself to a bit of mushroom. "How is Mr. Hambly today?"

She sniffed. "Not right as rain, I can tell you that."

She insisted on pouring tea before she withdrew. She seemed

to enjoy having company in the house. Finian didn't want to disappoint her by doing too much for himself, but he was used to being on his own. He sat at the table, relishing the sunlight streaming through the windows. He had opened the drapes before Ruthie had arrived and could do the job for him. He noticed a garden past the terrace, its established beds, fountain and statuary calling up images of times long past—times, he thought, that were no quieter than now.

He ate his breakfast, as delicious as it looked. He hadn't seized the moment to go to London out of a sense of priestly or brotherly duty, or even for fun in the big city. He had seized the moment out of mad curiosity, because he'd known about Aoife O'Byrne's show and Oliver York's fascination with her. Finian supposed his curiosity was the natural product of his friendships with FBI agents, but he wouldn't blame Emma Sharpe and Colin Donovan for his own decisions, good or bad.

After breakfast, instead of heading down the hall to find his host, Finian stepped outside, inhaling deeply the brisk morning air. Vines and branches drooped from trellises and trees, awaiting the return of spring. Raindrops glistened on an ornate, evergreen-painted round table and chairs set up on the yellow-stone terrace. The sun would soon dry the raindrops, but Finian had seen the forecast. Clouds and rain would move in again before nightfall. He would appreciate the sun while it lasted. The brutal Maine winter was an experience, but he was glad to get a break from the relentless cold, the nor'easters that brought wind, snow, sleet and freezing rain. He had learned to dread the words *wintry mix* in the forecast.

He crossed soft, wet grass to a black iron gate. Unlatching it took some doing, but he finally got it to creak open. He suspected it hadn't been used in a while. He stepped onto a pebbled path, his sturdy walking shoes suited to the conditions. He passed a stone fountain, a chipped statue of a graceful angel and mulched, carefully tended beds. Busy with the girls and work, he and Sally had only managed pots at their cottage in the Kerry hills but had dreamed of planting gardens. He'd wanted to hire a landscaper but she'd wanted to do the work themselves.

Ah, Sally.

Sometimes, still, his heart ached for her, but no longer did it undermine the peace he felt, the acceptance that his kind and loving wife had gone to God.

He went through another gate and found himself face-to-face with a gray-haired man in a worn jacket unzipped over a wool sweater. "You must be Father Bracken," the man said. "Martin Hambly. I'm sorry I wasn't able to greet you last night."

He didn't look as if he were in any condition to greet a guest now. His quiet formality stood in stark contrast to his ashen, ragged look. Being up and about was clearly costing him, but Finian greeted him with a smile. "A pleasure to meet you, Mr. Hambly. I was sorry to hear about your fall. How are you feeling this morning?"

"Dodgy but better than at this time yesterday. Ruthie is seeing to you? If there's anything I can do…" His voice trailed off, and he looked as if only pride were keeping him from grabbing hold of the fence to steady himself. He smiled feebly. "Apologies."

"Is there a doctor I can take you to in the village?" Finian asked with concern.

"I'll rally. A passing moment. I decided fresh air would be therapeutic."

"The sun is irresistible."

Martin's hands were trembling visibly, and he licked his lips, as if to keep himself from groaning aloud. Swelling and bruising on his neck disappeared under a bandage and his jacket collar. "I thought I might walk down to the dovecote where I fell, but that's a bit optimistic, I'm afraid," he said. "I can get back to my cottage without collapsing." He gave a look of pure distaste. "I hate to be a bother."

"I can walk with you—"

"No, no. Thank you, Father. I'll manage on my own. It's good for me. It was a rough night, but I'd have died in my chair if there were anything seriously wrong with me. I'm much improved this morning. Good to be back on my feet."

"Is there anything I can do?"

"I would like to thank the woman who helped me. She might have stayed at the pub last night. I remember little of my fall and its aftermath, but I remember her. If you happen to see her, would you give her my regards? She's American—young, with dark, curly hair and more energy than I could drum up when I was eighteen never mind sixty-two and bloodied. She handled herself well in an unexpected situation."

Finian would say it had been an emergency, not merely an "unexpected situation," but he was struck by the similarity of the description of Martin's rescuer with the woman asking about Aoife in the London gallery on Wednesday.

"This woman urged me to get medical attention, too," Hambly added, matter-of-fact. He touched a hand to his neck, his eyes half-closed. He shivered, almost like an involuntary shudder. He made an attempt at a smile. "Every minute is better, I assure you. A walk and sunshine do help."

Not enough, Finian thought. "You look as if you could drop here on the ground. Can I help you get back to your cottage?"

"I'll manage, thank you. Again, my apologies."

He staggered down a gentle hill toward a stone wall. Finian noticed a honey-stone cottage through a gap in the stone wall, tucked amid bare-limbed trees and shrubs. He waited, watching the Englishman until he reached the cottage and disappeared inside.

Oliver York grunted, approaching Finian from the main house. "Hambly is bloody stubborn, but I don't have to tell you. You've seen for yourself."

"Stubbornness can be a positive trait."

"Not when a head injury is involved."

Oliver was dressed in a heavy wool sweater, faded corduroy trousers and muddy wellies. He put his hand on a waist-high stone sculpture of Celtic knots and spirals. "I should pound this thing into dust. It's an early work. Total mess."

"I rather like it," Finian said.

"You would with all the Celtic symbols. I was going to do a cross, but I decided it would look too much like a tombstone marking the spot where we buried the dog." He nodded toward the cottage. "Martin's avoiding me. Did you notice how he got wobbly once he spotted me?"

Finian smiled. "He was wobbly before he saw you."

"He's frustrated that he can't remember the details of his fall, but it doesn't occur to him that's a good reason to see a doctor— not to mention the gash on his neck and a night in the elements. Lucky he didn't die of exposure. Imagine explaining *that* to the local police. Worse yet, to our FBI friends." Oliver drew his hand from the sculpture. "I have a stonework studio in the dovecote where Martin fell. I've hardly stepped foot in it this winter. I plan to shut it down. Martin can turn the entire dovecote into a potting shed. A puttering shed, my grandfather used to call it. My grandmother loved it there."

"Did you show your studio to Wendell Sharpe when he visited?"

"Now, why would I do that?"

So innocent, Finian thought. He knew, however, that Oliver had taunted Wendell Sharpe by sending him a small stone cross after each art theft, claiming the theft as his work. The stones were inscribed with a Celtic cross depicting a traditional, rudimentary image of Saint Declan, one of Ireland's patron saints, and his bell, which legend said had led him to the south Irish coast, where he had established a monastery and performed miracles.

Few people knew about the crosses. The Sharpes, of course, and the FBI, if only because Emma was both a Sharpe and an agent. And Aoife O'Byrne, because she had received one herself. It had ended up in the hand of a dead woman in Boston last fall. Finian hadn't seen Aoife since then. From his momentary encounter with her in London, he would guess she had recovered from her ordeal in Boston.

"Do you believe Martin's fall was an accident, Oliver?"

He narrowed his gaze, as if the sun were in his eyes, studying his guest, debating his answer. "No," he said at last.

"Perhaps the police should have a look at his injury."

"But I could be wrong," Oliver said, as if Finian hadn't spoken. "We have a ram who likes to escape."

"As rams are wont to do," Finian said.

"You and your brother grew up on a farm. Do you ever wish you'd stayed on the farm, Finian?"

"There are days."

"It seems like a simpler life, but it isn't. This farm covers its costs but I doubt it will ever turn a profit. Fortunately I don't need it to. I can't imagine if I did since I have no head for farming. I'm happy we can employ people who love it." He stood back from the statue and looked out at the rolling fields. "I like the views here. They comfort the soul."

"This was your grandparents' home," Finian said.

"Yes." Oliver squinted into the sun. "They took me in. They did the best they could with me after my parents were killed." He spoke quietly, keeping his gaze on the gentle hills. "I followed Martin everywhere in the months after their murder. He never once told me to buzz off. He was steady and uncompromising. He taught me to get on with it. Do the work, live my life. He refused to let me give in to self-pity. The British stiff upper lip and all that, I suppose."

"He seems like a good man."

"We never spoke of the investigation. My grandparents left it to the police and saw no benefit to supplementing their efforts. *Interference*, they called it. Discovering the perpetrators of my parents' murder and my torment wasn't their job. For them, there was no such thing as closure. There was only carrying on. It was a matter of will, and perhaps of faith, too."

Finian touched raindrops glistening on a Celtic knot on the sculpture. "They sound like good people," he said.

"The best. After they were gone, I had the means to hire private investigators, and I did. Martin didn't dissuade me. He simply asked me what I expected to accomplish. It was a sincere question, and he was deliberate about saying 'expected' rather than 'hoped.' I had no answer."

"Have you ever taken time to mourn your parents' death?"

Oliver shifted his gaze to Finian. "I mourned my parents in the ruins of the Scottish church where their killers left me." A coldness had come into his voice—an emotional distance that, Finian suspected, kept the small, terrified, traumatized boy inside him at bay. "I knew they were dead. I knew what had happened to them. Even at eight, I had no doubt, no illusions. I was never in denial."

"Then you cried for them," Finian said.

"Ha. Tears. As if they equal mourning. Have a good sob and all will be well."

"Does that mean you didn't cry?"

Oliver smirked. "So asks a priest, a man who himself has suffered terrible loss. You don't fool me, Father Bracken. You know there is no cure for my grief, by willpower, faith or the arrest and conviction of the perpetrators. My grief is with me every moment of every day, no matter that I do get on with my life."

"It's a part of you."

"It's a permanent injury to my soul. I live with it as I would an amputated limb."

Finian nodded and stepped back from the sculpture. "Yes. I see that you do."

Oliver pointed at him, then laughed, an unexpected, cheeky laugh that lit up his eyes. "Touché, my friend." He made a face.

"Can you wear that priest getup for a walk into the village, or do you have sweats and tennis shoes tucked in your bag? I thought we could wander to the pub and see if anyone there knows anything about this woman who rescued Martin yesterday."

"I have good walking shoes. I can leave whenever you're ready."

"Excellent. I'd like to find this woman and thank her myself." Oliver scooped up a small clump of sodden plant debris and tossed it into the garden. "I'll meet you at the side door in fifteen minutes."

He eased off back toward the house.

Finian lingered by the Celtic sculpture. He admired traditional Celtic symbols more than he understood them. He felt at home and himself when he saw them on a cross, a work of art, a bit of jewelry. He had visited Trinity College in Dublin to see the Book of Kells, a priceless medieval illuminated manuscript that was arguably the greatest example of early Celtic Christian art in existence. The sculpture didn't compare, but it wasn't supposed to.

He reminded himself that he and Oliver York weren't friends. Oliver had few, if any, real friends, apart from Martin Hambly and the rest of his staff.

Was Oliver in love with Aoife O'Byrne? Did he want to find out if Finian harbored any romantic feelings for her that could ultimately lead him out of the priesthood?

Was she the reason Oliver had extended the invitation to his Cotswolds farm?

Or was the man only looking to connect with people, however awkwardly?

He had peacemaking to do—with himself, with others, perhaps with God—and maybe he thought inviting an Irish priest here to his farm could help.

Finian touched the cold stone, the last of the raindrops drying in the sun. He traced the edge of a Celtic knot. It was as if Oliver had channeled the eight-year-old boy in the Scottish ruins when he had carved the symbols into the gray stone. It was that horrific experience, no doubt, that had propelled him into his solitary study of mythology, and into adopting a different identity.

Oliver Fairbairn. Oliver "fair child."

Finian turned back through the dormant garden.

He wished he could help Oliver. Right now, the best thing he could do was to walk to the village pub and see about the American woman.

The pub was a cluster of small buildings and a walled courtyard set off the village green, complete with ducks, bantams, a playground and a shallow brook with its own little footbridge. The sun was fighting gray clouds when Finian and Oliver entered the pub, cozy with low, beamed ceilings, a wood-topped bar and an open stone fireplace, lit against the February chill. Breakfast had finished being served in a separate room.

Oliver sat on a wood stool at the bar. This was his show. Finian sat next to him and kept quiet as Oliver chatted with the waitstaff and, then, the proprietors, a cheerful young English couple. Oliver was comfortable, good-humored and friendly, but, at the same time, reserved if not distant. His relationships, Finian realized, bounced on the surface, never went deep.

But he got what he wanted.

The American woman had stayed there one night. She'd had breakfast yesterday morning—prior to discovering Martin—with another guest, a man, also American.

Separate rooms.

Oliver had more difficulty prying their names from his friends, but he finally did, at least from the husband. The wife wouldn't budge.

Naomi MacBride and Ted Kavanagh.

Finian didn't recognize the names but he stuck on the descriptions of the pair. "Oliver, I saw them in London."

"Where in London?"

"They were at the gallery. Aoife's show. They didn't speak with each other." Finian spoke in a low voice. The waitstaff and the couple had returned to work in another room, and he and Oliver had the bar to themselves. "They fit the description of the pair who were here."

"FBI agents," Oliver said, with certainty.

"You saw them, too?"

"Mmm. I told Emma. She scoffed."

Oliver ordered two coffees and moved to a rough-wood table by the fire, motioning for Finian to join him. Reluctantly, Finian eased onto a cushioned bench opposite his British host.

"Did you speak with them?" Oliver asked.

"No, I didn't, I'm afraid."

"FBI agents," Oliver said again, as if that explained everything.

Finian frowned. "Where did you see them?"

"They were in the park near my apartment."

"Wouldn't Emma know if two FBI agents were…" Finian faltered, searching for the appropriate words. "Wouldn't she know if two agents were interested in speaking with you?"

Oliver grunted. "There's no indication they wanted to speak with me, is there?" He glanced at the fire, eyes narrowed, his keen intelligence in evidence. "They must have known I was still in London when they came here." He didn't look at Finian. "What does that tell you?"

"They wanted to see your farm? Speak with Martin without you?"

"Perhaps."

Finian reminded himself that the Englishman possessed a calculating mind that had helped him avoid arrest for a decade. No doubt he was alert to dangers, tricks and pursuit.

Their coffee arrived, delivered by the husband of the proprietor couple. Oliver thanked him and asked about business—the
pub was bustling, the inn naturally quiet this time of year. They
chatted about a quarrel over upcoming road improvements in
the village. In other words, Finian thought, Oliver was com-
municating that he wasn't pursuing more information about
the two Americans but also that he wasn't further explaining
his interest in them.

The proprietor withdrew, and Oliver poured coffee for himself then Finian. "I once dressed up as a priest. I missed my
wellies, and the collar drove me mad."

"Dare I ask why you dressed as a priest?"

He poured cream into his coffee. "For my mythology studies."

Finian doubted it. More likely for one of his heists.

Oliver drank some of his coffee, looking at ease, perhaps a
touch excited by having the names of the pair arguably following him. "You should consider leaving the priesthood, Finian.
You're going to get into trouble with your superiors. Mark my
words. What will they do? Exile you? Or are you already in
exile in Maine?"

"I follow my calling."

"Mmm. What if you discover that Aoife O'Byrne is your
calling?"

The fire crackled behind him, as if it were a warning. Finian
drank some of his own coffee. It was strong, hot, very good. If
only he could relax and enjoy himself, but he didn't thrive on
danger and adventure quite the way Oliver York obviously did.

"What about you and Aoife, Oliver?" Finian asked.

The question didn't seem to surprise him. "Am I in love with
her, do you mean? Well, who wouldn't be? She's beautiful, talented and temperamental, and she doesn't need love."

"We all need to love and be loved," Finian said simply.

"Isn't that why we have God?" Oliver held up a hand. "Sorry.
No theological discussions. I'm on the trail of FBI agents. What

if one or both pushed Hambly down that hillside? What if one did without the knowledge of the other? What does that say?" He paused, tapping the table with one finger as he considered. "What if they didn't do it but they know who did?" He took a breath. "I suppose neither could be responsible and they're on the trail of who is—someone who is responsible for other misdeeds."

"This is England. The FBI has no jurisdiction here."

He laughed, incredulous. "Oh, yes, and that will stop them."

"You're cynical," Finian said mildly.

"They could be after an American. I'll allow that. I wonder where they are now." He was silent a moment, then sat up straight. "Back to this notion of love. Honestly, I don't know if I would recognize love. Feeling it, giving it. I've been turned inward. I can't explain."

"Your parents and grandparents loved you, didn't they?"

"With all their hearts. I never doubted it, but that doesn't mean I took it in."

"Studying mythology must help you understand human nature."

"Keeps me busy, anyway." Oliver held his cup to his lips but didn't drink. "I know you're aware that I have...a past."

"Yes."

"Emma and Colin almost had me in Boston in the fall. Oliver Fairbairn nearly undid me. He can be a dolt." He drank some of his coffee and smiled. "Tweedy types often can be dolts, don't you think, Father Fin?"

"You realize I don't care for 'Father Fin,' don't you?"

The Englishman's green eyes sparked. "I expected as much."

But his mood darkened almost instantly, visibly as his shoulders slumped and he seemed transfixed by the flames. Finian found Oliver's vaults from cheekiness and soul-baring impossible to predict and suspected his English friend did, too. For a man so accustomed to being solitary and self-contained, soul-baring—openness, honesty—was a new experience, a foreign concept. Even without two Americans following him, such a change would be bound to make him volatile, uncertain, awkward.

"Aoife doesn't say she knows about my dual life but it's obvious she does."

"If she has no evidence…"

"No one has evidence." It obviously wasn't a point up for discussion. "You're the man she pines for, Fin. She likes to pretend if only you would come back to her that the two of you could have a cottage on the south Irish coast and small children running about. You'd peg out your washing on Saturday mornings and tumble down to the village pub together in the evening."

"Aoife has a full life in Dublin," Finian said, then smiled. "I doubt she has ever pegged out her washing."

"But she longs to. She longs to live in a quiet Irish village and lead a simple, traditional life. If she had to do it over again, I think she would stick to painting walls and the occasional shamrock for tourists and never mind being an internationally recognized artist."

Finian wasn't convinced, but he said nothing.

"I was always meant to be an only child. My parents had no desire to have more kids. It was to be the three of us." Oliver glanced out a small window next to their table, set into the thick stone edifice of the old pub. "I wonder how that day would have gone if I'd had a couple of brothers and sisters. Would we have ganged up on the bastards? Would they have chosen a different family to rob and murder, or would they have killed us all?"

"I wish I had answers for you."

"I wish you did, too, my friend." Oliver kept his gaze on the window. Chickens roamed on the pebbled driveway, near the courtyard entrance. "I cowered that day. My mother did her best to protect me. I hid behind my father's desk in the library. If I hadn't—if the two men had discovered me in the midst of their killing—I believe they would have killed me, too. They were on their way out of the apartment, no doubt afraid to linger after what they'd done. When they saw me…" He paused. "Taking me wasn't a planned act. They didn't have a chance to think."

Finian waited for him to go on, but he didn't. "I'm sorry, Oliver," he said quietly.

"Thank you." He shifted from the window. "I sometimes wonder if they're dead. I don't know which would be preferable. Dead, or out there, one day to be arrested and tried for their crimes."

"Would you recognize them?"

"I don't know. I like to think so. You lost your family in an accident. I don't know if it's any better. Such a tragedy can feel like God is coming after you."

"I know it can," Finian said.

"My parents and I were caught in the wrong place at the wrong time with a few sick, drugged-up blokes who wanted money. They thought the apartment was empty." Oliver pushed back in his chair but didn't get up. "This is a morose conversation for a sunny English morning. Change the subject, shall we? Turn our attention to the matters at hand. What do you think is going on with our Emma if she doesn't know about these two Americans?"

"Perhaps they aren't FBI agents, Oliver."

"I suppose it's possible. What if we have a fight among FBI agents on our hands? Or worse." Oliver's expression lightened. "I say *we* because you saw them in London. No reason to think they're following you, is there?"

"I can't imagine."

"Your friend Special Agent Donovan won't be pleased that you're here, will he?"

"I suspect not."

"I told Emma I invited you. Do you suppose she told him?"

"Without a doubt," Finian said.

"What do you do now, then, Fin? Call Colin about our American pair or take a long walk on the Oxfordshire Way?"

"I can do both. At the moment, I'm relieved Colin and Emma are across an ocean."

"So am I," Oliver muttered, then laughed as he got to his feet. "You have no idea how relieved."

"I'm getting an idea," Finian said, also getting up from the table.

"Better the FBI hounding me than bloody MI5."

Oliver didn't expand on that provocative statement as he came around the table and waved to the proprietor, who obviously kept a tab for his eccentric guest.

When they exited the pub, the sun was still shining, the day warming to springlike temperatures. Oliver took a deep breath. "It's good to be away from London. I was tempted to invite Aoife to join us. What do you suppose she'd have said?"

"One can only imagine."

"Ah, yes."

As they crossed the green, a lad who worked at the pub joined them. He angled his cigarette, keeping the smoke away from Finian and Oliver. "I hear you were asking about the two Americans who were at breakfast yesterday," he said. "That's the only time I saw them together, but I saw the man—Kavanagh—out by your farm on Wednesday afternoon, Mr. York."

Oliver's brow furrowed. "What time was this?"

"It must have been close to five. I was on my way in to work. He was chatting with a courier." The lad shrugged, flicking ash off the tip of his cigarette. "I assumed he was asking for directions."

"Where exactly were they?" Oliver asked.

"By the gate to the track that leads to the dovecote."

Oliver thanked him. He nodded to Finian, and they continued on through the green. "The courier arrived *after* Hambly fell," Oliver said, pensive. "Where was our FBI agent then, I wonder? Well. We shall see. When we get back to the farm, I'll draw out a good walking route for you, Fin."

"I'd like that. You'll give Mr. Hambly the name of his rescuer?"

"Oh, yes. I will describe Special Agent Kavanagh to him, too."

"We don't know if he's an FBI agent—"

"*I* know." Oliver turned up the collar to his jacket against a stiff breeze. "After your walk, my friend, we can discuss Irish saints and Irish art, and you can tell me what you learn about Naomi MacBride and Ted Kavanagh from Special Agent Donovan."

14

Colin was on the interstate, heading north out of Boston, when his phone buzzed. He expected Mike or his mother, or even Emma, not Finian Bracken. He gritted his teeth as he answered. "Why are you hanging out with Oliver York?"

"It's perfectly innocent. I can call back later if I've caught you at a bad time."

"It's not a bad time, Fin. What are you doing in England in the first place?"

"I joined Declan on a business trip to London."

"And you just happened to end up in the Cotswolds with York?"

"It's a bit more complicated than that. We ran into each other."

"All right." Nothing Colin could do now, since Finian was already at the York farm. "What's up?"

"Oliver believes two FBI agents are following him."

Two?

"Talk to me," Colin said.

Finian explained. He was calm, deliberate and precise. The goings-on in England weren't his first law enforcement issue since he and Colin had met on a dock in Rock Point last June. Finian had just arrived in the United States for his yearlong assignment. He had the means to go back to Ireland, give up the priesthood—live a quiet life—but so far, he was still serving struggling St. Patrick's Church and coping with Colin and his brothers. And with Emma and the Sharpes.

"I can try to find the courier and ask him what he and Mr. Kavanagh talked about," Finian said. "Perhaps if I'm not with Oliver—"

"Don't, Fin. Stay out of this. Where are you now?"

"Walking. Oliver set me off on a route. I have a feeling he didn't want me around when he spoke with Martin Hambly—you remember him, don't you?"

"I told him that he and Oliver remind me of Batman and his stalwart manservant."

"I don't know Batman," Finian said. "Before I set off on my walk, Oliver told me the courier picked up a package he sent to the rectory."

"*Your* rectory?"

"Yes. It's addressed to Emma."

Emma hadn't mentioned it when she'd called Colin Wednesday night. But why would she?

"Martin Hambly put the package out for the courier before he took a fall," Finian said. "Oliver asked me if you can find out if it arrived. It's a small matter, Colin. No need to trouble yourself."

"What's in the package, Fin?"

"*Nonsense* is the word Oliver used. He told Emma about it when he spoke to her Wednesday evening. Oliver likes to tweak the Sharpes, doesn't he?"

"Yes, he does."

"I can ask him about the package's contents."

"Do not do that."

Colin heard his Irish friend take in a breath. "As you wish."

"I don't like Hambly's fall," Colin said. "Do you believe him when he says he doesn't remember the details?"

"I do, as a matter of fact. He hopes he will remember more once he feels better."

"But he won't see a doctor."

"Would you in his place?"

Colin didn't answer. Traffic wasn't bad heading north out of the city, even during morning rush hour. "How long are you planning to stay at York's farm?"

"A night or two. I'm due back in Maine soon. You'll check on the package? Do you think Emma picked it up?"

"She's at the convent."

"Oh, yes. Her retreat. I wouldn't want to interrupt her. The package was due to arrive yesterday. She might have picked it up before she went on to the convent, but it's hardly an urgent FBI matter."

Maybe, Colin thought. And Emma definitely would have picked up a package from Oliver York, assuming it had arrived.

"Do you know who these two Americans are, Colin?" Finian paused. "You at least have an idea, don't you?"

"An idea. Fin…" Colin inhaled. "Stay out of this."

"Whatever *this* is," Finian muttered.

A tractor-trailer truck whizzed past Colin. He had no reason to believe the man who had identified himself to the English innkeepers as Ted Kavanagh wasn't, in fact, Mike's FBI agent friend. Same with Naomi MacBride, the former State Department analyst. He'd dug up photos over coffee but wouldn't send them to Fin Bracken in England. His Irish friend needed to wind up his visit to the Cotswolds.

Finian knew he was hanging out with an unrepentant art thief.

"How far are you walking?" Colin asked.

"It's an eight-mile loop."

"Do it twice," Colin said.

After he disconnected, he jumped off the interstate and pulled into a gas station. He texted Mike.

Where are you?

Hurley's.

Where is Naomi MacBride?

Across from me. Plum Tree is next.

Call me when you get free of her.

Mike didn't respond. Colin knew he wouldn't.

He was reasonably confident his older brother would call when he could.

Colin got out of his truck. He'd gas up and get more coffee.

His phone buzzed.

Finian again. This time, a text.

I stopped at the pub and spoke to the waiter again. A second man picked up the woman. Thirties, fair, well dressed.

Name?

Didn't get one.

Okay. No more sleuthing. Got it?

Yes. Be well.

Colin slipped his phone back into his jacket pocket. If the second man Finian had described was Reed Cooper, then he, too, was either en route to Maine or there already. But what were Reed Cooper, Naomi MacBride and Ted Kavanagh doing in Oliver York's Cotswolds village?

And what did all this have to do with Mike?

Colin pushed the questions aside. He'd be in Rock Point in an hour. First he'd check on York's package. He didn't want to bug Emma at the convent—he took her lack of response to his text as a hint—but he would get in touch with her if he needed her to provide answers about this mysterious package.

Then he'd head to the Plum Tree.

Time to meet Mike's friends.

15

Seeing Naomi again was affecting Mike more than he wanted to admit. She spun out of Hurley's ahead of him, leaving him with the bill and his two youngest brothers.

"Have fun," Andy, the lobsterman brother, said.

Kevin, off duty as a state marine patrol officer, just shook his head.

Naomi had held her own with them over breakfast. As if there'd been any doubt. Mike had thought Hurley's made more sense than the inn with his folks, but now he wasn't so sure.

Not a good start to the day.

She beat him back to his truck. She looked as if she'd just come in from London with her black trench coat, skinny jeans and ankle boots. He'd heard her shower running about an hour after he'd rolled out of bed. He'd stood at the window, trying to focus on the view of the harbor but instead seeing her in the shower with him three years ago.

Not good.

She was funny, irreverent, open by nature, sneaky by trade, insatiably curious and smart. She'd lost her father to a senseless IED and had done what she could to keep her mother from falling apart. She'd graduated from Vanderbilt with a double major in history and political science. After Vanderbilt, she moved to Washington and started work for the State Department. Eventually she'd ended up in Afghanistan.

When they'd first met, Mike had told her if she dyed her hair red, she could play Orphan Annie. Just an offhand comment. He hadn't meant much by it, certainly hadn't meant to demean her skills and stature as a civilian intelligence analyst. She'd called him a jackass and threatened to rain hell on him if he said anything like that again.

He hadn't had to worry about intimidating her then, never mind now that he was an ex-soldier, an expert these days in canoeing, kayaking, wilderness camping and locating seals and puffins on the Maine coast.

She squinted out at the harbor, sparkling in the morning sun. Last night's unsettled weather had cleared, leaving behind a cloudless sky and sharply colder temperatures. "It's breathtaking, Mike. Good breakfast, good view. Can't ask for more than that, except maybe grits on the menu and sixty degrees warmer." She turned to him. "Ready for the Plum Tree?"

"Whenever you are."

They got into his truck. He started the engine.

"Your truck could use heated seats," she said.

"I hate heated seats."

"Not me. I love them. Sums up the differences between you and me, doesn't it?"

Probably it did.

She snapped her seat belt on. "Was Andy the lobsterman brother or the marine patrol officer brother?"

"Lobsterman."

"And he's the one seeing the local woman who is doing the marine biology internship in Ireland. You have an interesting family. Do you ever go winter camping with your brothers?"

"Sometimes."

"I'm not sure *winter* and *camping* should be in the same sentence in Maine. It sounds cold."

"It's not cold if you're prepared."

"Not cold enough to kill you if you're prepared, maybe."

Mike didn't try to explain the appeal of winter camping. He took the coastal road north out of Rock Point. He'd call Colin after they got settled at the Plum Tree. Mike wanted to see Reed first. He could tell Colin didn't like this get-together. Couldn't blame him. For all Mike knew, Colin had Naomi's flight information. For sure he would know by now she had stayed in Rock Point last night. Kevin if not Andy would have told him.

Law enforcement officers, Mike thought.

"You know what, Mike?" Naomi gazed out her window. "I don't regret visiting Rock Point. It helps me understand you better. Why you and I didn't work."

"Okay."

"You don't care, do you?"

"No."

She turned to him with a smile. "You could have hesitated."

He winked at her. "I'm not the hesitating type."

"Forget it. You haven't changed." She made a face. "Sorry. That came out like an accusation and it wasn't meant to. It's just another fact. I'm sorry I called you a jackass last night, too. High emotion on top of a very long day, and jet lag is a recipe for blurting out the wrong thing."

"I didn't notice much difference from when you aren't tired and jet-lagged."

"Nice, Mike."

He'd thought so but he noticed her sarcasm. He'd thought he was taking her off the hook for whatever she was worrying about having said wrong. He supposed he should have known better. Trying to talk to Naomi had always spun him dizzy.

The road took them close to the water but summer homes and businesses thinned out here. The Plum Tree was located past a headland where a lighthouse once stood. Now there was just the keeper's house and a few summer homes, most of them small and fairly ordinary—not like the mansions down in Heron's Cove.

"It's beautiful here even this time of year." Naomi sighed, watching the scenery. "Makes more sense why Reed picked Maine. I love the rocky coastline. Very picturesque. Does Maine have any sand beaches?"

"Down here," Mike said. "Wells, Orchard Beach, Kennebunkport. Heron's Cove has a decent beach. Not as many up north but there are a few small ones."

"Somehow I don't see you on a sandy beach. Do you even own a swimsuit?"

Mike didn't answer. She was goading him, or having a little fun for herself. Either way, he wasn't indulging her.

He turned into a long, paved driveway that wound between snowbanks to a Maine cottage-style building with weathered gray shingles and white shutters. An attractive sign decorated with what he assumed were plum blossoms announced that they had arrived at the Plum Tree Inn.

"Hard to take Reed and his guys seriously when they pick a place with a giant moose out front," Naomi said, nodding to a metal statue by the inn's front entrance.

"That's a life-size moose," Mike said.

"No kidding? Damn. What do I do if I meet up with a real one?"

"Let it go on its way."

"Will do. I won't need to be told twice."

Mike knew she wasn't afraid of moose any more than she was of him. She hopped out of the truck the second he pulled to a stop and got her bag, slinging the thick strap over one shoulder.

He grabbed his duffel bag and met her at the rear of the truck. They could be a couple checking in for a romantic getaway, except the Plum Tree was closed for the season.

"I hadn't planned to show up with you," Naomi said.

"You'll figure it out."

"Reed's a good guy."

"You need him," Mike said.

Naomi rolled her eyes. "No, Mike. Reed needs me. He's new at being a private contractor. I'm not new at being a crisis management consultant."

"I stand corrected."

He started across the parking lot. She stayed up with him, despite her city boots and the sting of the icy wind off the water. Wind hadn't been a problem in the protected harbor in Rock Point. They passed the moose, the metal twisted and shaped to create the appearance of motion. At the right angle, it probably could almost look like a real moose.

"I like him," Naomi said. "I think you're exaggerating about the size, though. Are there moose where you live?"

"Yes." He didn't bother to tell her he wasn't exaggerating about the size. Naomi wasn't thinking about moose, and he didn't want to be.

When the front door to the attractive inn opened, Mike recognized Jamie Mason, the former Special Forces soldier who had stopped in Rock Point. Jamie was in his midforties, grayer, balder and paunchier than Mike remembered but not anyone he would want to underestimate.

Naomi greeted Jamie with a big smile and a hug. Old friends. Mike hadn't remembered they knew each other.

Jamie's eyes narrowed on Mike. "Long time, Mike."

"Yep."

"I hear you live up in moose country."

"Bold Coast for a bold guy."

Jamie ignored him.

"You're in moose country right now, Jamie," Mike added.

"Lucky us," he said, holding the door for them.

Naomi leaned close to Mike as they entered a small, carpeted lobby decorated in seacoast blues and grays, with reproduction Early American furnishings. "I can rest my case," she said in a low voice. "You haven't matured."

He shrugged. "Demonstrating I have a light side."

"Light moments do not make a light side."

Jamie had them leave their bags in the lobby and pointed them down a carpeted hall. "Last room on your left. The library. Reed will meet you there. I'll let him know you've arrived."

The library was in a small room that opened onto a covered porch and overlooked the water, glittering and blue under the morning sun and cloudless sky. Floor-to-ceiling shelves covered one wall and contained books, board games, puzzles and playing cards. There were comfortable-looking chairs and a love seat by a fireplace, and a few wooden card tables with folding chairs tucked under them.

A rail-thin man was shaking a Yahtzee cup onto a card table. He dumped the dice onto the table and grinned, eyes crinkling as he whooped. "Three deuces, two fives. Full house. Yay for me."

Mike recognized the devil-may-care way that was pure Buddy Whidmore, tech expert, adventurer and Vanderbilt dropout—one of those guys too smart and restless for school. Buddy had been in Afghanistan, too, at least for a time. Mike wasn't surprised to find Buddy currying favor with Reed Cooper. Buddy liked action, just not too much action.

"Buddy—I didn't know you would be here." Naomi laughed. "This party just keeps getting better."

He set his Yahtzee cup on the table. "To think we could be meeting in Nashville instead of the frozen north. Your cheeks are pink from the cold, Naomi. Or is it the company?" Buddy tossed a die into the cup and grinned at Mike. "Mike Donovan. Damn. Great to see you."

"Buddy."

"How are you? Been ages."

"Doing fine, thanks." Mike hated small talk and wasn't any good at it. "You?"

"Still doing my thing. I stay out of war zones these days, though. I keep thinking I'll take on a regular job, but I'm a solo entrepreneur at heart. I like the freedom to come and go, work remotely, pick and choose the projects that excite me. It's great. I was in Dubai last month on business. Ever been to Dubai, Mike?"

He nodded. He wasn't talking about Dubai.

"Naomi and I both travel a lot, but we get together in Nashville for barbecue and bourbon when we can. Couldn't do that with most desk jobs I'm qualified for. You, Mike? Is it true you're a wilderness guide?"

"True."

"Not much firepower required in that job, is there?"

Mike didn't answer.

Buddy put away his Yahtzee game. He had on a bright plaid flannel shirt, jeans sunk low on his thin hips, a Predators cap and canvas shoes that would give him cold feet if he stayed outside for long. He shoved the game box onto a shelf. "Reed's setting up a room for a lunch meeting. He's got folders and everything. I feel like I'm in a bank, applying for a mortgage."

Naomi eased over to French doors that opened onto the porch. "It's so pretty and romantic here with the snow, ice, rocks and ocean. I can picture myself sitting by a roaring fire with a stack of books and a mug of hot cocoa." She looked back at Mike. "Does that describe your life, Mike?"

He decided he had been out of his mind to come here. "Sure."

She grinned at him. "Liar. The stack of books, maybe. I don't see you with hot cocoa." She turned to Buddy. "I'm just back from London and still a little jet-lagged."

"Did you work nonstop as usual?" he asked her.

"I took a few good walks."

Reed Cooper entered the library. "Like to Scotland and back. I've never seen anyone who loves to walk the way you do, Naomi." He strode over to Mike and shook hands with him. "It's good to see you. Thanks for coming. Damn—you haven't changed a bit. I know it's only been a few years but it seems like forever."

"Good to see you, too, Reed," Mike said.

"I hope we didn't catch you in the middle of skinning a moose."

"Working on my canoe lately."

"One of the tools of your trade, I guess. You won't be needing a canoe for a while. May? June?"

Mike shrugged. "Depends."

Naomi eased onto a love seat. The grace with which she moved always took Mike by surprise, given her high energy. "I'll sit quietly and let you all get reacquainted. Or do you want me to clear out?"

"Please, stay," Reed said. "How was your flight?"

"Fine. I caught up on movies and resisted alcohol since I knew I'd be seeing you all today and I didn't want a hangover."

Reed didn't look amused. He'd had a limited sense of humor when Mike knew him in the army, and that obviously hadn't changed. Naomi wouldn't care. She'd keep up with the smart remarks if it suited her. It was her personality, but it was also her way of establishing her independence and authority.

She jumped to her feet. She couldn't have been sitting for more than ten seconds. "I'm going to find Serena Mason and get her to point me to the girliest room in this place. I hope it's the warmest, too. I didn't have time to go back to Nashville and pack my winter clothes. Not that I have clothes suited to a Maine winter. Did you swing through Rock Point on your way up here, Reed?"

"No, but I want to see it."

"Rock Point," Buddy said, as if trying to imagine such a place. "Land of the Donovans. Home sweet home, huh, Mike? Don't you have a big family?"

Mike wasn't talking about his family, either. He hadn't dealt with the kind of dynamics that were bubbling in this room in a long time. Not his thing. He kept quiet.

Naomi glanced back from the doorway. "Three younger brothers," she said. "I met the two youngest Donovans at breakfast this morning. We ate at a place called Hurley's. I'll leave you to contemplate that. See you guys later."

She slipped out of the library. When she was out of sight, Reed turned again to Mike. "She hasn't changed, either. She's the same Naomi MacBride I met in Kabul when she announced we had both gone to Vanderbilt and had a bet with a coworker that I was a frat boy, which I was. She's smart, sarcastic, not sure who she can trust. How do you feel about her being here?"

"Not my call," Mike said.

"That's not what I asked, but never mind. Have a seat. Jamie's bringing coffee. The inn's regular cook is catering for us. Food's excellent. You want anything to eat, or did you and Naomi—"

"I'm all set."

Buddy started for the door. "Why don't I go find another fire to sit by for a while? You two are a couple of former soldiers who haven't seen each other in several years. I'll let you get reacquainted. I'm already in love with this place. Reminds me of *Murder, She Wrote* reruns. Let's hope Jessica Fletcher doesn't show up, though. Talk about a sign for bad crap happening." He was halfway to the door when he gave Mike a little salute. "Really great to see you, Mike."

He headed out, and Reed gave a small laugh. "Buddy's a character. See, Mike? You can relax. We're a friendly group. We're in Maine. We're not in a war zone."

As if Mike needed reminding. "Jamie was in Rock Point the other night."

"My idea. Thought you might be there. I hope it wasn't provocative. We pulled this weekend together on the fly. As you can see, I'm running my own outfit now."

"I'd heard you'd gone out on your own."

"We're small but we're getting off the ground in a big way." He walked over to the fireplace, next to the love seat Naomi had vacated. "We work with private individuals, corporations, non-profits and nongovernmental agencies. We put people's minds at ease about their security so they can get on with their work. We already have a few clients. I did work for another contractor. I have a solid reputation. We're meeting here to review training and tactics, see where the holes are in staffing. We'll be here through the weekend. It's low-key."

"Funny time of year to pick Maine."

"You know why we did, Mike. We want to talk to you."

"Kill two birds with one stone," he said, keeping any skepticism out of his tone.

"Exactly. I'm a Southerner but we're fifty-fifty warm weather and cold weather guys. Don't worry, I'm not going to ask you to lead us over hill and dale through the snowy Maine countryside. I'm sure you could—I'm sure there's none better—but I want you to have a look at my team, let me talk to you about what we do."

"Why?"

"Because you're the best and you're not done yet. You're bored trekking into the Maine wilderness with rich people with too much time on their hands. I understand you do outfitting, too. That must be rewarding. Filling backpacks with energy bars and poop bags." Reed cleared his throat. "I'm sorry. That wasn't what I meant."

It was, but Mike didn't take offense. "It's okay. It's close enough. I'm not bored, though."

"The Bold Coast sounds perfect for you. You're close to family but not too close. Your mother told Jamie you helped plant a hundred tulip bulbs at their inn in the fall." Reed glanced back from the fire. "Tulips, Mike."

"You're not in Maine just to talk to me about coming to work for you."

"You and I have unfinished business," Reed said quietly.

Naomi.

Reed sat on the love seat, throwing one leg over the opposite knee. "Jamie and Serena got in on Tuesday. They're my entire administrative staff. That gives you an idea of how small we are right now. We're limiting the number of full-time employees. Most of our operators will work on a contract basis. But we can talk about all that. You'll like this place. It has old photographs of lobstermen on the wall in the bar. I wouldn't be surprised if there was a Donovan or two among them."

Mike wouldn't, either. "When did you get here?"

"Last night, late. I was going to stay in Boston but I came on up here."

"Who else are you expecting?"

"A couple of guys you don't know will be in on Saturday, but we can get started without them. Buddy will lead us through some tech stuff. We can't do this work without tech know-how. It's the world we're in nowadays. I'd like to hire him full-time, but you remember Buddy. He likes his freedom. He's doing well financially and knows his way around computers and the internet as well as anyone I've ever known, but he thrives on danger and adventure—not the typical profile of someone with his expertise."

Mike went over to the French doors. The porch would be a good spot in warmer weather. One of the photos on the inn's website showed the porch with hanging flower baskets and cozy wicker furniture. Now the furniture was covered with tarps, and there were no flowers.

"Have you and Naomi stayed in touch?" he asked, glancing back at Reed.

"Some. I worked for another firm until last fall. She's always looking for good contractors who have the right fit for her clients. Once we're fully staffed, I'm sure we'll do more business together. She's good, Mike."

"Always has been."

"I'm newer at this work than she is. She can be a huge help." Reed leaned back against the soft cushions. "She's a reassuring presence at often difficult times. It's what clients want in a security consultant. She puts clients at ease. I do, too, but in a different way. You'd scare the hell out of them, Mike—until they got into trouble. Then they'd look to you." He paused, staring at his hands. "Like Naomi did three years ago."

"She didn't look to me. I just was the one there. What are her liabilities?"

"Same as always. Trust. That's why she's still a one-woman show."

Mike didn't think it was that simple. "What about Ted Kavanagh?"

"He's here somewhere. He says he wants to talk to me about post-FBI work. I don't know that I believe him, but I invited him to join us. It can't hurt to have someone to help us navigate law enforcement. I'm a soldier. I ran into Kavanagh in London." Reed got to his feet, as if he were suddenly restless. "He says he's on vacation."

Mike frowned. "You have doubts?"

"It doesn't matter. There's no reason for me to be under FBI suspicion. I have nothing to hide. Feel free to ask all the questions you have, Mike. Don't hold back." Reed smiled. "Not that you would."

"What were you doing in London?"

"Naomi was meeting with a group of volunteer medical professionals preparing to head to a hot spot in Africa. She invited me to talk to them about what we do. They're a good group. Smart, dedicated men and women who should be able to focus on fighting diseases, not on whether they're going to be hacked to death in their beds."

"And you can make that happen," Mike said, not making it a question.

"Yes."

Reed's confidence in himself and the people he led had always been unshakable. Mike had never served under him but knew a number of men and women who had, and he respected their faith in Reed.

"You are staying, aren't you, Mike? You're not just dropping off Naomi and leaving."

"I'll stay but no promises."

"I wasn't sure what you'd be up to nowadays. Thought you might be settled down with a wife and little kids. I want a family one day—when the time is right."

Jamie arrived with coffee and chocolate-chip cookies warm out of the oven. He set the tray on a card table then headed out without comment.

Mike helped himself to one of the cookies. He hadn't had as much at breakfast as Naomi had. He took a bite of his cookie but wondered what the hell he was doing here. Cookies. A country inn. He poured coffee.

Reed took one of the cookies. "Jamie and Serena's daughter started at West Point this fall. They only have the one. Empty nest now. They were ready for something new. They're not fussy about a job description. They'll pitch in and do what needs to be done."

"Good people to have," Mike said.

"I think so. Ask any questions you want to, Mike. That's why I'm here."

"You came straight from London. Why not go back to Nashville for a few days?"

"No time. This was more efficient. It'll be an interesting few days. A change of pace for you." Reed popped his cookie into his mouth. "I drove Naomi to Heathrow yesterday. One of those endless days with the five-hour time difference. I met her in a small English village. She said she was there for a quick break in the country before her flight."

"You sound skeptical," Mike said.

"Maybe." Reed paused, looking out at the ocean, relatively tranquil under the late-morning sun. "I don't want to see her hurt. Whenever I hear her name, I hope I'm about to find out she's quit security work and gone into something else. Opened a bar in Nashville, hit the lecture circuit. Anything but this work." He sucked in a breath. "She wouldn't appreciate my protective impulses."

"Probably not."

Reed continued to stare out at the water. "When I saw her in action in London, I saw how good she is—how many lives she's saved doing what she does best. It can be a heavy burden."

Mike shrugged. "Maybe she likes heavy burdens."

"That would explain why she fell for you," Reed said with a laugh, then winced as he pulled his gaze from the view. "That was really bad humor. I'm glad you're here, Mike. If I'd asked you to visit us in Nashville instead of coming to Maine myself, you'd have told me to go to hell. Am I right?"

"Still might tell you to go to hell."

"Aren't you even a little flattered that I want you on my team?"

Mike grinned. "Yeah, Reed. I'm flattered."

Reed laughed, shaking his head. "Don't think I forgot what a bastard you can be. I tell myself it's part of what makes you good."

"Did you ask Naomi to join you here as a way to get me down

here? You could have let her go back to Nashville and had her join them via Skype."

"I knew you wouldn't be able to resist once you found out she would be here." Reed walked back to the table and poured himself coffee. "But it's not the reason I invited her. We have work to do on her volunteer doctors."

Mike's phone vibrated. He checked the screen. Another text from Colin. Where are you? Call me. I'm counting to ten.

Mike typed a quick response. Fifteen minutes.

Good. Next up is BOLO.

No doubt in Mike's mind his brother meant it and would sic every cop in Maine on him if he didn't get in touch.

"Is someone looking to book a kayak tour come summer?" Reed asked.

"Too early. My brother Colin."

"The FBI agent."

"Correct."

Reed seemed to expect more of an explanation, but he shrugged when he didn't get one and drank his coffee as he grabbed another cookie. "We tough guys need our cookies, don't we?"

Naomi joined them, heading straight for the tray of cookies and coffee. "My room is great, Reed. Very pretty. In fact, it's called the Lady Slipper. It's a New England orchid." She chose a cookie, getting melted chocolate on her knuckle. She licked it off. "Tomorrow I eat celery. Maybe for the rest of my life I eat celery."

"I thought we could go snowshoeing this afternoon," Reed said.

"Snowshoeing?" She seemed incredulous. "I saw on the inn's website there's a health club. Maybe I'll check it out later. You guys can stay fit as fiddles without stepping foot into the winter cold. I, on the other hand, only chase bad guys on paper and the internet. Sometimes on the phone, but rarely these days."

"Didn't they teach you to shoot at the CIA?" Mike asked.

"Culinary Institute of America? I didn't go there." She bit into her cookie. "Anything you need from me, Reed?"

"The truth," he said lightly. "The whole truth and nothing but the truth."

"Nothing but the truth I can do. I don't know the whole truth about anything. One of my assets is recognizing that fact." She sounded pragmatic, without a hint of defensiveness. "Jamie says we're meeting over lunch. I suppose I could head out for a walk in the snow and ice with the brisk wind off the water in my face. That ought to jump-start me. Jet lag never used to bother me. It's only after I read you need a day for each hour of time change that I started to notice it. Something to be said for being oblivious, isn't there?"

Mike had a feeling she wasn't just talking about jet lag, but he wasn't asking.

Reed shifted to him. "Why don't you get settled? Call your brother back. At least stay tonight. Have lunch and dinner on us. Hear what we have to say. Then decide what you want to do."

"Sounds good."

Mike left Reed and Naomi in the library and headed down the hall to the lobby. Serena Mason, a sturdy, efficient woman, greeted him with a room key. "Second floor," she said. "You're next door to Naomi."

At least he hadn't had to ask to be put close to her.

Naomi's room was, in fact, called the Lady Slipper. Its name was on a brass plaque on the outside of the door. Mike let himself into a room called the Lightkeeper. Sure enough, it had a model of a lighthouse on the bedside table and a print of the Cape Elizabeth lighthouse on the wall. It wasn't a "girlie" room, but it wasn't what he was used to. He figured he would stay tonight, at least. He couldn't put his finger on what was bugging him, but something was off—with Reed, with Naomi, with this last-minute weekend in Maine.

He set his bag on the bed. Naomi could be running her own game, manipulating Reed and his team for her own ends, whether to enhance her reputation, profit margin or ego. She wasn't the most straightforward, easy-to-read person Mike had ever met. She lived and worked in a world very different from the one he lived in.

He checked his cell phone. Enough coverage to make a call.

Colin picked up on the first ring. "Tell me who's at this get-together."

"You investigating these guys?"

"No."

Okay answer as far as it went. Mike figured out he was on a need-to-know basis with whatever was on Colin's mind, and his younger brother clearly wasn't answering a lot of questions. "I don't have all the names." He gave Colin what names he did have. "Cooper, Kavanagh and MacBride were in London until yesterday. Jamie's the one who stopped in Rock Point. He and his wife got in on Tuesday."

"You all knew each other in Afghanistan?"

"Correct."

"Anything happen back then that I need to know about?"

Not a question Mike wanted to answer. "Our last joint mission had problems but everything worked out okay."

"Anyone killed?"

"Three bad guys we wanted alive. Cooper, Kavanagh, Mason and MacBride were involved."

"And you," Colin said. "Hard feelings?"

"It's in the past."

"For whatever that's worth. Any loose ends that could come back to haunt you?"

"There are always loose ends. No reason to think they'll be a problem now or in the future."

"All right. Not a good time for details. Mike, are you think-ing about working for Cooper?"

"He's gone to a lot of trouble to meet with me."

"Red-carpet treatment?"

"I wouldn't go that far. This isn't about my ego. Reed's, ei-ther. He's ambitious but he's pragmatic. Is Kavanagh a problem? He's an active FBI agent, isn't he? Didn't quit?"

"As far as I know, yes, he's an active agent."

"Then he can arrest the lot of us," Mike said. He meant it as a joke but noted that Colin didn't laugh.

"Did you run into Emma when you were in Rock Point yes-terday?"

"No. Isn't she with the nuns?"

"I meant before she headed to the convent. She's staying there again tonight. A package was sent to her at St. Patrick's rectory. Never mind. I just got in to Rock Point. I'll head up there to meet your friends."

"Feel free."

Mike looked at the lighthouse print. He thought it was a wa-tercolor but didn't know enough about painting to tell. When he left the army, a psychologist friend suggested he take up painting to process his experiences. He had moved into his grandfather's cabin and never considered painting anything more complicated than a canoe or a wall.

"Have you talked to Kavanagh?" Mike asked his brother.

"No. You?"

"I haven't seen him yet. We're all supposed to meet over lunch."

"Mike…"

"Tell me what you're looking for, Colin. I'll do what I can to help."

"I'm going to text you a photo of Kavanagh. I want to be sure we're talking about the same guy. Have a look. Tell me if it's him. Then delete it."

"I like it when pressing Delete can keep me safe," Mike said, then disconnected.

In thirty seconds, he had Kavanagh's photo.

He texted Colin. That's him.

Thanks.

Mike deleted the photo as promised. He didn't know if identifying Kavanagh had been good, bad or neutral news to Colin. Whatever the case, it didn't change what Mike was doing for the afternoon.

He washed his hands and splashed his face with cold water. He returned to the bedroom. He didn't bother to unpack. He could take his brother's advice and clear out, head back up to the Bold Coast. He wasn't worried about stranding Naomi. She had friends at the Plum Tree who could see her back to the airport and Nashville.

You'd love Nashville, Mike, she had whispered to him in the dark, laying on her middle Tennessee accent. *Spring comes early and lasts and lasts, and the music, bourbon and barbecue are the best.*

No ocean.

Long, lazy rivers and deep lakes.

I like long, lazy and deep.

Mmm. She'd given a soft laugh, turning to him, her skin hot. *You can sit out late into the night on the riverbank and watch the fireflies.*

Homesick?

Not right now. Not with you.

She had touched him then, and they'd made love late into their own night.

Mike stood at the cold window and looked out at the water, ice and rocks. The Maine coast was his home, and it was where he belonged.

16

Emma dropped to the floor for a third time in what she esti-mated was the past half hour. She was breathing hard and sweat-ing—warm, at least, if also expending fluids she couldn't afford to lose. But she was more confident than she'd been in the night.

One more try and she'd have it.

At first light, she'd realized there was a half loft above her. The window was opposite it. That meant she'd have to leap sev-eral feet to reach it, but it felt more viable than scaling the wall up to the window.

First she had to get up to the loft. There was a partial ladder, with only a top rung. She'd tested the stability of the ladder and loft on her first attempt. They'd held. She was confident they wouldn't collapse or crumble under her. On her second attempt, she'd tried leaping up and grabbing the top rung of the ladder, then swinging herself up to the loft. That hadn't gone well. Yet another reason to do pull-ups, she thought.

On the third attempt, she'd found a nick on the ladder's ver-tical support that she could use as a foothold, making it easier to hoist herself up to the top rung and then onto the loft. She'd managed to get high enough to see out the window. The old glass was cracked, dirty and caked in the corners with cobwebs and dead flies, but she could see through it to ocean, waves rolling toward her. It was like being in an infinity pool. She couldn't see the land on which the shed was perched. Even if the shed was built close to the water, there had to be land below the window.

Ignoring her sore leg muscles, Emma sank onto the floor next to the door. If her attacker returned, she wouldn't be caught by surprise. The heavy wood door itself was her only weapon. The shed was completely empty. She hadn't found so much as a rock in her search of the place once it was light enough.

She *had* found three soft, warm, natural sheepskins.

What's in the package, Oliver?

A present for you. A surprise. You'll love it.

Oliver York's present.

Only Oliver.

The sheepskins had been cast aside on the floor next to the door, along with packing materials. Nothing of use there, either.

Emma assumed they were English sheepskins, presumably from sheep raised on the York farm in the Cotswolds. She'd spread them below the window. If she fell trying to reach it, the sheepskins would at least cushion her landing.

She would check the door one more time, but she doubted it would budge. What was on the other side? A house filled with armed men? She had no idea. If she went out the window, would someone see her, hear her? Would she be met by gunfire?

She hit the door with her elbow. "If you're out there, let's talk," she called, keeping her voice steady, without any hint of panic or frustration. "Let's work this out."

No response.

Up to the loft, leap to the window. Break it open. Take her chances.

That was her only way out.

17

Naomi kicked off her ankle boots and stretched out on the bed in her Lady Slipper room. The bed was comfortable but not as comfortable as the bed in her room at the Rock Point Harbor Inn. It was only the middle of the day, but it felt like night. She glanced at the bedside clock. Twelve fifteen. Okay. That was only 6:00 p.m. in England. Jet lag wasn't her only problem.

She flopped against the pillows and put her feet up on the bed. The cold had to be what was affecting her thinking. She was normally a strategic thinker who could see possibilities and angles with dizzying clarity, but right now all she saw was mud.

That and Mike Donovan's smile.

And his eyes.

And his thighs.

Damn, he had a great smile, great eyes and great thighs. How was she supposed to not notice? Even if she and Mike had never slept together, or if they were meeting today for the first time, she would have noticed.

She groaned and sat up straight. Mike wasn't the same Mike she'd known in Afghanistan—made love to in Washington.

While that Mike had been a skilled soldier, he'd also been tender, homesick and so ready to fall in love.

This Mike was skeptical, distrustful and not at all tender.

Well, what had she expected?

Reed, Jamie and Serena were preparing for the lunch meeting. Or maybe the Masons were preparing, and Reed was off with Mike shooting or kicking ass or some damn thing. Kavanagh could have joined them. He was an FBI agent. He could shoot and kick ass. She didn't know about Buddy. He didn't have military or law enforcement training, but he must have picked up a few self-defense skills, at least, during his time in war zones.

Naomi yawned. She knew how to shoot and fight, too. Technically. Her role as a consultant didn't necessitate she own a gun, and therefore she didn't. Operators decided what weaponry they needed to do their job. Ideally, whatever weapons they chose wouldn't be required.

She hadn't practiced hand-to-hand combat in months, except with a big old snake that her mother had found in her garage. Nonpoisonous. They'd escorted it elsewhere.

Wherever everyone else was, the meeting would start in fifteen minutes. From what she'd seen in Afghanistan three years ago and in London this past week, Reed wasn't one to fool around, let chitchat take hold and turn into endless blather that bled away an afternoon.

A knock on the door drew her out of the thoughts. She jumped up, relieved to have company. She didn't care if it was whoever cleaned the rooms. She welcomed a distraction. But when she checked the peephole, she saw Buddy Whidmore shifting from one foot to the other. She had to admit she'd hoped for a different distraction. Buddy was an energy drainer. He didn't mean to be. He just was, with his manic energy and sharper-than-tacks, faster-than-a-whirlwind mind.

She let him in, but she couldn't get a word out as he burst

past her. "What are you, crazy, Naomi?" He spun around at her. "Messing with Mike Donovan again."

"I'm not messing with anyone."

He dropped a manila file folder on the foot of her bed. "I brought this for you—slipped an extra out of the conference room in case you want an early peek at what Reed's got cooked up for us. I know you're not yourself. I don't want you to have to go in there cold and let those guys get you rattled."

"Why would I get rattled?" she asked him, not buying into his drama.

"Reed. Mike. Kavanagh. The Masons. Memory lane, Naomi."

"Old friends."

Buddy laughed, looking less agitated. "I guess that's another way to look at it. Don't get me wrong, I like these guys, and I'd trust them with my life—in fact, I have trusted them with my life. But you, Naomi. You're the only woman, except for Serena, and she's ex-army and administrative."

"Serena Mason could run the Pentagon," Naomi said, not sure what to do with Buddy. Ask him to sit down? Her room had a single upholstered chair. There wasn't a desk. People didn't come to the Plum Tree to work.

"I wish I had Serena and Jamie looking after me," Buddy said. "They can do the work of ten people without breaking a sweat. I bet they already know I swiped the file and I'll have a bill under my pillow for a replacement folder. Reed's got plenty of money, but he's cheap. Have you noticed?"

Naomi smiled. "He says he's a good steward of his and his investors' funds."

"In other words, he's cheap. You're not an investor, are you?"

"In Cooper Global Security? No. Thanks for the file, though."

"Biggest risk I've taken so far this year, swiping a file you're going to get handed to you in a few minutes. I've been working on a new productivity app. It's kept me at my laptop most of the winter. I was so into it, I canceled a camping trip to Chile."

Naomi sat on her bed. "You're the one who should be talking to Mike."

"Mike the wilderness guide. I still see him decked out in night-vision goggles and enough weaponry to take out a small country."

"Now he picks wild blueberries at his cabin."

Buddy frowned. "What?"

"Never mind. You need to see Rock Point while you're here. It'll explain Mike."

"I don't need Mike explained. Do you? Why would I do that? You're the one with the happy history with him." Buddy put up both palms as if in self-defense. "Don't hit me. You know I'm being sarcastic to emphasize a point that is designed to help you come to your damn senses."

"What makes you think I'm not in possession of said damn senses?"

He shook his head. "Nah. No way, Naomi. I saw you with Mike when you got here. You can't hide it. He's got you stirred up."

"Buddy."

"None of my business?"

"None."

"All right. I won't go there, but now you know you can't fool me. I know." He walked over to the door out to her small balcony. "It gets darker than the pits of hell out here at night. I don't know if I made a mistake coming here."

"It's not a prison," Naomi said. "Hang out, enjoy yourself and then go home and forget Reed if he doesn't have anything to offer you."

"You're right. I'm letting myself get worked up for no reason. I gave Reed a buzz when I heard he was going out on his own, to let him know I'm available if he needs tech support. He invited me here. It was like getting invited to the prom by the star cheerleader."

"Buddy, you have a lot to offer."

"Cybersecurity. Cyber everything, really. It's not sexy. I sit in front of a screen all day. All night sometimes, too." He smoothed a bony hand over his longish hair. "I guess I'm in awe of guys like Reed and Mike."

Naomi decided to steer the subject in a different direction. "I haven't seen Ted Kavanagh yet. Have you?"

"Yeah. In the lobby." Buddy fiddled with the pull for the shades. "You know he and I have stayed in touch since Kabul?"

"I figured as much."

"Mostly I email him and he doesn't answer. Every now and then he'll email me back to let me know he appreciates hearing from me. I get a lot of ideas about this and that—mostly tech stuff—but I can't always tell the good ones from the bad ones. I don't have your filter, Naomi. You always seem to know what to do."

"I appreciate that, Buddy, but it's not true. We all fumble sometimes. Are you some kind of informant for Kavanagh?"

"Informant?" He shuddered. "No. What would I inform on? I just stay in touch. You know how it is with me. For every hundred 'sure' leads I send him, two pan out."

"But those two are pure gold, Buddy. Pure gold."

"I wouldn't argue with that." He glanced around the room. "Think Reed bugged our rooms?"

Naomi groaned. "No, Buddy, I don't think Reed bugged our rooms."

"Gotcha." He grinned, pointing at her. "You were going spook on me. Think about it, Naomi. I'm working on a *productivity* app. It's a glorified to-do list for people who hate to-do lists. I hear things and try to connect dots, but what would I know these days that an FBI agent could use?"

He had a point. Buddy's value as an independent consultant had never been his limited intelligence capabilities. Almost certainly he was here now, talking to Reed, solely because of his considerable technical skills.

"Is this productivity app going to make you money?" Naomi asked.

"Tons." He abandoned the blind pull. "You trust these guys, Naomi? Do you feel safe here?"

"Yes, of course. Look, Buddy, I have a job to do. That's what I trust. Reed's not watching my back. He's looking to watch my clients' backs."

"Is Mike watching your back?"

"No. Reed invited him. I didn't."

"But do you trust him?"

"You're putting too big an emphasis on trust, Buddy."

"Who *is* watching your back, Naomi?"

She smiled. "Well, gee, Buddy, I thought you were."

"Me? I can watch your banking accounts. That's about it. Sorry. Another lame joke."

"You're better with numbers than I am. I might want you to check out my accounts when I have more than rent and grocery money in them."

"Not getting rich?"

"Nope. You?"

"Ha," Buddy said. "Maybe with this app, but what would I do with a million bucks?"

Naomi couldn't tell if he was serious. "Who watches your back, Buddy?"

"Nobody needs to. I have eyes in the back of my head. I also don't have any enemies except imaginary ones, and maybe a couple of gamer jerks who are sore losers." He rolled his thin shoulders. "I should head back to my room. I'm staying tonight, but I don't know if I'll last the weekend. I'm in the moose room. It's not called that, but it's got a picture of a moose above the bed. You've got flowers, I see." He studied her painting but seemed preoccupied. "Naomi...do you feel like this whole weekend is a setup? Something Reed's cooked up to get us all in one place and then lower the boom?"

"Lower what boom?"

"Afghanistan."

"That was three years ago. We've all moved on. Reed's getting his company up and running. He wants to deploy his first set of operators. It's a huge responsibility. He's an achiever. He won't want to fail."

"People tend to get hurt when he fails," Buddy said.

Naomi had no argument.

"Reed wants to hear what I have to offer. He admits he's weak on tech stuff. You don't mind if I talk with him, do you?"

"Of course not. You go where the work is." Buddy's comment surprised her. It wasn't as if she had an exclusive contract with him. "Reed's got a lot of balls in the air, but he can handle it."

"He likes it that way. Think Mike will want to work for him?"

"I don't know. I'm staying neutral. It's none of my business who Reed hires."

"Mine, either, I guess. Thanks, Naomi. You have a calming way about you. I forget that." Buddy smiled. "It's good seeing you. Weird that we have to come way the hell up here to Maine to see each other when we live twenty miles apart."

"We both stay busy."

He narrowed his eyes on her. "You sure you're okay?"

"Other than jet lag, yes, just fine." She grinned at him. "Always scares me when you get solicitous. I figure I must look like death warmed over or something."

"Not you, Naomi. Never." But his humor didn't reach his eyes. "You really don't think Reed's up to anything? Deliberately stirring up the past to see what happens?"

"I don't care if he is, frankly. I only care if Cooper Global Security can help my doctors."

"Laser-focus Naomi. Good for you. I'll see you downstairs in a few minutes."

After Buddy left, she waited sixty seconds before she allowed herself to open the purloined file. Waiting was good discipline, and it forced her to think. Why had he bothered grabbing the file? But she knew. Buddy was awkward, and he'd used the file as an excuse to knock on her door—when the truth was, he didn't need one. He could have knocked on her door and told her he wanted to chat with her.

She opened the folder, leaving it on the bed. A simple agenda was on top of a half-dozen sheets of paper. Normal stuff. No surprises. The rest of the pages described Cooper Global Security and its history, mission and principles. Naomi didn't notice anything out of the ordinary or even that she didn't know already.

"Buddy, Buddy."

Had he bothered looking at the file when he'd grabbed it?

She sighed, shaking her head. He was brilliant and awkward, and it would be easy to feel sorry for him—but she didn't. Feeling sorry for him would be patronizing, and he had the life he wanted. He did work he loved and was good at, and it paid well and gave him the freedom to travel and have adventures. Naomi had no doubts that if Buddy Whidmore decided he wanted a relationship—a family—he would find a way to make it happen.

He was the one with the laser focus.

She felt scattered, unsettled. Jet lag didn't explain it. Seeing Mike again didn't, either. They were factors but not the source of her unease.

She shut the folder. She needed to get downstairs for Reed's meeting. She had a bad habit of pushing everyone away when she was under stress. She needed to behave.

As she headed out of her room, she reminded herself she was in Maine in a professional capacity. She'd told Buddy the truth. The past was past, and Reed Cooper could help her doctors—whether or not Mike Donovan joined Cooper Global Security.

Let Mike and Reed do their dance. The outcome made no difference to her.

She had work to do. *That* was her focus.

Ted Kavanagh was the only one in the meeting room off the inn's main dining room. He looked all business in his coat and tie. "No ugly sweater today, I see," Naomi said as she joined him.

"Hello, Naomi." He stood by a buffet table with plastic-covered platters of already-made sandwiches, vegetables, fruit and more cookies. "I think Serena might gun me down if I sneak a half sandwich early. Think she'll let me live if I sneak a grape?"

"A green one, maybe. There are more of those."

He grinned. "Last I saw you, you were waxing rhapsodic over porridge in an English country inn."

"Actually, it was over the blackberry compote." Naomi poured iced tea from a pitcher. Dead of winter, and there was iced tea. "Did you fly into Boston, T.K.?"

"Yeah. Same flight as Reed."

"Did you tell him about your visit to the Cotswolds?"

Kavanagh shook his head. "We didn't talk. He flew first-class. Not me. Coach all the way."

She handed him the tea and poured another glass. "Am I supposed to keep our breakfast yesterday secret?"

"Up to you. I'm not the one playing with fire."

"Isn't that what FBI agents do for a living?"

He didn't respond. Mike entered the room, followed by Buddy, Reed, and Jamie and Serena Mason. Serena unwrapped the platters but didn't stay for the meeting. Naomi eyed the food but for the first time in the past two days wasn't hungry. She took her iced tea to the table. Reed sat at the head of the table but let everyone else take seats at random.

Naomi told herself she wasn't surprised when Mike sat directly across from her. Of *course* he would. He could keep a better eye on her that way.

Buddy sat next to her and Kavanagh across from him.

Jamie didn't sit. He stood in the corner by the door, like a bouncer.

Naomi couldn't think of a good reason to have Kavanagh at the meeting—unless he wasn't with the FBI anymore and Reed knew it. She trusted that Reed wasn't doing anything illegal or deliberately provocative, but, from her experience, not all clients wanted a federal law enforcement officer in their business. A former fed was one thing, but she wasn't about to tell Reed to kick Kavanagh out of the room or ask him to explain the FBI agent's presence.

She wondered if Mike had mentioned Kavanagh to his FBI brother but gave herself an immediate mental shake. She was *not* talking to Mike about FBI agents.

Reed started the meeting. "Welcome to Maine. Thank you for coming. We won't be long here. I've included information in your folders on who we are and what we do. Review it at your leisure. Feel free to ask any questions as we go along, or find me later." He opened his own folder, in front of him on the table. "This isn't on the agenda, but why don't we start with each of you describing your life over the past seventy-two hours, before you arrived here? That will help break the ice, so to speak, and get us reacquainted. Naomi, why don't you go first?"

She dived in with an answer. "A meeting in London, a night in the Cotswolds, a night in Rock Point just down the road from here, and now here I am."

Reed gave her a small smile. "Can you give us a bit more detail?"

"I met with a volunteer medical group in London. For a break, I walked to a Mayfair art gallery. Then I took a walk in St. James's Park. That afternoon, I hired a car to drive me to the Cotswolds. So pretty. You were there, Reed. Don't you think it's incredible scenery?"

"Very nice," he said, his eyes half-closed on her.

She picked up her iced tea but didn't drink any. "After break-fast, I took a walk in the countryside and ended up saving a man's life. That was yesterday morning. The man might have survived without me, but he was in a jam. Hypothermia, head injury. He said he slipped on a wet bank above a stream, but he was muddled. I don't think he remembers what happened."

"You didn't mention this when I picked you up," Reed said.

"True, I didn't."

"Why not?"

She shrugged. "Still processing whether it was relevant." Out of the corner of her eye, she saw Kavanagh shift in his chair. She drank some of her tea and set her glass back on the table. She was avoiding Mike's eye. He probably knew it. "The in-jured man was British. Martin Hambly. I got him settled into a dovecote that's been converted into a potting shed. I'd never been inside a dovecote. They were quite the rage a few hundred years ago. Pigeon houses, basically. Think you guys could eat pigeon?" Naomi didn't wait for an answer. "Doesn't sound ap-petizing to me. Anyway, I handed Hambly off to a farmworker. Johnny. Didn't get a last name."

"Where was this?" Kavanagh asked.

"I was on a public path that goes through private property. Turns out the dovecote is on the farm owned by a wealthy Brit named Oliver York." Naomi kept her gaze on Kavanagh, but he had no visible reaction. "*Turns out* is a bit misleading. I knew it was York's farm."

No one at the table spoke.

Naomi decided to continue. "Oliver York is something of a mystery. When he was eight, his parents were murdered and he was kidnapped and held in a Scottish ruin until he escaped. It was a celebrated, tragic case in Great Britain. What, one won-ders, has he been up to since then?"

"Why do you care?" Reed asked.

"I got curious when I saw York on Wednesday at a London

art gallery that's showing works by Irish artist Aoife O'Byrne. It took some doing but I figured out who he was."

"And you're interested in this artist…why?"

"If you're about to recruit Mike here for your team, then I suspect you know why."

Reed's face darkened. "Don't play games with me, Naomi."

"Who's playing games?"

Reed made no response.

"The O'Byrnes have a history with the Sharpes." Naomi looked across the table at Mike. "Did you meet Aoife when she was in Boston last fall?"

"She's none of my business."

Mike's tone suggested she was none of Naomi's business, either—or, by extension, anyone else's at the table. She wished now she had grabbed half a tuna sandwich or a couple of celery sticks, just to have something else to do—a reason to keep her hands moving. She didn't want these guys to see she was shaking. She settled for another sip of her tea.

Kavanagh tapped the unopened folder in front of him. "For those who missed it, Aoife O'Byrne was caught up in a murder investigation that involved Mike's brother Colin and his fiancée, Emma Sharpe, both FBI agents. Her grandfather, Wendell Sharpe, is a private art detective who investigated an art theft at the O'Byrnes' home in Ireland. For the record," he added, his voice clipped, deliberate, "I was in the Cotswolds yesterday. I was aware Oliver York has a farm there. I was there because I was concerned Naomi had gone on a tangent. Seems I was right."

"What about you, Reed?" Naomi asked. "Were you in the Cotswolds so you could pick me up and invite me here, or were you worried I was on a tangent, too?"

"I didn't know why you were there, Naomi," Reed said.

Mike's gaze was firmly on her, but he said nothing.

She shrugged. "Maybe I wasn't on a tangent. Maybe I was meant to be in that quaint English village so I could save the

Brit's life. I've had an eventful seventy-two hours. If it'd been a month ago, I'd be telling you how I helped my mother clean out her sewing room."

"Glad things worked out for you with this injured Brit," Reed said. "Let's move on. Unless Naomi here has anything else to add."

"The gooseberry jam I had with my croissant was from the York farm. It was delicious."

Reed gave an audible sigh. "You have to remember that the rest of us don't have your convoluted brain. We're straightforward. Maybe that's why we need each other. Agent Kavanagh, do you have anything to add about this Cotswolds sideshow?"

"I was there. Otherwise, not a thing."

"What did you do after breakfast?" Naomi asked him.

"Checked out and drove to Heathrow. Anything else?"

"What's a Cotswold?" Buddy asked, then chuckled to himself. "Lame humor, I know. Sorry. Want to hear about my last seventy-two hours? I was in Tennessee, typing like a maniac so I could finish up a few things and fly up here yesterday—which I did. Mike? You next?"

"Worked at my cabin."

He didn't elaborate, and Reed didn't seem to expect him to.

"I'm on leave," Kavanagh said. "I saw Naomi and you, Reed, in London."

"You're here on your own time, then?" Buddy asked.

"He's always an FBI agent, Buddy," Reed said. "Am I right, Agent Kavanagh?"

"You are right," he said.

The meeting got started. Naomi steadied her breathing. Bringing up Oliver York and the injured Hambly hadn't yielded any answers, but the response of the men at the table didn't sit right with her. Reed's question about the past seventy-two hours didn't sit right, either.

She got up, hungry now, and put a cheese sandwich and a few

vegetables on a plate, resisting more cookies. She returned to her seat, aware of Mike watching her. She would focus on the work at hand. Whatever was going on wasn't straightforward and simple. She had to be patient.

"Tell us about your volunteer doctors," Reed said.

That she could do.

At the end of the hour-long meeting, Reed stood, his arms crossed on his chest as he addressed the rest of the gathered group. "Reputation is key to the success of any crisis management company, but reputation is earned. I saw that with the previous company I worked for. They worked hard to earn their reputation, and then they guarded it fiercely. False accusations can not only ruin reputations, they can ruin lives. I've dealt with them. I likely will again."

"Anything lately?" Kavanagh asked.

"Yes. That shouldn't surprise or alarm anyone, though." Reed paused, but no one filled the silence before he went on. "I'm always vigilant. So should you be. If any of you are dealing with any threats—direct or implied—I want to know. Blackmail, extortion, envy, frustrated ex-spouses, disgruntled competitors. People, in short, who wish you ill."

"I have a long list of people who wish me ill," Buddy said. "World's full of jerks."

Kavanagh sat forward. "Anyone dealing with an actual threat needs to bring it to the attention of law enforcement."

"And to me," Reed added.

"Because of your company," Kavanagh said.

"That's right. We're not law enforcement officers, nor are we vigilantes. I need to know if there's trouble on the horizon for the sake of all of us involved in Cooper Global Security." Reed dropped his hands to his sides and smiled. "Enjoy your time here. We will talk more. I'm going out snowshoeing in a little while. I noticed a trail along the water. There's enough equipment for whoever wants to join me."

Naomi left the room first. If the guys wanted to go snowshoeing, they could have at it. She slipped into a lounge down the hall and sat next to a low fire burning in a sturdy, prosaic brick fireplace.

Who was threatening Reed Cooper?

Was someone threatening him?

She'd never get it out of him unless he wanted to tell her. If anything, the meeting had added to her misgivings instead of alleviating them.

She felt Mike's presence a split second before she looked up at him. "Tempted to go snowshoeing?" she asked.

"Not right now. Colin's on his way."

"Here? Great. Then we can have two FBI agents in the house."

"You can tell him about Oliver York." Mike pointed to a side table. "Reed stocked a couple of good whiskeys."

"Your priest is a whiskey expert. Father Bracken. He's Irish. He was at the gallery in London." Naomi held up a hand. "Don't go nuts. I didn't talk to him. I'm sure it was him, though. I learned about him when I looked into Aoife O'Byrne. You know how it is. You pull on one string and a whole ball of knots starts to untangle."

"I don't know how that is."

"It's probably like following a moose trail in the wild."

Mike's deep blue eyes settled on her. "Right. It's like that."

"Sorry. I'm not demeaning your current life."

"Yes, you are."

"All right. I didn't intend to demean your current life." She wasn't that repentant. She eyed the bottles on the sidebar. "I don't see any Bracken Distillers whiskeys."

Mike lifted a bottle of Redbreast 21. "Father Bracken would approve. Did you speak with anyone at the gallery?"

"Just one of the workers. T.K.—Agent Kavanagh—followed

me there. I saw him and left. He was on my nerves. He showed up at my hotel on Tuesday, probably because of Reed. I wasn't expecting him. Reed made no secret that he wanted to recruit you. I did some digging and learned about Aoife O'Byrne and the Sharpes and all the rest."

"You weren't checking on me for Reed?"

She shook her head. "Kavanagh might have been. After I left the gallery, he followed me into St. James's Park and chewed me out there. I was having a look at Oliver York's apartment. T.K. thinks I'm playing with fire."

"He knows you well, then," Mike said, sounding neutral— which she knew he wasn't.

Naomi rolled her eyes. "If I were as reckless as you guys think I am, I'd have been the one with the head injury and hypothermia in England instead of that Brit." She nodded to the Redbreast. "It's a good sign Reed wants you on his team badly enough to stock quality whiskey. I'd take that as an act of good faith, wouldn't you?"

"I take it as good whiskey."

"You're in concrete-thinking mode. Got it. It's too early for Redbreast, although I could make a case for it since I'm still somewhat on English time. A few sips of Irish whiskey, curl up by the fire for a nap. That could work."

"You could go snowshoeing with Reed."

"Oh, joy. Remember my issue with wool socks? As in I don't have any."

"That's just an excuse," Mike said.

"Now we're getting somewhere." But her attempt at humor failed, came across to her as defensive, even shrill. She needed to throttle back after the intense meeting. "Are you going to wait here for your brother?"

"He'll find me."

"I wouldn't be surprised if we're experiencing the 'private contractor' effect. Not all contractors are perfect. Some have crossed lines that got a lot of attention. I'm careful, and I know guys like Reed do good work and serve a real need. He prevents bad things from happening if he can and deals with them if he can't. Always better to prevent problems versus having to send in the cavalry."

Mike nodded. "Agreed," he said, leaving it at that.

Naomi felt blood rush to her face. He had been the cavalry for her. The rough man with the gun. "We're not omnipotent or perfect," she said quietly, suddenly wishing Mike had stayed out on the Bold Coast. "Are you tempted to join Cooper Global Security?"

"I'm here to listen to what Reed has to say."

"He's good or I wouldn't have had him meet with my medical professionals."

"It's not about that. What about you? Tempted?"

"Me? I'm an independent consultant. Self-employed."

"Don't you think he asked you here because he wants to hire you to work for him exclusively?"

"He hasn't said as much. If I went to work for him, then I'd have a boss. I've had bosses. I do better when I don't. Clients are different. I work on their behalf but not for them."

"Mind of your own," Mike said.

Mind of your own was code for *loose cannon*. He would always believe she had acted precipitously in Afghanistan when he had rescued her. He knew as well as she did that precipitous and courageous sometimes went hand in hand, but he had his own way of looking at things.

"I did what I had to do three years ago," she said, trying not to sound defensive.

"What you thought you had to do."

Nothing to be gained from going further. She picked up the Redbreast. "No peat, right?"

"No peat."

She set the bottle back on the table. "I drink bourbon at home.

Are you going to tell Colin—Agent Donovan—about my visit to the gallery and the injured guy at the York farm?"

"You can tell him when he gets here."

She sank into her comfy chair. Soft cushions, a hot fire, the prospect of whiskey, the lingering fatigue of jet lag and the raw nerves of being around Mike Donovan when he was on a quiet, purposeful tear. Not a good combination.

"I was wondering whether to dress for dinner," she said. "Did you check out the dining room? Nice. I have this little knit dress I roll up for emergencies. Tights, boots, a scarf and earrings, and I'm good to go. What about you?"

"No little dress I roll up."

"You know what I meant."

"I'm not thinking about dinner."

"What are you thinking about?"

"Do you know all about us, Naomi?"

"Not all. Some, though. It's my job."

"I'll ask you again. Reed hired you to look into me?"

"No. I wouldn't be surprised if he either hired or green-lighted Kavanagh to do a background check, though. By the way, Aoife O'Byrne was at the gallery. I didn't speak with her, either. She's a very attractive woman as well as exceptionally talented. It was obvious she didn't want to talk to Father Bracken or Oliver York. I don't think they saw her."

Mike leaned forward. "Stay out of my family's business, Naomi. For your own sake."

He got up and left the room. When he was out of sight, Naomi said to hell with the early hour, splashed Redbreast 21 into a glass and took it to the French doors that opened onto the porch. The waves of undisturbed snow looked inviting. Probably not a good idea to go snowshoeing for the first time in her life after drinking whiskey. Jet lag or no jet lag. Mike Donovan or no Mike Donovan.

Once she finished her whiskey and her heartbeat returned to

normal, she would head up to her room, take a long, hot bath and wish she were somewhere else. Home in Nashville. Sewing with her mother. Still in London, working on security and crisis management for her medical professionals. When she first got into this business, she hadn't believed anyone would want to hurt nonpolitical, volunteer medical professionals dedicated to helping people. Her naïveté hadn't lasted long.

It wasn't until she had finished her splash of whiskey that she remembered she had worn a little knit dress in Washington on one of her days with Mike.

Heat rushed to her face that had nothing to do with alcohol.

She was remembering Mike removing the dress later that same evening...

He *couldn't* think she had brought it up as a reminder of that night, could he?

She thought of his lingering gaze.

Yeah, he could.

She thought about the little knit dress she'd brought with her to Maine.

It was a different one from three years ago.

18

Heron's Cove, Maine
Friday, 1:30 p.m., EST

Colin felt a certain uneasiness when he used Emma's key to let himself into the empty, revamped main offices of Sharpe Fine Art Recovery. He'd driven down to Heron's Cove after striking out in Rock Point, but there was no package from Oliver York here, either. He went out to the back porch, where, five months ago, Emma had painted at an easel while he spied on her from his brother Andy's boat, bobbing in the river below the house. He hadn't thought he'd fall in love with her, but he'd been attracted to her—green-eyed, smart, thoughtful and not like any FBI agent he'd ever met. He'd thought she kept secrets. Was this missing package one of her secrets?

He stood on the top steps. The river and the marina next door were quiet. They would bustle with boats of all kinds in the warm-weather months. Even now, there was more activity than there'd been at St. Patrick's Church and the rectory when he'd stopped there. He'd had a quick look around. No package.

He hadn't expected Emma's car at his house in Rock Point. He assumed one of the nuns had picked her up and taken her to the convent, but it struck him as odd for her not to drive herself. But what did he know about a convent retreat? *Her* convent retreat? He'd gone out of his way not to intrude. He hadn't asked her for details, and she hadn't offered any. He told himself he was giving her space, but the truth was, he hadn't wanted to dig into details. He was fine with Emma's past with the Sisters of the Joyful Heart, but that didn't mean he wanted to know everything about it. Let it stay on the surface. He didn't need to dive deep into her life as Sister Brigid.

He'd checked the house in case she'd come home from her retreat early, but she wasn't there. The bed was still made up, the heat still turned down low.

He looked down at the undisturbed snow in the Sharpe yard. He wanted to talk to Emma about the package Oliver York had sent her and their art thief's latest antics, and about Finian Bracken's visit to the Cotswolds. Was she enjoying her retreat? Was it pulling her back into her past—into whatever had driven her to think she should become a nun? Or was it finally freeing her of the hold it had on her? Because there was a hold, whether or not she wanted to acknowledge it or couldn't quite define it.

Damned if he could, either. He just knew she needed this time and wanted to stay out of her way.

Nuns.

He gritted his teeth. He couldn't think about Emma as a nun. She was the woman he loved and would marry in a few short months. She wasn't a nun now. That was what mattered, what he had to remember.

Maybe the package from York hadn't arrived yet. In Colin's experience, the simplest explanation was often the correct explanation.

He wished Emma would get in touch but recognized that it shouldn't bug him that she hadn't. He needed to put the damn package out of his mind and head to the Plum Tree and Mike and his friends, find out why Ted Kavanagh and Naomi Mac-Bride were on York's trail, and how they'd picked it up in the first place.

The Sharpe porch had a roof but wasn't fully enclosed, and he could feel the wind, icy and cold. He noticed a movement down by the hedges that separated the yard and a parking lot behind an inn next door to his left, close to the mouth of the river.

He recognized Sister Cecilia, Emma's friend. The young nun lifted the hem of her midcalf coat above her knees and stepped into the snow in the backyard. She waved to him. "Colin—I didn't expect to see you. Oh, dear. I've snow in my shoes. Not much of a path, is there?"

"Hold on. I'll come to you." He trotted down the porch steps and crossed the yard on a narrow footpath that had been hastily shoveled through the knee-deep snow. "Hello, Sister."

"It's so nice to see you, Colin." She shivered, her arms crossed on her chest against the cold. The wind tangled her hair. She wore only her wide headband, no hat. No gloves, either. "I wasn't expecting to be outside this afternoon. Is Emma here with you? We must have our wires crossed. I thought we were going to meet at the studio in town for her painting lesson."

"Is that part of her retreat?"

"Her retreat? Didn't she…" Sister Cecilia hesitated, pulling her hands up inside her coat sleeves. "Emma canceled her retreat at the convent."

Colin went still. "When?"

"Yesterday afternoon. She stopped at the shop here in town and told me she was canceling. Then she called Mother Superior and told her. I thought we were still meeting today for a painting lesson, but she didn't show up. She's working on a series of watercolors of Ocean Avenue. I thought maybe that's where we were supposed to meet…" The young nun glanced behind her, toward the ocean, then turned back to Colin. "I walked a little ways up Ocean Avenue, but I didn't see her. Then I came here."

"What time did she stop by to see you yesterday?"

"Just after five o'clock. She wasn't upset or anything. Honestly, I wasn't surprised she decided to cancel her retreat at the convent, even at the last minute."

"Have you been in touch with her by email, text—"

"I tried calling but it went straight to voice mail." Sister Cecilia shivered again, her pale eyes on Colin. "You two... You haven't been in touch with her?"

"Not since yesterday morning."

"We would know if she'd been in an accident, wouldn't we?"

"I'm sure we would," Colin said, trying to reassure her—and maybe himself, too.

"It's icy up on the water where she was painting. If she went up there and slipped and hit her head..." Sister Cecilia inhaled. "Someone would have seen her."

He touched Sister Cecilia's upper arm. "Did you walk or drive from the studio?"

"I walked. I got myself worked up and struck out on foot without thinking about the weather. I only came through the backyard here because I know Emma often paints on the porch. The marina is one of the waterfront scenes she wants to paint."

"Let's go inside." Colin struggled to keep the tension out of his voice, his own fears at bay. He needed Sister Cecilia as calm as possible so that she could remember details. "We'll find Emma."

She nodded. "I know we will."

He appreciated her certainty. He let her go ahead of him onto the path across the yard. He had his cell phone out, hit Yank's number. "Anything from Emma?" he asked when Yank picked up.

"Isn't she at the convent?"

"No."

Yank inhaled. He would fill in the blanks. If Colin was calling, it meant Emma wasn't answering her phone and he couldn't find her. "I'll check with the team," Yank said, disconnecting. Details could come later.

Wind gusted off the water, whipping hair into Sister Cecilia's face as she mounted the porch steps. The back door was still unlocked. She glanced at Colin, and he nodded. She went inside, saying nothing, clearly worried. He called Kevin's cell phone number. "Hey, Colin," his youngest brother said, no hint of worry in his voice. "You in town?"

"Heron's Cove. Have you seen Emma?"

"Before she headed to the convent? No. What—"

"Mike, Andy, anyone else mention seeing her yesterday or today?"

"No. What's going on, Colin?"

"I don't know. She canceled the convent and missed a painting lesson with one of the sisters in Heron's Cove. We can't find her."

"You're at the Sharpe offices?"

"Yes. I have Sister Cecilia with me."

"I'll be there in ten."

Colin went into the freshly renovated Sharpe kitchen. Sister Cecilia touched his arm. "I'm okay, Colin. Please don't worry about me. Do what you need to do. I'll try to make sure I've remembered everything."

He thanked her and called his mother. "Hey, I just got into town." He forced himself to keep any tension out of his voice. "You and Emma still on for your lunch tomorrow?"

"As far as I know. She's at the convent again tonight. I expect we'll connect in the morning. Are you going up to the Plum Tree to see about Mike and these friends? Colin, I'm afraid they want him to be one of their mercenaries. Your father cautioned me that most private contractors do good work. I don't know."

"I'm on my way up there. I have a couple things I need to do first. I'll catch you later."

"Colin—"

He pretended not to hear her and disconnected.

He stood in front of the sink and stared out the window, clutching his phone, trying not to get ahead of himself. Emma could have taken a cab to Portland for the day. Since everyone thought she was at the convent, she could be enjoying a digital holiday. Picking out wedding shoes.

He needed facts.

Kevin would have told him if the police had an unidentified injured female on their hands.

Or a dead one.

Sister Cecilia got two glasses down from a white-painted cupboard. Colin stepped aside, and she filled the glasses with water, setting them on the counter. She gave him a weak smile. "You don't have to drink it."

"Thank you, Sister."

He wanted to ask her if Emma had mentioned the package, Oliver York, Reed Cooper, Ted Kavanagh, Naomi MacBride, Mike, the Plum Tree Inn—Aoife O'Byrne, Finian Bracken, London, the Cotswolds…

Colin took a breath, stopping himself. He knew better than to let his mind ping here, there and everywhere. He didn't have enough to get crazy yet, anyway. Emma's car was in Rock Point, but the Plum Tree wasn't far. For all he knew, she'd hooked up with Kavanagh and hitched a ride with him.

Colin texted Mike. Have you heard from Emma?

No. Isn't she with the nuns?

Canceled. He didn't explain further. On my way soon.

His fingers were cold, shaking. Not good. He drank some of the water Sister Cecilia had poured. She was outwardly calm, but she'd had a difficult recovery from her encounter with a killer in September. She had permanent scars from where she'd been cut, tortured.

"I hope I'm not worrying you unnecessarily," she said quietly.

"Nothing would make me happier."

"I know what you mean. I hope you find Emma at a spa, getting her toes done."

Sister Cecilia took her water glass to the kitchen table and sat down.

Kevin arrived, coming in through the front door. Colin introduced him to Sister Cecilia and filled him in. He could see the questions in his youngest brother's eyes. They would be the same hundred questions Colin would have in Kevin's place.

"How do you want to handle this?" Kevin asked.

"Talk to Sister Cecilia. Keep this quiet for now. If someone..." Colin got control of himself. "It's possible someone grabbed Emma."

"Colin..."

"Yeah. I know, Kevin."

Both knew the drill if she'd been snatched. Proof of life. Pinpoint her location. Rescue her.

Simpler to say than to execute.

"Can't jump ahead," Colin added, more to himself than to his brother. "I'll head back to the rectory and the house to see if I missed anything obvious there, and I'll check with Finian and York about this package."

"If she was grabbed at either place—"

"Yeah. Seal them off. Find any witnesses."

Kevin nodded. "We'll do this your way," he said.

Colin started toward the hall door. "We'll stay in touch."

He knew Kevin was aware he wasn't getting everything. That the rest—whatever it was—could wait until they were sure Emma wasn't cross-country skiing with friends.

He swallowed, tasting bile. She wasn't cross-country skiing.

He turned to Sister Cecilia. "Thank you, Sister."

"I hope I didn't mess up and she's waiting for me at the studio."

Kevin touched her shoulder. "Let's go up there and have a look."

Colin left them and went out through the front.

He tried Emma's cell phone again as he got back into his truck. Straight to voice mail. No response to his earlier texts.

"Emma. Damn."

He put his phone in his jacket pocket and started his truck.

The church and rectory were unchanged from his earlier visit. No one was around. With their Irish priest on vacation at home in Ireland, parishioners had less reason to stop by. The church secretary wasn't working today, or she'd taken advantage of Finian's time away and booked some herself. Colin didn't know. He didn't keep track of the day-to-day workings of his hometown's Roman Catholic parish.

He was more attuned to anything out of the ordinary than he had been an hour ago. Looking for it. He noticed prints in the snow in front of the church. Dog, probably.

His phone buzzed with a text. Kevin. Checked with couriers. Package delivered yesterday about 4 p.m.

It wasn't here, Colin thought. Someone had picked it up. Emma would have been arriving in southern Maine around then. She'd be curious about what Oliver York was sending her, but she'd also consider it her job to find out. She wouldn't leave the package for anyone else. She'd pick it up herself.

Colin treated the rectory as if it were a crime scene. He knew he had to take this one step at a time. He also knew Kevin wouldn't let him get too far in before he forced his brother to step back and let the local and state police take the lead in finding Emma.

First things first.

He scanned the walks, snow, ice, porch and garage for anything he could have missed earlier. Prints that could be hers.

Parts of the package from England. Signs of injury or struggle. Blood, a dropped scarf or phone.

There was nothing.

Had someone beat Emma to the package?

He got back in his truck. He had to gather the evidence and see which way it pointed. Tunnel vision wouldn't help.

Except this was Emma.

Kevin called as Colin started the engine. "She's not at the sisters' shop," his brother said. "I called Hurley's, in case she walked down there from your house and let time get away from her. No luck. We'll find her, Colin."

He drove back to his house, pulling in behind Emma's car. As he got out, Yank called. "I'm on my way to the airport. Padgett's heading up there. Keep us informed."

"Yank, we don't have anything that confirms she's in trouble."

"Let's hope she's not. We can all have a beer at Hurley's. Padgett's never been to Hurley's." But Yank's voice was clipped, his concern unmistakable. "Go up to this inn. Talk to Kavanagh. Find out what the hell's going on up there." A slight pause. "Don't go in with guns blazing. It won't help."

"If Kavanagh stirred up York…"

"Don't go there. I'm betting her phone got busted and she's not worrying about it right now, since she knows we all think she's with the sisters. She's probably visiting a friend, enjoying her long weekend."

Colin knew he didn't have to tell Yank that Emma never would have left Sister Cecilia hanging. She'd have found a way to cancel their lesson. But why not indulge in a few seconds of wishful thinking? In wishful-thinking mode, Sister Cecilia would have missed Emma's message canceling their lesson.

He hung up with Yank and walked up to Emma's car. He inspected it without touching it, but he didn't see anything out of the ordinary—no package, no signs of a struggle or any problem.

Emma…

Colin sucked in a breath, knowing she was in trouble. Feeling it. Did she know he would find her?

Because he would.

There was no question in his mind, no other option. He would find her.

19

Finian inhaled deeply at the fear he heard in his American friend's voice. "What else can I do?"

Colin didn't respond right away. Although he refused to give details, it was clear that something was terribly wrong, and whatever it was involved Emma and, at least potentially, the situation with the American pair, Naomi MacBride and Ted Kavanagh. This obviously was a difficult call for Colin. Finian was glad he'd been in the guest suite, alone, when his phone rang. So far, he hadn't been much help. No, he didn't know what was in the package Oliver had sent to Rock Point for Emma. No, Finian didn't know who else knew about the package. It had been picked up on Wednesday afternoon, before the American woman—Naomi MacBride—had discovered Martin Hambly at the dovecote yesterday morning.

"MacBride checked into the pub on Wednesday," Colin said.

"She had time to go to the dovecote? Did your waiter put her at or near York's farm then?"

Finian understood what Colin was getting at. Could Naomi MacBride have pushed Martin Hambly down the stream bank, or possibly have seen the package, then intercepted it in Rock Point? Leaving it behind in England would make sense given her flight to the United States and tight airport security and customs. She could wait and intercept it upon its arrival at the rectory.

What did she think was in the package? Or did she know?

"The waiter didn't mention seeing her at the York farm," Finian said. "He did see the man who was with her at breakfast—Ted Kavanagh."

"The waiter's positive it was Kavanagh?"

"Seems so. He says Kavanagh spoke with the courier. I can ask him to confirm—"

"No, Fin, don't ask," Colin said. "No prowling around. My advice is to think up an excuse and get the hell out of there. Go back to Ireland or come home."

Finian didn't remind him that Ireland was home. It wasn't a time to get bothered by semantics. "Don't worry about me, Colin. Are you sure there's nothing I can do to help?"

"Say a prayer for Emma, Fin." Colin's voice was ragged, choked.

"I will. Take care, my good friend."

It was a moment before Finian realized Colin was gone. He held his phone, aware of raindrops striking the windows in the guest suite. The day's sunshine had lasted until midafternoon before giving in to clouds and rain. Ruthie Burns had promised to light a fire for him, but he'd assured her he could manage.

What's happened to Emma?

Finian steadied his breathing, then left the suite, his phone still in his hand. He walked down a chilly hall to the living room. He found Oliver standing by the fire, staring at the flames as if transfixed. Could *he* know what had happened to Emma?

Could he be a part of it, even? Finian dismissed the questions. He would focus on what he knew and not speculate about what he didn't know.

Oliver stood straight, as if he were deliberately jerking himself out of his thoughts. "Martin's remembered something. He's at the pub. Care to go down there with me?"

"Of course."

"Excellent. We'll take the Rolls."

Oliver was a mad driver, but fortunately it was a short distance to the village pub. Finian was downright relieved his host had hired a car for him for the drive from London. They went inside together. The pub was crowded with locals, but Martin had secured a table by the fire. He was nursing a pint, looking stronger. He held up a hand as Finian and Oliver joined him. "Not a word about mixing alcohol and head injuries," he said.

Oliver grunted, sitting across from Martin. "You wouldn't keep your mouth shut if I were the one with the bashed-in head."

"You're not," Martin said. "Be grateful and leave me alone. Besides, I've a gash not a concussion. I'll have a roguish scar, nothing more, for my ordeal."

Oliver turned to Finian. "We'll have whiskey, shall we? You choose."

Finian remembered Oliver was partial to Scotch and ordered Talisker for them both. Martin stuck to his pint. They waited to continue their conversation until the waiter—the same lad who'd spotted Ted Kavanagh at the York farm—delivered their glasses.

Oliver clinked his glass onto Finian's. *"Sláinte."*

Finian mumbled *"Sláinte"* in return. He noticed Oliver's furrowed brow, but he withheld comment and turned to Martin. "Have you remembered how one manages to get a gash on the back of one's neck while falling down a Cotswolds stream bank? It wasn't the snowdrops that did it."

"A sharp rock would do." Martin glanced around, but no one

seemed to be paying them any mind. He frowned at Oliver. "Keep your voice down. I don't want to have to make a police report, and neither do you."

"The bloody FBI are involved now," Oliver said. "They can notify the local police with or without our knowledge."

Martin shook his head knowingly. "They won't if one of their own is out of control. I think it might be this Ted Kavanagh. I decided to retrace my steps on Wednesday to see if it would help jog my memory. I remember that I picked up amaryllis bulbs in the village that afternoon, then decided to walk past the church on my way back to the farm. I went over there…" He paused, still clearly in pain from his injuries. "I ran into a man there who identified himself as an FBI agent. Special Agent Ted Kavanagh. He showed me his credentials but I didn't take a close look. He didn't have a card with his contact information."

Oliver frowned. "Our Agent Kavanagh gets around. Did he ask for me to get in touch with him?"

Martin shook his head, then shut his eyes, as if waiting for a wave of pain to pass. He opened his eyes again, his face noticeably grayer. "He knew about you, and he mentioned Agents Sharpe and Donovan."

"Well, well," Oliver said, leaning back against his bench.

"It felt like a fishing expedition," Martin added.

"Obviously this encounter was before your mishap," Finian said. "We're putting together a fairly reliable timeline. We know Agent Kavanagh stayed here Wednesday night and spoke that afternoon with the courier who picked up the package we sent to Emma—Agent Sharpe. Do you remember seeing the courier?"

"No," Martin said. "I don't remember anything about the package. It's driving me mad."

Oliver tapped the rim of his glass with the tip of one finger. "The courier apparently didn't notice anything amiss. I suspect you were ass-over-teakettle down the bank by then, Martin. Are you certain you don't remember what happened at the dovecote?"

"My memory of the fall hasn't fully returned," Martin said, his tone even.

"I'm not getting impatient," Oliver told him.

"Yes, you are."

Oliver scoffed, "I'm feeling the urgency of the situation. I know badgering you won't help your memory return."

"You'd badger if it would help."

"Most assuredly," Oliver said, unapologetic, his eyes twinkling as he lifted his glass and took a sip of the Scotch. "You'd badger me if our positions were reversed. Don't deny it."

"I don't," Martin said, wincing, clearly in pain. "This is a bridge too far given my condition, I'm afraid, but it's good to be out and about. I'll remember more. I know I will. I can feel it."

"Assuming there's anything else to remember," Oliver added.

Finian drank some of his Talisker, debating how much to tell the two Englishmen about Colin's call. Colin hadn't expressly forbidden him from saying anything. In fact, Finian could argue that his friend had implied he was to use his own judgment. He finally decided there was nothing to be gained from being circumspect.

He sat forward, feeling the fire. "Colin Donovan called from Maine a little while ago. The package was delivered to the rectory yesterday as scheduled but has disappeared, and, I gather, Emma Sharpe along with it."

Martin blanched. "Good heavens."

Oliver set his glass on the rough-wood table. Flames from the fire reflected in his eyes. "Tell us everything, Finian. Let us help if we can."

Finian explained what he knew about Emma's convent retreat and its cancellation, and the situation in Rock Point. He abandoned his Scotch for the moment. After all, what did he know about Oliver York and Martin Hambly? How deeply involved had Martin been in Oliver's thefts? How far would Martin go to preserve the York reputation?

"What was in the package?" Finian asked finally.

"The contents are utterly harmless and of value only to the intended recipient," Oliver said. "If some idiot believed otherwise…" He didn't finish. "Dear Emma. I saw her once in Dublin, after she'd left the convent but before she joined the FBI. She had no idea. Still doesn't. I was considering consulting her grandfather."

Spying on him, he meant. Finian let it go. "I knew of Wendell Sharpe and Sharpe Fine Art Recovery prior to finding myself in Maine and meeting Emma. There's a logical if roundabout connection. Father Callaghan, the priest at St. Patrick's, chose Declan's Cross as one of his destinations on a trip to Ireland prior to his sabbatical. He knew of Declan's Cross because of the Sharpes. I happened to be there at the same time as Father Callaghan. He was staying at the O'Byrne House, which had just opened as a hotel."

"The brainchild of Aoife's sister, Kitty," Oliver said.

Finian debated again. He wasn't sure how much Hambly knew about the suspicions surrounding Oliver. "Kitty and Aoife inherited their uncle's house and all its contents upon his death a few years ago. They recently had art that was stolen from the house ten years ago returned intact." Finian listened to the pops and hisses of the fire. "The thief is still at large."

Oliver lifted his glass and took another sip, then set the glass down again, firmly. "Sheepskins," he pronounced.

Martin frowned at his employer and friend as if he'd lost his mind. "Sheepskins?"

"That's what's in the package. Three sheepskins, one for each side of Colin and Emma's bed and one for wherever they want to put it." Oliver gave a quick smile. "Sorry, Finian. Let's assume the sheepskins are for the postmarital bed. I wouldn't want to offend."

As if Finian didn't live in the contemporary world. He made no comment.

"Anything else in the package?" Martin asked.

Oliver waved a hand. "I enclosed a cross I created in my studio at the dovecote. It's a traditional Saint Brigid's cross but instead of being made of rushes twisted together, it's made of silver. It was a difficult piece to make. Rushes would have been much easier. Emma called herself Sister Brigid during her days as a nun. Along with Saint Patrick and Saint Columba, Saint Brigid is one of the patron saints of Ireland. She's a fascinating figure. The cross is my best work but I'm no artist. Its only value is the silver."

"There's nothing provocative about the package contents, then?" Finian asked.

"Sheepskins and a Saint Brigid's cross?" Oliver looked mystified. "What could be provocative about that?"

"Unless they could be used against Agent Sharpe somehow," Martin said, half to himself.

"How?" Oliver asked, clearly skeptical.

Martin shrugged. "Sometimes it only takes the belief and even just the suspicion of wrongdoing to cause trouble."

Finian considered Martin's point. If someone was trying to undermine Emma, or tie her to Oliver York in some unsavory way—prove she was covering for him, or had known about him for years and hadn't done anything to stop him—it could explain the past forty-eight hours. More important, it could help lead to her whereabouts.

What if she was in hiding, trying to figure out her next move? But Finian couldn't imagine her leaving Colin in the dark. The anguish in his friend's voice had been genuine, Finian thought. He was convinced the call hadn't been part of an elaborate ruse, whatever else was going on between his two FBI agent friends and Oliver.

"I'm giving up metal and stonework," Oliver said. "It's time for new pursuits."

Meaning he was giving up art thefts, too? Finian had no intention of asking him outright, not here, at least.

"I would hate to think a simple, well-intentioned gift of authentic Cotswolds sheepskins and a beautiful silver Saint Brigid's cross could cause harm to anyone," Oliver added with a heavy sigh.

Martin pushed his empty pint glass aside. "I suspect we're caught in the middle of something else that's going on, and so, perhaps, is Agent Sharpe. What can we do to help, Father Bracken?"

"Permit me to call Colin and tell him what's in the package."

"Done," Oliver said. "But you know he'll tell you that you can't trust me and you should go back to Ireland."

"He already has." Finian shifted to Martin, who looked as if he wanted to curl up by the fire for the night…or several nights. His skin had gone ashen, the bruising on his neck blossoming now into splotches of dark blue, purple and yellow. "A visit to the dovecote could help you remember more details of your fall, just as retracing your steps to the church did. Do you think you'd be up to it in the morning?"

"I'm up to it now if it would help," Martin said.

"It's dark and it's raining," Finian said. "Let's go at daylight."

"Brilliant." Oliver smacked the table with the palm of his hand. "We'll all go."

Martin didn't look as enthusiastic about having Oliver join him, but he said nothing. He refused Oliver's offer of a ride back to the farm. Martin had wanted fresh air and had walked on his own to the pub, but he would get a ride back from a friend, after he finished nursing his pint—and, Finian suspected, a whiskey, once he and Oliver had gone on their way.

"Tell me about Saint Brigid," Colin said, alert and intense when Finian called to tell him what else he'd learned.

He sat in front of the fire in the living room while Oliver fetched glasses and more whiskey. Ruthie had left a plate of cold meat, cheese, grapes and apples, but Finian wasn't hungry and doubted Oliver was, either. The news about the package contents and Martin's encounter with Agent Kavanagh hadn't gone over well with Colin—largely, Finian suspected, because they gave him no clue as to where Emma was.

"Saint Brigid's story is intertwined with myth, legend and folklore," Finian said. "She shares many of the same characteristics as the Celtic goddess Brigid. A traditional Saint Brigid's cross is made of reeds. It's often placed above a door to protect the house from fire. Saint Brigid was a contemporary of Saint Patrick. It's said he heard her final vows when she entered the convent. She was a woman of great learning, spirituality, compassion and charity. She founded many convents but is most known for her convent in Kildare. *Cill Dara* in Irish. The Church of the Oak. The oak, of course, is sacred to pagan Celts."

"She's the patron saint of farmers, isn't she?" Colin asked.

"Farmers, babies, the children of unwed parents, the children of abusive fathers, sailors, poets—it's a long list. Saint Brigid also founded a school of art in Kildare that produced some of the most elaborate illuminated manuscripts of the time. The Book of Kildare is said to rival or exceed the Book of Kells in beauty and craftsmanship, but it disappeared three hundred years ago. Some say it actually is the Book of Kells. No matter now." Finian tried to ease his death grip on his phone. "I don't know if any of this helps, Colin."

"I don't, either. I doubt we're dealing with someone who's fixated on Saint Brigid. Did anyone else know about the cross?"

Finian had asked Oliver that same question on their return from the pub. "Oliver says he didn't tell anyone, including Emma. His studio is locked but there is no alarm system."

"And Kavanagh—he didn't mention the package, the cross, sheepskins?"

"Not to Martin, at least not that he recalls. His memory is still uncertain."

"All right. Thanks, Fin. I have to go."

Oliver appeared with the whiskey and glasses as Colin disconnected and Finian pried his fingers loose from the phone, setting it on the side table.

"The iconography, mysteries and legends of Brigid of Kildare and the possible whereabouts of our missing Emma." Oliver opened the whiskey, a newly introduced Bracken Distillers expression that Finian's twin brother, Declan, particularly liked. "That will keep us occupied well into the evening."

"Oliver, if you have any idea what's happened to Emma—"

"I wish I did, Finian."

Without further comment, Oliver poured the whiskey.

20

Mike was chatting with Serena and Jamie Mason in the lobby, getting a feel for Cooper Global Security and its president and CEO from their point of view, when his mother called. He excused himself, ignoring Jamie's grin. "A call from Mom, huh?" Serena elbowed her husband, reminding him that she'd give anything if she could talk to her mother, who'd died last year.

Mike stepped outside. "What's up?"

"Mike, what's going on?" Rosemary Donovan had her mother radar on. "Franny Maroney was just here with Emma's cell phone. She found it while she was out walking. It was on a sidewalk near St. Patrick's. She said Kevin was out there."

"Have you talked to Colin?"

"Yes. I called him first. He said to tell you he would be delayed. He and Kevin are on their way over here."

Mike didn't bother asking why Franny hadn't given Kevin the phone when she saw him. Franny was the widowed grandmother of Andy's girlfriend, Julianne, a marine biologist doing an internship in Ireland. The Maroneys had their ways.

"Mike," his mother said, "if you know what's going on—"

"I haven't heard anything. If something's up, Kevin and Colin are taking care of it. If you need to know, they'll tell you."

"I already know."

Mike wasn't arguing with her. He got off the phone with her and called Colin. "What do I need to know?"

Colin didn't answer at once. "I can't find Emma."

"Talk to me."

"She canceled the convent and missed an appointment with Sister Cecilia. Car's at the house."

And now Franny Maroney had found Emma's phone. It could mean a lot of things, not all of them bad, but Mike could guess where Colin's mind must have gone. His had gone there, too. Emma was in trouble. Mike listened intently as Colin told him about the package Oliver York sent to the rectory and Finian Bracken's side trip to the York farm.

"I know Naomi MacBride and Ted Kavanagh were there yesterday," Colin said. "I need to see about Emma's phone. Give me an hour. Mike…" His brother inhaled. "Would you recognize a Saint Brigid's cross if you saw one?"

"Sure. Franny Maroney had us make Saint Brigid's crosses in Sunday school when I was ten. She keeps one over her front door. Wards off evil spirits or something."

"If you run across a silver Saint Brigid's cross, call me. Keep this quiet. I'll get there as soon as I can."

Colin was gone. Mike slid his phone into his jacket pocket.

A Saint Brigid's cross?

He thought of Emma. They hadn't hit it off at first. He'd pictured Colin with a woman less complicated, and he hadn't wanted to see his brother hurt. But he'd seen Colin's love for her—and her love for him—and had throttled back on his distrust, and she'd won him over.

He could see her over the holidays, baking pies with his mother, laughing at all of his father's stupid jokes.

Mike's throat tightened. He liked Emma. He hoped her disappearance would turn out to be miscommunication. A phone she hadn't realized she'd dropped. A call she didn't know she needed to make.

Wherever she was, Mike wanted her back with Colin, safe and sound.

He went down the hall to the library. Reed was at a table, working on his laptop. "I'm finishing up a few things before I strap on my snowshoes," he said. "We should be able to get in a good trek before sunset. Am I going to burn down the place with that fire? Feels hot."

"It's fine," Mike said.

"I like it here this time of year better than I thought I would. It's a good choice after London. I think it's going to work out for us to provide security for Naomi's doctors." Reed tapped a few keys then looked up at Mike. "You should join us. The pay is good, and the work is good. Do what you're good at. You'd work on a contract basis, not as a full-time employee. You can do your wilderness guide work in summers. Work with us when you can."

Mike stepped away from the fire. It was hotter than what he was used to, but it wouldn't burn down the place. "Other people know how to do what I do."

Reed shook his head. "I don't trust other people the way I trust you."

"If you trust me, then you can tell me what's going on."

"What do you mean?"

"What did you make of Naomi's tale today?"

"About the Brit who fell? I had nothing to do with that," Reed said, dismissive. "Doing this work, Mike—it's who you are. You can keep people from getting hurt. I'm not in this just for the money, although the money is damn good."

"You're here because of your company," Mike said.

"Why else?"

"You brought an FBI agent."

"I didn't bring him. He came. I'm wide-open to talking to Kavanagh or anyone else with his kind of résumé."

"Reed, if you're in some kind of trouble, you should talk to Colin. He'll be here soon."

He shifted to the fire, his cheeks flushed from the heat. "What if our FBI agent is the problem?"

"Then all the more reason to talk to my brother."

"I was speaking hypothetically. There is no problem, Mike. I like how you think. I like that you ask questions and don't take anything for granted or at face value, but one thing at a time." Reed pointed at the fire. "Sure it's okay?"

"I'm sure," Mike said.

He returned to his room and grabbed his coat. He stood still, listening, but he didn't hear Naomi in her Lady Slipper room. He'd left her in the lounge, contemplating whiskey and snowshoeing, when he went to talk to the Masons. He hadn't noticed where she'd gone from there.

He headed back down to the lobby and ducked outside to meet Colin when he arrived. He might not always appreciate his mother's instincts, but he trusted them—and he'd heard the tension in his brother's voice himself.

Ted Kavanagh had the trunk of his rental car open. "I didn't know if I would be staying the night," he said when Mike approached him. "Might as well."

"Need a hand with anything?"

"All set, thanks." He got out a battered, soft-sided suitcase and set it on the ground. "What's on your mind, Mike? Having Reed and the rest of us here on your home turf has you on edge, doesn't it?"

Mike shrugged. "From the sounds of it, it would have been

easier to fly me to England. Who are you investigating, Agent Kavanagh?"

"I love that kind of question. The only good answer is for you to trust me."

"Why should I trust you? Because you're an FBI agent?"

"That's a place to start."

"Colin's on his way here. Are you investigating him, Agent Kavanagh?"

"My presence here has nothing to do with him. I don't have to explain myself to you." Kavanagh shut his car trunk and picked up his suitcase. "Look, Mike, I get where you're coming from, but you need to focus on what's good for you. Figure out if you have a future with Cooper Global Security."

"Will do, Agent Kavanagh." Mike tried to keep the sarcasm out of his voice, but he'd decide what he needed, not this FBI agent. "Naomi didn't report the incident with this guy in England to the local police. Do you have an obligation to report it?"

"I'm not a witness. I was already on my way to Heathrow when she was helping this guy. What, do you think Naomi attacked him?" Kavanagh frowned, studying Mike. "Do you think *I* attacked him?"

"I think you know more than you're saying. Doesn't mean you're lying."

"Butt out of my business, Mike."

Mike didn't know Kavanagh well from Afghanistan, but he was inclined to cut him some slack because he was an FBI agent. "Have you stayed in touch with Reed since Kabul?"

"I've stayed in touch on and off with everyone but you, Mike. Look, I'll give it to you straight. I've had a tough couple of years on the job. I'm looking at new opportunities."

"Reed's outfit is one of them?"

"Maybe. He and I got on well in Afghanistan. I want this thing to work out for him. He's one of the good guys and he does good work. I know something about private contractors, and I've no objection to Reed going out on his own." Kavanagh shivered, the cold turning his nose and cheeks red. "Reed was right when he said trust and reputation are everything in this work. I wouldn't want him tainted because of his old loyalties."

"To me, you mean," Mike said, toneless.

"It's not a knock on you if I did, but I don't mean anyone specifically. More guys are arriving tomorrow—more ex-soldiers with solid résumés. I'm not ingratiating myself with Reed, but if I could keep him from making a mistake, I would. I would do the same for Naomi, too. She has a sterling reputation. One wrong move could ruin her."

"That's why you followed her to this English village? You were keeping her from tripping over her own shoelaces?"

"Maybe I was."

"You don't like the idea of Reed recruiting me," Mike said.

"That's up to him. My opinion? Your heart's not in the work, Mike. I can see it. There's a difference between now and when you were in the army."

"No argument from me."

"Naomi's heart was never in the work. She's always been chasing her father's ghost. She knows what she's doing and she does it well. Her commitment is real but it's not like Reed's. He's in this to win. He wants to go big."

"You told Naomi she's playing with fire," Mike said.

"She is. She needs to stick to her volunteer doctors and clients like them—people she can feel good about helping. You can tell her. Maybe she'll listen to you."

Mike doubted that.

Kavanagh nodded to the inn's entrance. "A chair by a fire is calling to me. I'm going to take a nap. How's that for excitement? Jet lag didn't use to faze me but I'm beat."

"You'll miss snowshoeing."

"Hard to believe you have a sense of humor, Mike. Tell your brother I said hello."

"I'm not stopping him if he wants to get you up from your nap."

Kavanagh grinned. "I think I know the mood he's in. Is his fiancée with him?"

"She's taking a long weekend with friends."

"That opens up more questions than it answers. See you later, Mike."

Kavanagh went into the inn. Mike shoved his hands into his jacket pockets, although he wasn't cold. He wasn't jet-lagged, either. He didn't need a damn nap.

If having Colin as a brother and Emma as an imminent sister-in-law nixed his chances to work with Reed, that was fine with him, Mike thought. Did everyone else here believe it would be fine with him?

Didn't matter.

Back in November, he figured Oliver York, aka Oliver Fairbairn, for an art thief the Sharpes had been hunting. He didn't have to know the details, and he didn't care one way or the other if York was arrested—by the Brits, the FBI or some other law enforcement agency. His fate was of zero concern to Mike. *Unless* it affected the safety and the good reputation of his brother and his fiancée.

And Naomi?

As she'd pointed out, they were even. She'd saved his life. He'd saved her life.

In between, they'd made love a few times.

He gritted his teeth, remembering her laughter. He could see her under him, biting her lower lip as they made love. The woman who'd shown up at his parents' inn was the same Naomi MacBride he had fallen for three years ago. Smart, fearless and more vulnerable than she would ever admit—to herself or anyone else.

We're all vulnerable, Mike thought. It wasn't a big deal to him. It was a fact.

He wasn't falling for her again.

★ ★ ★

Ten minutes later, Mike was in Naomi's room. He'd grabbed a passkey at the front desk. Serena and Jamie weren't keeping watch, and he knew his way around inns. Plus he didn't care if he got caught.

The bedding was rumpled. He chose not to picture Naomi taking a catnap.

He checked her suitcase. No wheels, but a ton of zippers and compartments. Usual stuff for a business trip to London. He didn't unzip her packing cube with her lingerie. If she had something illicit tucked in there, so be it.

Her laptop was in its own compartment, in a padded sleeve. He left it there. It would be password protected, and he only wanted to do a quick check for anything obvious. Anything that suggested she was cooking up trouble—or in trouble.

He found a brochure of the Aoife O'Byrne show at the gallery in London, with her photo and bio and "Oliver York? Finian Bracken?" handwritten on the back.

Fin Bracken was at Oliver York's farm, where Naomi had found a man injured. The package had gone out by then. Now it was missing, and Emma was missing.

Mike didn't find a Saint Brigid's cross in Naomi's suitcase, or anywhere in her room.

He went to a glass door that opened onto a balcony. His room didn't have a balcony—not that it was balcony weather. He noticed a movement below him and smiled. *Naomi.* She was on the walkway out from the main back porch with a pair of snowshoes and poles. She tossed them all onto the walk and put her hands on her hips as if she didn't have a clue what to do next. But she'd figure it out. She might not be thrilled with the cold New England winter, but she was game for anything.

Buddy, the Masons and Reed descended the porch steps with their own snowshoe sets. Mike decided to join them. Snowshoeing would burn off some frustration while he waited for Colin, and he wanted to keep an eye on Reed's crew.

He headed downstairs. He didn't need to change clothes. He'd be fine in what he was wearing.

"This wind will cut you in two," Naomi said when Mike eased in next to her on the shoveled walk. "It only gusts every now and then." She lifted a snowshoe, her nose and cheeks pink with the cold. "Serena checked lost-and-found for boots. Not very fashionable and a size too big, but better than my London boots, don't you think? And, miracles of miracles, there was a pair of wool socks. I don't know how clean they are but I'm not going to think about that."

"Our resourceful Naomi," Reed said with a laugh. He had snowshoes on and was standing in the snow next to the walk, his poles secured properly on his wrists.

Naomi pointed down to the water, at a trail winding atop the rocky coastline. "It looks romantic, doesn't it?" She squinted at Mike. "We'll count on you to call 911 if we go down."

The trail would be tougher going in boots than on skis or snowshoes, but the snow wasn't that deep. Ice would be a bigger problem given the proximity to the water. But it wasn't as if they were off for a full day's trek. Thirty minutes and they'd be back by the fire, with hot cocoa and whiskey.

Thirty seconds onto the trail, Buddy's snowshoe came off. "Mike? Any tips?"

"Back strap needs to be on the heel."

Buddy grinned. "Duh."

The wind gusted, and Serena swore and pointed at the inn with one of her poles. "I surrender. I'm going back in and sitting by the fire with Ted. You all have fun."

Mike amended his assessment. If they lasted twenty minutes, that would be a good day.

Fine with him.

He scanned the area for a spot one of them could have Emma

hidden away, then warned himself against such thinking. It was one thing to be on alert. It was another thing to jump that far ahead of the facts.

Regardless, they would all be back by the time Colin arrived.

21

Emma stood as close to the edge of the loft as she dared and took the leap, grabbing hold of a rafter above her and swinging feetfirst to the window. She anchored her feet on the half-rotted sill, her arms hooked around the sturdy crossbeam. She'd considered removing her boots before climbing up to the loft but decided the risks of them causing her problems getting out of the shed were less than the problems of being outside in her stockinged feet.

She kicked the glass with the heel of her boot. The glass cracked immediately. When she gave it another hard kick, the entire window dislodged unexpectedly, falling into the snow. A few pieces of glass splintered on the floor near where she'd placed the sheepskins.

Her arms ached, the beam cutting into her as she steadied herself, maintaining her balance. Flailing out of control wouldn't help.

She could see the rot now around the window. She hoped her weight wouldn't collapse the wall, but she would have to take her chances. Cold air seeped in through the opening. She welcomed it as a sign of imminent freedom.

Moving quickly but deliberately, she eased herself into the opening, still hanging on to the beam as she scanned the ground under the window. Snow had drifted in front of the shed, probably from blowing off the roof. That was good, she thought. Deeper snow would help cushion her landing. She would have to take care to avoid the remains of the fallen window, especially any broken glass.

"No time like the present," she said aloud, then swung into the window.

In one swift motion, she launched herself into the cold air, letting go of the beam and dropping into the snow more or less feetfirst. She rolled onto her side, getting snow in her face, down her back, up her sleeves. She was breathing hard, but she'd managed to avoid injury. Snow she could handle.

She let snowflakes melt on her tongue, grateful for the moisture after hours without water, and got her bearings. The shed was about fifty feet from the water's edge. The door would be on the opposite side, presumably facing the road.

Catching her breath, Emma moved out of the thigh-deep drift into snow that was closer to knee-deep. She took in the disturbed snow from her fall, her footprints, the broken window. If her attacker returned, it would be obvious she had escaped.

The cedar shingles on the exterior of the shed were stained brick red, faded in the Maine sun. It took a moment to orient herself. She was north of Rock Point, near an old, abandoned lightkeeper's house and small seasonal homes—off the main road, along a narrow back road that dead-ended at the lightkeeper's house.

Why here?

Emma let the question go. Questions—and answers—would have to wait.

She needed to get moving.

She spotted a six-inch shard of glass sticking up out of the snow and decided to take it with her, in case it came in handy.

Holding it in one hand, she walked through knee-deep snow to the front of the shed and a plowed driveway that, as she'd expected, went right up to the door. Although empty now, the shed was probably used for storage. She wondered if the owner realized it was in such bad shape. At least her escape through the window had exposed the rotted window casing.

She squinted against the snow and sunlight at a small, cedar-shingled house across the one-lane road. The shades were pulled, suggesting it was a seasonal home. Emma suspected the shed was part of the same property. In summer, she'd be able to flag a lobster boat or wave to kids checking out tide pools down on the rocks. The tide was low now, adding to the quiet, the sense of isolation.

She debated breaking into the house, but it was unlikely she'd find a working landline. A waste of time and energy for no good reason.

She noticed the shed door was tied tightly shut with bungee cords. Her attacker had taken more time and care locking her in than tying her up, but she could see the logic behind it. It had been dark, with no worries about passing boats, cars or lovers enjoying a moonlight walk down to the water.

There was no need for her to unlatch the door now. She knew what was inside, and the sheepskins and packaging materials were no help to her.

This all could wait.

She licked her lips, but they were chapped and sore from dehydration and the cold. A hint of what the rest of her was like, Emma thought. She noticed a twinge in her right hip where she'd banged it on her way up to the loft. Otherwise she felt strong, able to walk to the main road and find a way to alert local police.

And Yank, her team.

Colin.

Holding on to her bit of glass, she walked in the middle of the one-lane road out to the main road that wound along the coast-line. She came to a cluster of small summer houses and turned onto the road toward Rock Point, a cold wind in her face. Late February meant the road was quiet—but did it matter? With her attacker unknown to her, possibly returning, did she *want* to flag down a passing car?

She heard a vehicle behind her, out of sight on a curve, and ducked off the road, over a snowbank and behind a spruce tree. She stood quiet. She didn't recognize the car and let it pass by her. It wasn't that far to Rock Point. She could make it on foot.

After another hundred yards, she heard an oncoming vehicle—a truck, she guessed. She eased off the road again, but there was no spruce tree to hide behind this time.

Then she smiled as the truck came into view. "I'd know that truck anywhere."

She staggered back onto the road and waved as the truck came to a hard stop.

Colin jumped out. "Emma," he said through clenched teeth, running toward her.

She laughed, sinking into him, feeling his strong arms around her, lifting her. "I knew you'd come," she whispered.

"You're safe now." He breathed into her hair. "Emma…"

"I'm not hurt," she said quickly, standing back from him, hugging her coat around her. "I was taken at St. Patrick's rectory."

"Picking up a package from Oliver York."

"You know?" She tried to smile, but she was shivering, the cold and snow melting down her back, up her arms and in her boots affecting her. "Of course you know. I was locked in a shed. I escaped about twenty minutes ago."

Colin eased the piece of glass from her fingers. "I need to call Kevin. We were about to search between the rectory and the Plum Tree Inn."

"You'd have found me," Emma said.

He winked at her. "Damn straight we would have."

"Why are you on this road?"

"Mike is at the Plum Tree with friends he knew in the army. I was headed there."

"Mike?"

"The FBI agent Oliver York saw is there, too. Ted Kavanagh. Know him?"

She shook her head. "No."

"All right." Colin touched her arm. "You need water and rest. We can talk later." He kissed her on the forehead. "I love you."

She struggled to contain her emotions. They bubbled up, mixing with exhaustion and adrenaline, threatening to overwhelm her. "Oliver sent me sheepskins. Whoever grabbed me opened the package and tossed the sheepskins into the shed with me."

"Was there a cross?"

"Not that I could see. I covered every inch of the shed looking for any clues, anything I could use. I didn't search the exterior. Once I was out, I thought it best to get away from the shed. I can't say for certain a cross wasn't dropped in the snow or on the driveway." She clutched Colin's upper arm, feeling the hard muscle through his jacket. "Oliver sent me a cross?"

"A Saint Brigid's cross. He says he made it himself."

"It could have been stolen before the package left England."

"Lots of possibilities. Come on. I've got water in the truck. I'll fill you in on what's been going on while you were plotting your escape."

Colin stayed behind her, spotting her as she climbed into the passenger seat. She thought he was about to say something, but he shut the door without comment. Emma found a bottle of water on the seat but couldn't grasp it well enough to open it.

When Colin came around and got behind the wheel, he took the bottle without a word, twisted off the cap and handed it to her. "Go slow," he said.

She resisted the temptation to gulp, or just to tilt her head back and pour the entire contents of the bottle down her throat. Then she would puke it up, and she'd been through enough without that. She glanced at the time on the truck clock. Three fifteen. Later than she'd have said.

Colin turned the truck around, back toward Rock Point.

"How long have you known I've been missing?" she asked finally.

"Not long enough."

His voice sounded strangled, and she ached at what he must have gone through. "You didn't miss me sooner because I was supposed to be at the convent. I planned to let you know I canceled after I picked up the package. I wanted to see what Oliver had sent...what he was up to..." She sighed, feeling less parched. "Someone else had the same idea. All hell hasn't broken loose yet?"

Colin shook his head. "Kevin and I have been working together. Sister Cecilia missed you, but we weren't sure..." He didn't continue. "We hoped you were off with friends. Then Franny Maroney found your phone a little while ago."

Hence, the planned search. Emma looked out her window. She drank more water. Rehydrating was helping, clearing any brain fog. So was the sunlight, and being free, with Colin. Coming upon her hadn't been a coincidence. He'd been on the case, putting the pieces together, following the evidence.

She turned to him. "Whoever grabbed me can't know I've escaped."

"Do you have any idea who it was?"

"No."

His jaw was visibly tight. "Professional job?"

"I can't say for certain. I think whoever it is knew I might be at the rectory, or maybe hoped I would be, and was ready with bungee cords, a blanket, a place to stash me. An open trunk." She realized her voice was toneless, as if she were reading numbers off the truck dashboard. "I was jumped from behind." She touched her neck. "Blood choke hold."

"Hell, Emma."

"I was dizzy at first when I regained consciousness. It wasn't a fun ride in the trunk. Never mind the rest of it, the frost heaves and potholes were rough."

Colin didn't smile at her halfhearted attempt at humor. He called Kevin and told his youngest brother about her escape. The shed needed to be secured and searched. "But we don't want whoever attacked her to know she's out," Colin said.

Kevin seemed to agree. Emma knew he would want to interview her. She would, in his place. She needed information. What had happened since yesterday afternoon?

Only yesterday.

It seemed longer.

She drank more of her water then put the cap on the bottle. She was steadier. Hydration and warmth were already helping. She started to ask Colin another question but realized they had arrived at his house in Rock Point.

She pointed at a car parked behind hers. "Isn't that Padgett's car?"

Colin nodded. "He didn't waste any time getting here. Yank sent him. He's on his way, too."

"All this fuss for sheepskins and a missing Saint Brigid's cross," Emma said.

"For a missing agent," Colin said, turning to her, his eyes a black-blue in the afternoon light. "And whatever's going on isn't about sheepskins and a cross."

"No, it isn't."

"Are you okay, Emma?" He touched a fingertip to her cheek, his expression softening. "Padgett's a hard-ass. He's not going to have any sympathy."

Emma smiled. "I'm glad to see your sense of humor is returning."

"Who's joking?" But he grinned, then leaned over and kissed

her on the cheek. "If you need a break, let me know. I'll kick everyone out."

He jumped out of the truck. She pushed the passenger door open, but he was there before she got out. She took his hand, felt its warmth and strength. "I can manage on my own, but it would be bad if I fell flat on my face with Sam Padgett peeking out the curtains."

They went into the house through the front door. Kevin and Padgett were in the living room, on their feet, looking grim. Kevin swept over to her and kissed her on the cheek. "Good job, Emma," he said, then stood back. "Anything I can get you?"

"I'll want something to eat soon. First..." She unbuttoned her coat, collected herself. "Let's get through my story and all your questions."

Padgett handed her an apple. "I keep two in my car. Best thing for you after a night under lock and key."

"The voice of experience," Emma said with a smile.

Colin set her piece of glass on the coffee table. Padgett and Kevin looked at it but made no comment. Emma sat in a chair by the unlit fireplace.

"I know the shed where you were held," Kevin said. "It's part of a three-acre property that includes the house directly across the road. It's owned by an elderly widow from Boston. She's in a fight with her offspring about who inherits it. I doubt there's any connection between them and whoever grabbed you."

"An opportunistic choice," Padgett said.

Emma noticed her hands were filthy. She expected her hair was tangled, her face pale—both as dirty as her hands. The past twenty-two hours had been an ordeal. She sank deeper into the soft cushions of the chair, imagining a hot bath, a good dinner and sleep, with Colin next to her.

"Emma," he said.

She heard the concern in his voice. She shifted her position, the twinge in her hip less noticeable now. She was safe, and she had a job to do.

She bit into her apple and looked up at the three men. "This whole thing has felt opportunistic," she said, then told them, step-by-step, leaving out nothing, what had happened when she arrived at St. Patrick's rectory yesterday afternoon.

22

As deliberate and analytical as Emma was, she wasn't one to waste time. Colin knew this about her and could see she'd made up her mind about her next move. She'd finished her story and answered what few questions he and Kevin had—Padgett had stayed silent—then stood up from her chair. She was steadier, Padgett's apple in her hand. She'd taken two bites. "I'm going to England," she said. "I can be on a flight tonight if I get moving now."

"You're recuperating, and you're pissed off," Padgett said from his position next to the fireplace. "Not the best time to fly across the Atlantic."

"I need to talk to Oliver York and Martin Hambly myself. And Finian," she added, tight-lipped, adamant. She turned to Colin. "You can talk to the people at the Plum Tree who were in England. Naomi MacBride, Reed Cooper, Ted Kavanagh. Find out their movements, who they talked to, why—and what, if anything, they know about Oliver York. Let me know." She started across the living room toward the entry, then stopped, as if she'd forgotten something. "I need to be on the ground in this village where the York farm is located. I'll be of most use there."

Colin eased in behind her, warning himself not to jump in with his own opinions until he'd absorbed her arguments. Right now, he needed to be an FBI agent, not a fiancé. Or a brother, he thought, reminding himself Mike was at the Plum Tree.

"It doesn't have to be one of Mike's friends that grabbed me," Emma added. "I know that. I'm not getting ahead of myself."

"We'll have to pour you onto a plane, Emma," Padgett said. "You look like crap."

She smiled, seeming to take no offense. "I probably look worse than I feel. I don't have a concussion or other injuries that would keep me from flying. I can sleep on the plane. A quick shower and clean clothes, and I'm good to go."

Padgett glanced at Colin. "We need to check with Yank."

"You two check with him," Emma said. "I'll go upstairs and get ready."

She continued into the entry and marched up the stairs. Colin shifted to Padgett. "She's in no shape to drive herself to Boston, never mind fly on her own to England."

"You can't go. You need to get up to that inn and talk to your brother and his friends." Padgett sighed, already dialing his phone. He held a fast, curt conversation with Matt Yankowski, then slid his phone back into his suit coat pocket. "Yank sees the wisdom of having someone talk to York. He isn't wild about Emma flying to England, but he isn't going to oppose it—provided I go with her."

"Have you ever been to England?" Colin asked.

"Yes, I have. Three times. Rained each time."

"Pack an umbrella," Kevin said, then shifted to Colin. "You okay with this?"

"Not my call."

"Mine, either," Padgett said. "I'll get moving on the flight details. Tell Emma not to dawdle or we won't make Logan in time."

Colin headed upstairs. Emma was already out of the shower, her hair damp as she slipped into fresh clothes and dug a suitcase out of the closet. She moved stiffly, but she wasn't trembling, wasn't shivering. He noticed bruising along her neck, probably from the choke hold, but didn't point it out. There was more bruising on her wrists, where she'd been bound. He didn't point that out, either. Instead he relayed Yank's instructions.

"I'm fine with Padgett tagging along," Emma said, "but I'm not sitting next to him on an overnight transatlantic flight. He needs his own row."

Colin didn't blame her. "Are you up to this, Emma?"

She smiled. "Of course I am."

That was Emma Sharpe, ex-nun, art crimes expert, federal agent. She was strong, smart, stubborn and relentless. He understood her reasoning for wanting to go to England herself. No one knew as much about Oliver York as she did, except, perhaps, Wendell Sharpe. Colin wouldn't be surprised if Emma had her grandfather fly in from Dublin and meet her in England. Lucas, her brother, was in Dublin, too.

Just as well Sam Padgett was accompanying her.

Colin pushed back his tension. "Will you need to stop at the apartment for anything?"

"I have enough here. I doubt we'll need to stay in England more than a day or two. You're on your way to the Plum Tree?"

"I put it off to look for you."

"You can't see the shed where I was held from the Plum Tree. It's not far, but it doesn't mean Mike's friends are connected to what happened to me. They could have stumbled into the middle of something Oliver's cooked up or dealing with—although it doesn't sound as if these guys are stumblers."

"Always have to be careful about being driven by assumptions," Colin said, watching her zip up her overnight bag. He stepped forward and lifted the bag off the bed.

"Thank you," she said. "You'd rather I stayed here and painted, wouldn't you?"

He attempted a smile. "You'll be missing your lunch with my mother."

"Oh, that's right! I was looking forward to it. She wants to take me to her favorite restaurant in Kennebunkport. I'll call her on the way to the airport."

"She's not in a great mood. She knows we've been holding back on her."

"She's a wise woman," Emma said, some of the life coming back into her eyes.

"You should get checked out by a doctor," Colin said.

"I'd say the same thing to you if you were in my position. I'm fine, Colin. Really. I never would have made it out of the shed if I'd been seriously hurt in the attack, and I'm very happy to have jumped out of that window." She stepped toward him, the ends of her hair dripping into her white shirt collar. "I'd be dead if killing me had been the plan. Leaving me in the shed, not caring whether I lived or died, is different."

Not different enough, but Colin made no comment.

"Do you need to tell Mike to be careful?" she asked him.

He shrugged. "Mike is always careful."

"He's your brother, Colin," Emma said. "This is personal for you."

"And you? Don't you make it personal?"

"I'm a federal agent. Mike isn't."

"Mike can take care of himself."

"No question," she said. "I just want to be sure your head is screwed on straight."

"I'm seeing things very clearly, Emma."

She smiled then, unexpectedly, but said nothing. She started to take her suitcase from him, but he stood back with it, allowing her to go ahead of him into the hall. She didn't falter, but she did keep a hand on the rail as she descended the stairs.

Padgett was waiting in the entry. "Kevin left," he said, addressing Colin. "He said for you to stay in touch and he'll do likewise. It's good he's doing this your way for now, but I wouldn't hold my breath it's going to last. This bastard assaulted a federal agent on Kevin's turf."

"I can't say for certain if it was a man or a woman," Emma said.

"Point taken," Padgett said. "Speaking of turf—what about Kavanagh? Guy's got a solid reputation. He might be freelancing and bending the rules, but that doesn't mean he'll appreciate us interfering."

"Not relevant." Colin grabbed his jacket out of the living room. "Kavanagh has a lot of questions to answer. I want to know why he was in that gallery in London and then went out to Oliver York's farm."

"He might not know about our interest in Oliver," Emma said.

"Then what—he stirs up trouble by accidentally stepping into York's business? I'm not going to blow any cover Kavanagh's established for himself, but I'm not giving him free rein, either." Colin shrugged. "If this get-together at the Plum Tree is a reunion and a job fair, no harm, no foul. If it's more than that, we'll find out."

"Someone attacked Emma and locked her in that shed." Padgett picked up her suitcase. "We'll take my car."

"You'll have to hoof it," Colin said.

Padgett grinned. "That's why we're taking my car instead of Emma's car."

He went out ahead of her.

Emma turned to Colin and tucked her hand into his. He drew her close. "Emma," he whispered. "Be safe."

"I love you."

"I'd have found you. You know that, don't you?"

"I do. I did. Knowing it helped me get through the night."

He kissed her softly, then felt her hand slip out of his as she turned around and headed down the front steps. Padgett was already in his car, waiting for her.

Once they were on their way, Colin texted Mike that he was resuming his delayed visit to the Plum Tree. He'd already let his older brother know that Emma was safe, and to continue to keep her situation to himself.

Mike responded. Okay.

Colin still had his phone in his hand when Kevin texted him. Watching shed. Stay in touch.

Kevin would stay out of sight and let Colin know if anyone stopped by.

Colin got his truck key. He'd settle down on the short drive to the Plum Tree. When he arrived, he'd be Mike's brother, the FBI agent home in Maine for the weekend who also happened to have a few questions he wanted answered.

It'd work fine.

23

An attractive woman with dark, curly hair and hazel eyes greeted Colin by a moose statue in front of the Plum Tree Inn and told him they were just back from snowshoeing. Colin thought his head would explode. What the hell was he doing here? But he steadied himself and picked up a pole she'd dropped.

"You must be the second-born Donovan," she said as she took the pole, thanking him. "Mike said you'd be arriving soon. I'm Naomi MacBride. Good to meet you, Agent Donovan."

"Likewise, Ms. MacBride."

"Naomi, please. Mike's gone inside. He's looking for a Father Bracken–approved whiskey. His words." She grinned. "I think we got to him snowshoeing. If he tells you I almost fell in the ocean, it's not true. I *did* fall."

Colin couldn't help but like her. "Where was this?"

"On a trail on the other side of the inn. I thought I might as well take advantage of being here this time of year and get a taste of snowshoeing on the rocky Maine coast. Stunning views. The trail took us close to the water. Buddy Whidmore and I hit an ice patch and our snowshoes went out from under us. Buddy

avoided the water but I went in. Mike says it was just a tide pool."
She kicked a hunk of ice off her boot and grinned at Colin. "It
was salt water. Therefore, it was the ocean. Isn't that right?"

"Worth arguing. Sounds as if you had a good time."

"It was incredible. The perfect cure for jet lag." She squatted
down, setting her pole neatly beside her, and tugged a snow-
encrusted strap off the heel of her boot. "I had to borrow boots.
They're too big. I think that contributed to my fall. Not that I'm
looking for excuses, mind you. The boots did keep my feet dry."

"I don't know how you stayed dry if you fell in the ocean."

She laughed. She didn't seem to care one way or the other if
there were legitimate mitigating factors for her fall, or even if
it had been a real fall. She had nothing to prove. She kicked off
the snowshoe, using enough force that it skittered across the icy
walk and under the moose statue.

"It's going to be a while before you see daffodils up here,"
she said, laying on her Southern accent as she stood up. "Is there
anything I can do for you?"

"I understand from Mike that you're a crisis management
consultant. A lot of pressure with that work. It must feel good
to get a break."

"If you want to call this a break." She picked up her pole,
tucked it under her arm. "You're not here just to see Mike, are
you, Agent Donovan?"

Colin warned himself not to underestimate her. "Father
Bracken is a friend of mine. You saw him on Wednesday at the
Aoife O'Byrne show in London. He's visiting Oliver York at
his farm. I'd like to hear about this injured man you helped."

Naomi didn't seem surprised at the question. "Not much to
tell. If Mike repeated what I told everyone at lunch, that's all
there is."

"Was anyone else there?"

"Just Johnny, the farmworker, at least that I saw."

"Who else knows about this incident?"

"Everyone here. I have no idea who Martin Hambly and Johnny told. Oliver York wasn't there at the time. That's what Hambly said, anyway."

"Were you hoping to meet him?"

"Not particularly, no."

She scooped up her second pole. She seemed comfortable answering questions. Skilled, even. Colin remembered she'd worked as an intelligence analyst with the State Department under difficult circumstances.

Mike eased out of the inn. He had on a flannel shirt over a T-shirt and didn't look cold or stressed after the snowshoe trek. "I see you've met Naomi."

Colin wasn't sure how to read his brother's tone and decided he didn't need to.

"Mike and I go way back," Naomi said, collecting her errant snowshoe from under the moose statue. She tucked it under the other arm from the ski poles. "What else can I do for you, Agent Donovan?"

"A courier picked up a package on Wednesday at the dovecote where you found Hambly. Know anything about it?"

"Not a thing."

"Why did you go to the dovecote?"

"A public pathway goes past it. I thought it would have a good view of the farm. As it turns out, I didn't even notice the view. Hambly was in rough shape. I couldn't tell if he'd been attacked, if that's what you're getting at."

"So all this is a bunch of coincidences? London, Oliver York, Aoife O'Byrne, the incident with Hambly?"

"I doubt it, don't you?"

Colin noticed Mike stiffen but kept his focus on Naomi.

"But I doubt whatever is going on has anything to do with me," she added. "I just was in the wrong place at the wrong time. Or the right place, if you're Martin Hambly." She glanced at Mike. "Works out that way sometimes. One person's wrong place, wrong time is another person's right place, right time."

Mike picked up her second snowshoe off the walk.

Colin noted the tension between Mike and Naomi. There was clearly a subtext to her comments that Mike understood, and that Naomi knew he'd understand.

Not going there, either, Colin thought.

"I was doing research," Naomi said. "I knew Reed Cooper was planning to talk to Mike about contract work and one thing led to another. I don't have to follow an evidence trail. I can dive in and go with my instincts and training and see where they take me."

"Why Oliver York?" Colin asked.

"Mad curiosity once I saw him at the London gallery."

"It was out of your way to go to the Cotswolds before heading here."

"Well, I didn't know I was headed here until Reed showed up at my Cotswolds inn and told me about this get-together. That was after my walk to the dovecote. Reed drove me to the airport. I avoid renting cars whenever possible."

Colin studied her a moment. She wasn't defensive, he decided, but she knew she was on the hot seat. "You planned to fly home to Nashville that night. The Cotswolds were still out of your way."

"I'd never been to the Cotswolds. Have you, Agent Donovan?"

Mike inhaled sharply. Colin ignored him. "Not yet, no."

"Beautiful, classic English countryside." She adjusted her snowshoe and ski poles in her arms, her cheeks flushed, her eyes alert, focused on Colin. She tilted her head back slightly. "I thought the York farm might be a good place for Oliver York, aka Oliver Fairbairn, to hide and then stage the return of his stolen art. Although he's returned most of it in the past few months, hasn't he? Since that awful murder in Boston."

Colin and Mike both were silent.

Naomi blew a stray curl out of her face. Despite her breezy manner, her expression was serious. "If I could connect the dots, Agent Donovan, so can someone else."

"If you want to take her in," Mike said, "I can help with the handcuffs."

Colin shook his head. "Ms. MacBride is welcome to draw her own conclusions."

Naomi narrowed her eyes, shifting from Colin to Mike and back again. "What are holidays with the Donovan brothers like? You guys throw each other in the icy harbor for fun on Christmas Eve?"

Colin glanced at Mike, but his older brother kept his gaze pinned on Naomi, as if she were fulfilling every frustrating, negative expectation he had of her.

"Where all did you go in Rock Point yesterday?" Colin asked her.

She walked over to a pile of snowshoe gear next to the inn's entrance and tossed hers on top of the heap. She turned, grinning. "Getting snowshoes on and off is harder than snowshoeing itself. Winter's a lot of work up here. Mike knows what I did in Rock Point. He was with me the whole time."

"Not before your car dropped you off," he said.

She shrugged. "The driver had no reason to dawdle, but I'm not familiar enough with Rock Point to know if he drove me straight to your folks' inn." Her tone was matter-of-fact, but her stance suggested she was alert, on guard. "Mike took me to breakfast at Hurley's. Your two youngest brothers joined us. Quite an experience."

"You had breakfast with Ted Kavanagh in England yesterday," Colin said.

"He'd finished his full English by the time I joined him. He was drinking tea. Shocked me." A flicker of humor in her eyes. "T.K. and I worked together on a number of projects in Afghanistan. Apparently he arrived in the Cotswolds on Wednesday afternoon, about the same time I did."

"Which was?"

"Me? Four o'clock. I didn't know he was there. I didn't see him until breakfast. Ships passing in the night and all that. I had an early drink and bite at the pub and went to my room to do some work."

"Was Agent Kavanagh alone?" Colin asked.

"As far as I know."

Colin doubted he would get anywhere but decided to ask all his questions. "Did you see him at the York farm?"

"No. And we didn't discuss Oliver York or the York farm at breakfast."

"How did he get to the airport?"

"We didn't discuss travel arrangements, either."

"Did he know Reed was picking you up?"

"I didn't know Reed was picking me up. How would Kavanagh know? Reed told him and not me? I guess anything is possible, but I don't know what difference it makes."

Colin didn't know, either. He turned to Mike. "Do you trust her?"

He set her second snowshoe onto the pile. "I'll keep a close watch on her."

Naomi rolled her eyes. "My turn to go find whiskey."

After she headed inside, Mike took in a deep breath. "I tossed her room before I got word Emma was safe. I didn't find anything."

"Mike…" Colin looked at the moose statue, as if it could remind him of simpler days. He flashed on a camping trip with his brothers, peeking out from their tents to watch passing moose. He turned again to Mike. "You know I still want you to go back to the Bold Coast, right?"

"Not doing that. I can talk to the people here."

"You're not a trained interrogator."

Mike grinned. "The hell I'm not. How's Emma?"

"On her way to England with another agent."

His older brother narrowed his eyes. "I'll let you tell me what you can. I'm not asking questions. I take it she's okay if she's flying tonight."

"She got a few scrapes and bruises and survived a choke hold. She says it's nothing a few ibuprofen can't handle. She cleared herself for her flight."

"You wouldn't have cleared her," Mike said.

"I have to trust her. She was in trouble for longer than I realized. That's hard to take."

"For you. Emma's cool. In a few months, you and I will be standing in a convent garden, watching her walk down the aisle to marry you. It will happen."

"Yeah. Thanks."

"What about Yankowski?"

"In Virginia."

"Probably a good place for him to be right now."

Colin debated before he continued. "We're still looking for the Saint Brigid's cross Oliver York sent to Emma."

Mike nodded. "Got it. Kevin's on this thing?"

"Yes. Be careful, Mike. What do I need to know about you and Naomi MacBride?"

"I participated in an operation that got wilder than it should have because of bad intel. Kavanagh and Naomi were involved. Naomi saved the day but exposed herself. A couple months later, she was grabbed by some very bad people. My guys and I rescued her."

"Mike. Hell."

He shrugged. "I was a soldier. I did what I had to do."

"What about Reed Cooper?"

"He was at a desk. He's ambitious. He expected to make a career in the military and move up, but he quit not long after

I did and went to work for one of the big private contractors. Now he's out on his own."

Colin absorbed the information. "Anyone else here who was involved in this business in Afghanistan?"

"Everyone, one way or the other."

"Unfinished business?"

"Not for me. I walked away from all the unfinished business."

"All right. Let's go in. Introduce me to the rest of your friends."

Ted Kavanagh grabbed a black-iron poker from a rack of fireplace equipment on the library hearth. Mike had introduced Colin to Reed Cooper, Buddy Whidmore and the Masons then left him alone with Kavanagh. Now it was two FBI agents having a friendly chat. Colin supposed it could be the case, but it wasn't.

Kavanagh clutched the poker. "I don't need you meddling in my business."

"I'm visiting my brother."

"These Southerners keep it hot in here."

It *was* hot.

"I should have gone snowshoeing, cooled off," Kavanagh said. "I grew up in Michigan. I did enough snowshoeing to last me a lifetime."

"I need to know what you're doing here, Ted."

"What if I tell you it's none of your damn business?"

"You can do that," Colin said, sitting on a small sofa opposite Kavanagh by the fire with his poker.

"I'm here on my own time with old friends. That's all there is to it. I don't know Mike as well as the others. He was a direct combatant. Reed and the Masons weren't, at least not when we met. Obviously Naomi and I weren't, either. Buddy did some freelance tech work for us." Kavanagh's tone suggested he'd told Colin more than he deserved to know. "I got in touch with

Reed when I heard he'd gone out on his own, and we met in London. Now here we are."

"With a trip to a London art gallery and the Cotswolds in between."

"I figured Reed would be interested in Mike. I took a look into the Donovans of late and decided to check out Aoife O'Byrne. I had some gallery worker look down her nose at me when I pronounced Aoife wrong. It's *Ee-fa* not *A-oh-fee*. Whoops."

Colin smiled. "You aren't the first."

"Oliver York is this Oliver Fairbairn character, isn't he? The mythologist who consulted on the art theft documentary. Tough, what happened to York as a kid. Anyway, I realized Naomi was following the same trail I was, and we ended up in York's Cotswolds village at the same time." Kavanagh pulled back the screen on the fireplace, stabbed ineffectually at the burning logs, then set the poker back on the rack and replaced the screen. "Neither of us wants Reed to step into anything that could hurt him."

"Or by extension you. You should have called Emma Sharpe or me."

"Ah. Right. Sorry."

He wasn't sorry. Colin glanced around the library, mentally comparing it to other Maine inns he knew, including the one his parents now ran. He'd never paid much attention to the Plum Tree. Just another place on the coast. He'd already looked out at the water, then to the south. Emma was right. The shed couldn't be seen from here. The place where she'd spent the night alone, cold, little food, no water—wrestling herself out of bungee cords, recovering from a choke hold.

"I'm being defensive," Kavanagh said with a sigh. "Look, I obviously stepped into your territory. It was inadvertent, and I admit I had questions about what I found. Emma Sharpe seems smart and knowledgeable about art crimes. At the same time..." He stopped, shaking his head. "Never mind."

"Go ahead, Ted. Say it."

"I'm glad you two are happy, Colin, but she will end your career."

It was about what Colin expected Kavanagh to say. "Well. I asked."

"Naomi accused me of bird-dogging her. I didn't follow her to the gallery or to St. James's Park but she thinks I did. We were both on the same scent, for different reasons. I did follow her to the Cotswolds—I got it out of a bellman at her hotel. Sometimes she doesn't know when to quit."

"Is that how she ended up helping Martin Hambly?"

"The injured Brit? Yeah. That's exactly how. It's classic Naomi MacBride. Is that why you have your knickers in a twist?"

"That's part of it," Colin said.

"Naomi didn't make her movements secret. Someone else interested in Oliver York could have beaten her to the dovecote. I know York's that Sharpe thief, Colin. Another thief could have knocked Hambly on his ass. A journalist. Scotland Yard. Lots of possibilities that don't include any of us here. The answers you're looking for are in England and with the Sharpes."

"You're supposed to be in a hammock on a beach."

"Still could happen," Kavanagh said with a shrug. "Look, I don't blame you for having alarm bells going off. I get it, but I have no reason to suspect anyone here is in danger or putting anyone else in danger—unless something's happened that I don't know about."

Colin didn't respond. Instead he got to his feet and opened the door onto the porch, then glanced back at Kavanagh. "Let's step outside. Get some air."

Kavanagh hesitated, then followed Colin onto the porch. The air was cold and dry, with no wind. Colin hadn't taken off his jacket since coming inside. Kavanagh didn't have one on, but he seemed to appreciate a jolt of cold air.

"How deep is your Emma in with this thief, Oliver York?"

Kavanagh asked. "And don't tell me he's not a thief. Have you been in contact with him, or with his manservant or whatever the hell he's called? You know these people. I don't."

"I haven't spoken with York or with Hambly," Colin said. "You spoke with Martin Hambly on Wednesday afternoon. After that you spoke to a courier at the York farm. He was coming from the dovecote where MacBride found Hambly the next morning. You were there right around the time Hambly ended up half-dead on the stream bank."

Kavanagh gave him a grudging smile. "You've been busy, I see. No wonder you have the reputation you do. Nothing nefarious happened. I chatted with Hambly about the village church and amaryllises. He had a flowerpot in each arm. Then I took a walk. I ran into the courier truck on its way out of the dirt track that leads to the dovecote—which I didn't realize then. I asked the driver if that was the York farm. He said yes."

"Did the driver say anything else?"

"He told me to have a nice day."

Colin ignored Kavanagh's sarcasm. "What did you do after your conversation?"

"Walked past the farm a ways, then turned around and walked back to the pub and had a pint and dinner. I figured Naomi would be staying there but I didn't go looking for her. Whatever is going on that you're not telling me is about the Sharpes and their relationship with Oliver York. It's got nothing to do with these guys here. We need to trust each other, Colin."

"No, we don't," Colin said, keeping any animosity out of his voice. Just stating the facts.

His bluntness didn't seem to offend Kavanagh. "I can get you out of my hair formally," he said, matter-of-fact. "I'll call Yankowski myself. He'll tell you to back off."

"Do you want to work for Cooper?"

"My presence here is legitimate. That's all you need to know."

"You're an active agent, Ted. You aren't a solo operator."

"I've been on the job longer than you. I don't need you to tell me the rules."

"Back to the courier," Colin said. "He picked up a package at the dovecote. Do you know anything about that?"

He could see the question caught Kavanagh by surprise, perked his interest. "I don't, no. Why would I? Who was it for?"

"It was addressed to Emma in Rock Point."

"Okay." Kavanagh looked out at the ocean, the gray dusk light making him look paler, older. Finally he turned to Colin. "So, Oliver York sent a package to an FBI agent in Maine, and I happened to talk to the courier who picked it up. Want to tell me the rest, Colin?"

Colin debated then told him about Emma.

Kavanagh winced. "You've had a hell of a day. Damn. I'm sorry this happened, but this guy Oliver York has no business sending packages to a federal agent. He's a thief. You know it and I know it. Emma knows it. He can't be trusted."

"Who took her, Ted?"

"No idea. I know I didn't, and I know barging in here won't get you answers. Back off and let me do my job. What was in the package?"

"Sheepskins." Colin decided not to mention the Saint Brigid's cross. "They were tossed into the shed with her."

"Maybe she did the tossing. Set this up."

"Don't even go there."

"All right. Sorry. She's safe, though, right?"

Colin nodded. He hadn't told Kavanagh that Emma was on her way to England. He wasn't convinced he had Ted Kavanagh's full story about his interest in Oliver York and his trip to London and the Cotswolds, and now Maine.

"That's good," Kavanagh said. "If anyone knows when to rewrite the rules, it's you, Colin, but you need to know we're on the same side. It's good Emma's safe and out of this thing. You can bow out now, too. Mike's a big boy. He can take care of himself." Kavanagh grinned suddenly. "You look like you want to throw me off the porch headfirst into the snow."

"It wouldn't do any good, would it?"

"No. My ex-wife would tell you the same. Mind if I go back in? That hot fire is starting to sound like a pretty good idea."

They went inside. Colin left him in the library and headed down to the bar, all dark red leather and wood-paneled walls covered with old Maine photos. Tall windows opened onto another porch overlooking the water. Reed Cooper stood up from a table, where he had a laptop open. They hadn't had a chance to talk earlier. "Join me for a drink?" Cooper asked.

Colin shook his head. "No, thanks."

"Let me anticipate your questions. I didn't ask Agent Kavanagh or Naomi to look into Mike never mind you or the Sharpes. I picked up Naomi in the Cotswolds because I wanted to invite her here."

Reed Cooper was smooth—a private security contractor and a former army officer accustomed to dealing with a variety of federal agents. "Why this get-together now?" Colin asked.

"Because of the opportunity we have with Naomi's group of volunteer doctors. It was clear once I met with them in London this can happen. I'm here to make sure I do everything possible so that it does, and that we do our best for them. Having Mike on board would help me accomplish that mission."

"Good luck, then," Colin said.

"You're welcome to join us for dinner."

If he said yes, Colin figured if Kavanagh didn't shoot him, Mike would. Only a slight exaggeration. He shook his head. "I'm staying in Rock Point."

"Come by this weekend. A few more of us will be here. Bring your fiancée."

Colin thanked him and left. When he climbed into his truck, he texted Mike. I'm guessing your friends have their own agendas.

Mike's response was immediate. Nothing new.

Are you armed?

Glock. It's legal.

When Colin arrived back in Rock Point, he had a text from Emma. Made the flight. About to take off.

Padgett?

Five rows behind me. Insisted so he can keep an eye on me.

Colin smiled. He was liking Sam Padgett better and better. Safe trip.

Love you.

Love you, too.

Kevin's truck was parked behind Emma's car. His youngest brother got out and Colin rolled down his window. "Any news?"

"Thought you might like to take a ride out to the old light-keeper's house with me."

"Not worried about our kidnapper seeing us?"

"Nope. It's dark and isolated, and if we're there and he or she shows up, all the better."

"Sounds like a plan. We can take my truck. Anyone sees it, they'll think I'm sticking my nose in Mike's business. Hop in."

Twenty minutes later, he and Kevin had the bungee cords off the door to Emma's shed and were inside, looking at sheepskins, broken glass and her discarded trail-mix bag.

Kevin shone his flashlight on more bungee cords. "Those must be the ones that were on her hands and feet."

Colin remembered the marks on her wrists and ankles. It would have taken time and persistence to get free of the cords, even if they'd been haphazardly attached. He noted a fleece blanket next to the sheepskins and pushed back an image of Emma stuffed in a car trunk, struggling to breathe.

He and Kevin didn't find the Saint Brigid's cross that York said he'd tucked into the package. Emma hadn't missed it.

"We need a team in here," Kevin said, glancing around the shed in disgust. "Whoever grabbed Emma didn't care one way or the other whether she lived or died. They're not coming back, either."

"Doesn't look like it."

Colin resisted the urge to scoop up the blanket, as if it somehow could allow him to go back in time and comfort Emma in her distress. But he knew her. She'd have fallen back on her training and experience—and her time with the sisters, too. Her years with the Sisters of the Joyful Heart had taught her how to meditate and stay centered in a crisis.

Kevin looked as if he wanted to kick something. It wasn't like him. People called him the nice Donovan brother. "This doesn't feel professional," he said through clenched teeth.

"No, it doesn't, but that could be deliberate."

"To mislead us," Kevin said.

"Emma is fairly certain the attacker wore gloves. She felt them on her neck."

"Her phone's clean. No prints."

Colin sucked in a breath. "Get a team in here tonight if that's what you want to do. Let's see what they turn up."

Kevin gave a curt nod. "It'll be a long night," he said. "At least we know where Emma is."

"On a flight to London with Sam Padgett."

"Lucky her," Kevin said with a halfhearted smile as he and Colin left the dark, cold shed.

24

Naomi didn't dress for dinner. No one did. It turned out to be subdued, not the intense affair lunch had been. She wasn't hungry, anyway, and left the dining room after a few bites of salad and chowder, almost as good as the chowder she'd had last night at the Rock Point Harbor Inn. She needed space, and air. Time to think. She bundled up as best she could in her English jacket and made her way off the back porch. The shoveled walk ended at an icy path that led to a dock. It probably was no place to be on a dark February night, but she headed down there, anyway, mindful of every step. If she slipped and fell, she wanted at least to be able to yell for help. Better to be able to bounce up, no one the wiser.

Being rescued by Mike Donovan once in her life was enough. *More than enough.*

The light from the inn, stars and moon cast shadows on the snow and the ocean washing against and under the rickety, snow-covered dock, but she still wished she had thought to unearth a flashlight.

She stepped onto the end of the dock. No footprints. Was she the first one out here this winter?

The air was freezing, but she needed air after dealing with the alpha Donovans.

She heard someone behind her and turned as Mike came up the path from the inn. "Thought that was you," he said. "What are you up to out here?"

"I'm getting air." She kept her voice level. "You sound suspicious. Are you going to keep suspecting I've done something wrong?"

"Should I?"

"That's a hell of an answer."

"Maybe I'm just anticipating you'll do something wrong."

He walked past her and jumped onto the dock, no wariness about snow, ice, the old wood collapsing into the tide. He had on a canvas jacket open over his flannel shirt. He turned to her. "You need to tell me everything, Naomi."

"Everything about what?"

"How much do you know about this part of Maine? You don't like going into situations blind. Protective intelligence is your specialty. You make it a point to know as much as you can ahead of time. It's what you do."

"Do you think I have done something illegal?"

"Not what I said."

"But someone does," she said half under her breath.

Mike kicked a chunk of frozen snow and ice off the dock. Naomi didn't see where it landed but heard it plop into the water. "Don't get ahead of yourself," he said.

"Tell yourself that, too. Being back with Reed has you on edge. Having him and his guys here. Talking about Cooper Global Security and the work it does. It has you back in Special Forces mode, hyper-vigilant." She shoved her hands into her pockets and wished she had a hat. "There's a reason you live by yourself on the coast."

He glanced at her. "Yes, there is."

She hunched her shoulders against the cold seeping through her jacket. It wasn't suited to these temperatures. "This was a bad idea. I'm for warming up by the fire before dinner. Serena and Jamie are setting a table in the dining room with tablecloths and candles. No meetings. Reed's waiting for the rest of the guys to get here. Do you know any of them?"

"A few."

Mike wasn't going to say more. She knew him well enough to tell that much. She nodded at a white-capped swell coming at them in the moonlight. "I take back my claim of falling in the ocean."

"Were you exaggerating on purpose?"

She grinned. "I never exaggerate on purpose."

He took her by the elbow as they walked off the dock. He didn't let go when they reached the path up to the porch. She tried not to read anything into it. Mike was a wilderness guide now. Probably he kept people inexperienced with the Maine coast from falling on their butts all the time. All in a day's work for him.

Reed stepped outside as they mounted the steps to the porch by the bar. "Saw you two out here. I hope I'm not interrupting." He shivered. "It's probably a balmy day by your standards, Mike. I've never liked the cold. Have you ever been to Nashville?"

Mike shook his head. "No."

"Great city. We've rented offices near Vanderbilt—not far from where Naomi lives, as a matter of fact. My old haunts. Feels good to be back home. I guess you know that, though, since you've been back in Maine for a few years."

Naomi realized Mike had dropped his hand from her elbow. She turned up the collar of her jacket, hearing waves crashing on the rocks and giant chunks of ice below them.

"It was good to meet your brother," Reed added. "Will we have a chance to meet your other two brothers?"

"Maybe," Mike said. "Once I figure out what you're up to."

Reed laughed. "Cut-to-the-chase Mike Donovan. That's what I need—guys who will say what they think, not try to gauge what they think I want them to say. I hate ass-kissers. But I'm careful with people, Mike. Even people I trust the most. One mistake can ruin what we do. I'd be fine. I have plenty of money. A lot of these guys wouldn't be. I owe it to them to be cautious, as well as to our clients."

Naomi kicked a chunk of ice down the porch steps. The two men looked at her as if suddenly remembering she was there. She smiled. "I'm going to go back to my room and try the spa products."

"You do that, Naomi," Reed said.

"What do I tell the FBI if you two kill each other?"

"Nothing," Reed said. "The FBI doesn't investigate local murders."

Mike didn't seem as amused. Naomi left them and walked into the inn.

She spotted Buddy alone by the fire in the lounge. "Those two still aren't over you," he said, barely glancing at her. "Reed trusts you because it's in his interest. Mike doesn't trust you at all."

"You are so off base, Buddy. You have no idea."

He winked at her. "I'm not as clueless as you might think about such matters. Still clueless, mind you. Just not as clueless as you think." He laughed, looking at her now. "You have a lot of nervous energy. Sit. Have a drink. Stare at the fire. I'm having hot cocoa spiked with Bailey's. Want one?"

"No thanks." She decided he was right about her mood, though. She sat on a love seat opposite him. "You still look cold from snowshoeing," she said.

"I *am* still cold. It was fun, though. It's not like we never get snow in Tennessee. I just never go out in it. You did great today."

"Snowshoeing isn't that hard."

"It's the snow that gets you," he said with a grin. "I'm not

sure Reed and Mike appreciate how smart and tough you are.
I sometimes wonder if you know."

"I focus on my job. I've got some medical types packing for
humanitarian work, and I want them all to stay safe. Beyond
that..." Naomi pulled off her Barbour jacket. "I don't care."

"Keep saying that until you believe it."

She laughed. "I will. I'm not cold now," she said, splaying her
fingers in front of the fire. "Who all were you in touch with
before you came here?"

"Reed. That's it. And Kavanagh, of course."

"Not Mike?"

"Why would I be in touch with Mike?"

"I don't know. Were you?"

"No."

"Did you stop in Rock Point or Heron's Cove yesterday?
They're the closest towns to this place."

"Mike's from Rock Point. The Sharpes are from Heron's
Cove. Is that why you're asking?"

"Just making conversation, Buddy."

"Ha. Right. This have anything to do with what happened
yesterday in England?"

"*This?*"

"Whatever has you looking and talking so earnest."

She waved a hand, sitting back from the fire. "Never mind.
I'm keyed up from the presentation and then snowshoeing."

"You like these doctors."

"They do great work at considerable risk to themselves. The
head of the group was impressed with Reed. I want this to work
out for everyone."

"Do you think Mike's a good idea or a bad idea for the team?"

"That's not my call to make. Where is our FBI agent friend,
by the way?"

"Kavanagh? No idea." Buddy edged closer to the fire. "This
place would be a great setting for one of those mystery week-

ends. A live game of Clue. Colonel Mustard in the conservatory with the candlestick."

"Buddy, Buddy," Naomi said, relaxing now.

"Yeah. I know. Not with this crowd. More likely grenades and automatics than candlesticks."

She left him to his spiked hot cocoa and went out into the lobby. She and Serena were the only women at the Plum Tree.

Naomi spotted Kavanagh outside in the parking lot, smoking a cigarette next to the moose.

"I found a pack and some matches tucked in a drawer in the library," he said. "I decided not to resist. I haven't had a cigarette in three years. Since you went missing in Kabul, as a matter of fact. It's kind of like winter camp here, isn't it?"

"But you're not fooled."

"No, I'm not. Naomi, if the guy in England was attacked, you'll be a suspect. You should mind your own business once in a while."

"You arrived in the village around the same time I did."

"But I'm an American federal agent." He pointed his cigarette at her. "You're the intel expert sneaking around and asking questions."

"Are you calling me a busybody, T.K.?"

He laughed. "Now, I didn't say that. Reed put you up to checking out York? Checking out me?"

"No, he didn't. It's just what I do. How much contact have you had with our merry band since Afghanistan?"

"None until the past couple weeks."

"Not even Buddy?"

"Why, what's he saying?"

"Not much. He likes to provide tips. Makes sense he would stay in touch with you."

"Try to, maybe. I don't consider the occasional email staying in touch. And I never considered him a part of—what did you call us? Our merry band. That's good."

"Buddy probably has more to offer Reed right now than anyone else."

"He knows the cyber world. I've offered to put him in touch with the Bureau, but he likes his independence."

"He's always wanted to be one of the alpha guys," Naomi said.

"It's hard to top these guys. I'm an FBI agent, but Reed, Mike, Jamie and the rest of the guys coming in this weekend—damn. Maybe this isn't about recruiting Mike and solidifying a team. Maybe Reed pulled this weekend together because he wants to make sure Cooper Global Security isn't threatened by people who have axes to grind with him."

"Old scores to settle, you mean?"

Kavanagh drew on his cigarette, then exhaled the smoke away from her. "I know of at least one," he said, letting his gaze fall on her.

Naomi ignored a rush of emotion. Now wasn't the time. "Mike and Reed had other dangerous, difficult missions. The one you and I were involved with was just another day on the job."

"That's not what I'm talking about. I'm talking about you."

"Let's not talk about me. I've decided you must be for real or Mike's FBI brother would have called you out—might even have hauled you out of here for pretending to be an active federal agent."

Kavanagh winked at her. "No doubt." He tossed his cigarette into a snowbank and eyed the moose statue. "Think this fellow is life-size? Are moose really this big?"

"That's what Mike says."

Kavanagh grinned. "Maybe Mike will take us on a moose-sighting trip while we're here. Doesn't that sound like fun, Naomi?"

Chuckling to himself, he headed back inside.

Naomi watched the cigarette burn itself out in the snow. Had she set herself up for suspicion when she hadn't stayed with Martin Hambly? Should she have called the police herself? Maybe she'd let her suspicions about Oliver York and her urgency to get to Heathrow affect her judgment.

Now it looked as if she'd run.

Did Kavanagh know something she didn't know?

She scooted back inside and caught up with him. "The injured man in England—Hambly—he's all right, isn't he? You'd tell me if you'd heard anything, wouldn't you?"

"I haven't heard anything."

"Could you find out?"

Kavanagh eyed her. "Oliver York is Colin Donovan and Emma Sharpe's problem. Talk to Mike. He might know, or could put you in touch with them."

"Why were you checking on York?"

"Curiosity," he said, quoting her. "It can be a mixed bag, can't it?"

Buddy had vacated his spot by the fire. Then she saw him at the bar, getting a refill on his spiked cocoa. He waved to her. "Guess what, Naomi," he said, walking to her, carefully balancing his near-overflowing mug. "The National Weather Service is talking about a winter storm for southern Maine. They're expecting at least half a foot of snow in a few days. Imagine all of us stuck here."

"Six inches of snow won't faze people here, Buddy, but thanks for the heads-up."

"You'll be back in Nashville by the time the storm hits?"

"Drinking bourbon and checking if the crocuses are up," she said. "Enjoy your hot cocoa. I'm heading up. See you tomorrow."

"Sleep well. Let me know if you change your mind about cocoa and Bailey's."

She promised she would and took the stairs up to her room, her legs aching, her mind spinning. She passed Mike's door. What if she could sneak in there and have a look around? Was that a wise idea?

Why wouldn't it be?

She unlocked her own door and stepped into her room. It was cool, dark, quiet.

"I miss my Cotswolds chickens," she said, then backed out into the hall, shut the door behind her and went in search of a passkey.

25

Mike eased onto a bar stool next to Reed at the inn bar. A college basketball game was on the small television up on the wall, the sound on mute. The whiskey glass in front of Reed was almost empty. "I was catching the Vanderbilt score," he said.

"The Commodores," Mike said.

"Didn't take you for a college sports fan, Mike."

"I'm not. I just know the name of the Vanderbilt team."

"Because of Naomi," Reed said, his gaze still on the television screen. "It was you in Afghanistan and it's you now. It always will be you. Deal with it. For her sake if not your own."

"You might want to hold off on more whiskey." Mike tried to make his tone light but didn't quite pull it off. He noticed Reed was into the Redbreast 21, the bottle on the bar by his glass.

"I'm only saying out loud what we all know. You included, Mike."

He wasn't discussing his relationship with Reed. "You and Naomi are both in Nashville these days."

"There is no Naomi and me," Reed said. "There never was. There never will be. See that once and for all. If you were out of the picture—married, attached, whatever—that still wouldn't leave room for me. Forget that line of thinking."

"I don't have a line of thinking about Naomi."

"Now that makes sense," Reed said. "I knew when I met her in Afghanistan we were never going to be more than friends. It's not just on her end. It's on mine, too. She's like a sister to me. I'm not a monk pining away for a woman I can't have. I've put my romantic life on hold until I get this outfit off the ground."

"Any of the guys have sisters?"

"I don't lack for women, Mike, but if I need a matchmaker, you're the last person I'm calling."

Mike grinned. "Three brothers limits my matchmaking options."

"Your future sister-in-law, Emma Sharpe, only has a brother, Lucas, the heir apparent to Sharpe Fine Art Recovery. No sisters. The Sisters of the Joyful Heart don't count." Reed lifted his whiskey glass. "Then there's Julianne Maroney. Your lobsterman brother's love interest. When does she get back from Ireland?"

"Spring." Mike opened the Redbreast. "You've done your homework on my family."

"I always do my homework. I figure an objective look at the Donovans makes sense. You're blind when it comes to your brothers. I get that." Reed looked up at the television again, his glass still in hand. "Are you going to tell me what happened that brought your FBI brother here?"

"He's in town."

Reed gave an incredulous smile as he sipped his whiskey. "Consider, Mike, that what you're not telling me is a ruse by the FBI to worm their way in here to check out my operation."

"You're barking up the wrong tree, Reed."

"Maybe."

Mike got a glass from the side of the bar and poured some of the Redbreast. A *táoscán*, Finian Bracken would call it. An imprecise measure. Reed wasn't distracted by the basketball game.

He wasn't distracted by anything. "Dinner was good," Mike said. "Low-key. No tough questions from the boss."

"Boss." Reed chuckled. "I like that. My family was ecstatic when I left the army earlier than expected. They wanted me to start my own business. I don't think they had a private security firm in mind. Was your family pleased when you took off to the Bold Coast to be a wilderness guide?"

"I didn't ask."

Reed shook his head, his grin broadened. "You're such a bastard. Always have been. You're a solid, uncompromising SOB. You're the guy people want when the bad guys are coming for them. You're the best, Mike. Naomi isn't the only reason I got in touch with you. You know that. We need your skills. You're wasting yourself taking tourists to see moose."

"That's not all I do, and moose are cool."

"I also have a debt to be paid," Reed said quietly, no grin now. "I owe you. It would have been my career if you hadn't brought Naomi back in one piece that day."

"Glad I saved your career, Reed," Mike said, drinking some of his whiskey.

"That didn't come out like I meant. Too much whiskey." He seemed genuinely contrite. "I still get nightmares thinking of what could have happened to her. I should have known she was in danger."

"You don't owe me." Mike didn't want to think about rescuing Naomi—how close she'd come to torture, abuse and death. She'd been a high-value prisoner. But that was three years ago. Emma's ordeal had ended only a few hours ago. He set his glass on the bar. "What about Buddy and Kavanagh? Do you have a role for them at Cooper Global Security?"

"I could use Buddy but I hate being around him. It's not kind of me to say, but it's the truth. As for our friend Special Agent Kavanagh—I don't believe for two seconds he's thinking about leaving the FBI. That doesn't mean they're not thinking about kicking him out. I wish I could find out, but he doesn't work for me."

"Is he investigating you?"

"Actually, I wouldn't be surprised if he's investigating your brother and future sister-in-law. I'm being frank with you. We have a lot to do if we're going to be ready for Naomi's medical volunteers, but I also want everyone to relax and enjoy this place."

"You could have driven up to the Bold Coast or picked a place and asked me to meet you. Boston, Nashville. London."

"Would you have come?"

"Maybe," Mike said, blunt. "You provoked me into coming here by sending Jamie to Rock Point."

"It worked."

"Did you send Naomi there, too?"

Reed shook his head. "No, I didn't."

"But you want to make sure my family won't cause you problems if I come on board."

"The Donovans are an interesting lot, that's for sure."

"Then there's Naomi. You need her but you want to control her."

"In my world, Mike, *control* isn't a bad word. I'd like to know what's going on with her and this Oliver York character, and what Kavanagh's interest is—and yours. I don't want to get caught in the middle of a no-win situation." Reed turned to Mike. "Do you trust Naomi, Mike?"

Mike didn't answer. He dipped into his shirt pocket and withdrew the passkey he'd swiped earlier. "If I searched your room, Reed, what kind of trouble would I discover you're in?"

Reed gave him a thin smile. "The usual. Blackmail, extortion, threats to my life, liberty and pursuit of happiness."

"You're serious," Mike said.

"Yeah." Reed grabbed the Redbreast, splashing more into his

glass and then into Mike's. He took a sip of the whiskey. "How did you know?"

"You have the same look you did the day Naomi went missing."

"It's the usual fare. Par for the course given the work I do and starting a new venture. It could be the competition, former clients whose asses I saved, people I annoyed in the army. Hell, I wouldn't be surprised if my mother's behind a couple of the nasty emails. She'd like nothing better than for me to quit this work."

"She likes having you back in Nashville?"

"She says so. She'd like it better if I didn't work with men with guns and protect people with targets on their backs. I'm kidding about her threatening me. I don't have any threats that worry me. I stay on alert. Reputations in my world are fragile. Whispers, innuendo..."

"Someone determined to hurt you can do a lot of damage without any concrete evidence."

"Yeah." Reed set his glass on the bar, then grinned suddenly. "But who would want to hurt a nice guy like me?"

"Right."

"You don't have enemies, either, do you, Mike?"

He smiled, not into Reed's game. "There's a testy red squirrel who would like nothing better than to take over my cabin. We're sworn enemies."

"But you let it live," Reed said, not making it a question.

"We have rules of engagement. Well, I do. I think he'd take me out first chance he got. I don't give him any openings."

Reed laughed, but without any real heart in it. "One of the three guys killed in Afghanistan on that screwed-up mission was one of ours. An intelligence asset, as we like to say. I never told you."

Mike had guessed as much.

"He was one of the two Americans killed," Reed added. "He

wasn't supposed to be there. It wasn't just bad guys turning on bad guys."

"Our guy was caught in the middle."

"Naomi figured out they knew we were coming—you were coming. She warned you. Exposed herself in doing so and paid for it later, but the bad guys…" Reed exhaled, looking tired. "Could have been a lack of discipline. An argument that had nothing to do with us and turned violent. Their bad timing instead of ours."

"Why are you focused on this now?"

"We were all there. Stirs it up. And I need to know," Reed added, shifting his position on the stool so that he was facing Mike. "I need to know this isn't going to come back and bite me in the ass now that I'm out on my own."

Mike remembered walking into the carnage that day. Three dead. The FBI had been after the two dead Americans, but Mike had never felt he had the whole story. He and his team were after specific intelligence that would lead to the disruption of a major attack on civilians in Kabul. He'd always suspected the bad guys had been given a heads-up about the operation and had turned on each other, looking to find someone to blame. The remaining bad guys, alert to the mission, had tried ambushing Mike's Special Forces team. It hadn't worked, thanks to Naomi. She'd figured out they were walking into a trap.

A relatively straightforward mission had turned into a messy one.

"Was our deceased asset the one who alerted his drug-dealing, arms-trafficking friends that we were coming?" Mike asked.

"Maybe."

"Is this what this get-together is about, Reed?"

"The past? No. This is what happens when you drink too much whiskey on a dark winter night on the Maine coast." Reed grinned, looking ragged. "You start telling war stories."

"Not me. I read a book."

Reed laughed. "You could tell your red squirrel war stories."

"My advice, Reed? Ease up on yourself. You can't be perfect all the time."

"Neither can Naomi," he said quietly.

Mike pretended not to hear Reed's comment. He eased off the stool. "Kill the alcohol. Get some sleep. I'll see you in the morning."

"If I get a nasty email in the middle of the night, I'm calling you, Donovan."

Mike grinned. "Easy solution. Don't check your email in the middle of the night."

Naomi yawned at Mike when he entered his lighthouse room and found her standing by the window. "I found myself a passkey," she said. "Isn't that what you did with my room?"

Mike shut the door behind him. "What are you looking for?"

She pointed at the queen-size bed. "I thought you might sleep with a little stuffed baby moose. Packed it in your duffel bag as you left the Bold Coast."

"Didn't find one, did you?"

"I didn't get that far. I unzipped your duffel bag, saw a pair of boxers and almost ran screaming into the hall. Memories, you know? Not that they're the same boxers you wore in DC. Even you have to go shopping once in a while."

"Naomi."

"I pulled your drapes for you." She pointed at the window, the passkey in her hand. She tucked the key into her pants pocket. "I know I don't have any right to come in here and search your things. Call it payback for not trusting me if you want."

"Provocation," Mike said.

"I'm not law enforcement. I don't need a warrant."

"It's just illegal breaking and entering."

She angled a look at him. "Going to have me arrested, Mike?"

He sucked in a breath. She'd always driven him crazy. He

stepped away from the door, no idea what he was going to do now. He knew what he felt like doing but he kept his eyes on her. If he glanced at the bed, she'd know what he felt like doing, too.

"I didn't try to have you arrested," she said. "As if there was any chance that would happen since you're a Donovan and we're in Donovan country."

"That proves you don't know my family or Maine."

"No argument from me." She waved a hand in front of her chest. "My heart's thumping. I wonder why that is?"

"You didn't expect to get caught."

"That's a good reason. I expected to be in the tub right now. It's been a long two days. My heart didn't beat like this when I found that injured Brit yesterday. What do you think of Oliver York? Is he trouble for your brother—for Emma Sharpe? If he is, does that mean he's trouble for you?"

"More like for you, Naomi."

"Lucky me." She moved away from the window, running her fingertips on the top of his duffel bag on a luggage rack at the end of the bed. She'd zipped it back up. "You know York's an art thief, don't you?"

"That's your theory, is it?"

"A private theory. Interesting to think about how he pulls off his heists, where he has the art hidden—why Scotland Yard hasn't tossed his London apartment and his farm and arrested him. What do you think they have in mind for him?"

"I don't care."

"Oh, right. You stick to paddling your canoe into the wilds and never think twice about the rest of the world."

Mike remembered this mood of hers. This was Naomi Mac-Bride pushing people away. Rationalizing. Provoking. Not recognizing a friend when she saw one. It was all so much easier than taking the leap and getting close to someone—letting someone get close to her.

He couldn't play that game again.

"You dived in headfirst with Oliver York when you should have stuck to your own business."

"I didn't dive in," Naomi said, not particularly combative. "I meandered in. But I get now why you went alpha on me."

"Alpha, Naomi? What am I, a dog?"

"More like a wolf," she said, a spark in her dark hazel eyes.

"I'm just a guy."

"You pegged me as a magnet for trouble three years ago. I guess nothing I've done in the past twenty-four hours has changed that."

He shrugged. "Nothing good happens when you're in my life."

"That's such a load of BS, Mike. I saved your damn life."

"You did your job. I did my job."

"There were also a few nights of mad, wild, unforgettable sex." She tilted her chin up at him. "Or did you forget?"

"I didn't forget."

She was visibly taken aback by his answer, but only for a split second. "Never better sex, either," she said, defiant, daring him to deny it.

Mike stepped closer to her. He touched a curl that had dropped onto her forehead. "Are you done chasing demons, Naomi?"

"I never did chase demons. That's your fantasy about me. I did my job in Kabul to the best of my ability. I do my job now to the best of my ability. That's all I can do, and it's all anyone can ask me to do. If it wasn't enough for you—if I fell short— then so be it."

"It was enough. You didn't fall short." He skimmed a fingertip along her cheek. "I'm sorry if I ever led you to believe otherwise."

"'Never again, Naomi'?"

"That wasn't about you falling short."

"Then what was it about?"

"You got dragged out of a restaurant and thrown into a van by some very bad people because you had exposed yourself two months earlier to warn me."

"Warning you was a necessary risk, and it wasn't about you."

"I know that, but I couldn't let it happen again."

"Mike. Ah, Mike." She threw up her hands and let them fall to her sides. "I'm glad you and your team weren't among the casualties either day. But I know that going after those guys—walking into an ambush—and then rescuing me weren't your toughest missions. Not even close."

"It's all in the past."

"Easy to say." She touched his shoulder. "But thank you for rescuing me. You saved my life."

He shrugged. "I don't need your gratitude, Naomi," he said softly.

"Nor I yours," she said. "I should go run the tub."

"The guy in England. Hambly. What's your gut on what happened to him?"

His non-sequitur question obviously took her by surprise. "It wasn't an accident."

"Did he know it?"

"I think so, deep down. If he's loyal to Oliver York, he would be reluctant to have the police in there mucking around, even if the attack had nothing to do with art theft." She pulled her hand away from his shoulder. "Sleep well."

Mike brushed his fingers through the curls on her temple. "I'm not leaving you alone tonight. I can sleep on the floor."

She took an audible breath. "You don't have to sleep on the floor."

26

They ended up in Mike's bed, because once he kissed her, Naomi knew she wasn't going anywhere. She melted into him. The months—the years—fell away. He'd been the only man for her three years ago. Now. Forever. That was all she could think with any coherence as they disrobed each other, not slowly.

"I can't stop kissing you," she whispered.

"Then don't."

"I need to… Your belt…"

But he had it, and in seconds they were snuggled under a fluffy comforter, his skin hot and hard against her. She felt the same scars, and new ones. The same heat burned through her, as it had in Washington all those years ago. He hadn't known she'd be there. She hadn't known he'd be there. The surprise had been the lit match that had set them on fire, ending any resistance to the sparks that had erupted between them in Afghanistan. She'd told him she was quitting and wouldn't be back. It had been true when she'd said it.

"Naomi." He slid his palms up her sides, over her breasts. "Come back to me."

She smiled. "I'm here."

Neither spoke again for a long time. There was no need, with his touch, the feel of his mouth, his tongue, his finger on her, inside her, the heat and ache of desire sweeping through her. Even if there were things that needed to be said between them, she couldn't think of what they were, and they didn't matter, not right now.

They made love slowly, tenderly, a second time, and Naomi fell asleep in his arms. When she awoke, it was still night. She slipped out from the comforter, the cool air striking her heated skin. She walked to the window and peeked out at the stars and quarter moon above the ocean. The cold air seemed to make them brighter, sharper.

Mike joined her, putting an arm around her and kissing her on the top of her head.

"We're still impossible," she said.

"I know."

"It's always this way with us. In Washington, did we go on a date? No. We fell into bed."

"Life could be worse."

And has been, she thought. She smiled at him. "We could go kayaking or have a Netflix night. Shuck clams. Cook lobsters."

"We could do that."

"Not right now, though. We're both stark naked."

He laughed. "Naomi."

This time there was no falling into bed together. He scooped her up and carried her, pulling the covers over them and finding her again.

27

Padgett drove from Heathrow. Emma had more experience driving on the left, but he managed with only one unnerving incident at a roundabout. The near miss with a van didn't faze him, and she was too preoccupied to pay much attention. She'd slept on the plane, but fitfully, fighting bad dreams. In the plane's bathroom, she'd washed her face and hands, making sure she was as alert as possible for seeing Oliver York again. She'd done a few stretches, discovering new bruises and strained muscles. But it was a lovely morning in the Cotswolds, and she had no regrets about getting onto a plane last night.

Padgett still had understandable reservations about her being here at all given the circumstances, but she wasn't getting into it with him. She knew England, and she knew Finian Bracken and Oliver York. She needed to be here.

"Your parents are in London?" he asked her as he drove

through the pretty village of Burford, its shops and restaurants relatively quiet at nine on a Saturday morning.

Emma nodded. "They'll be there for a few more months."

"You can visit them if it turns out Hambly slipped on a cow pie."

"More likely sheep droppings," she said.

He grinned at her. "Hence the sheepskins."

"Sam…"

"Perked you up. While you're visiting your parents, I'll tour Oxford. I've always wanted to see Bodleian Library."

They'd passed through the edge of Oxford. "Any particular reason?"

"Oxford is one of my paths not taken."

"You are a man of many mysteries, Special Agent Padgett."

"Just your average small-town Texas boy."

As they wound past rolling fields and honey-stone houses, Emma sank into her seat. She'd texted Colin when they'd landed. He'd texted her back.

Not sleeping, obviously.

"Quaint," Padgett said when they came to the York farm. "Expect to see Mr. Darcy pacing in the garden."

"You read Jane Austen?"

"Saw the movie. Forced. Daughters of a friend in Texas. They made me watch the version with Colin Firth. It lasts forever. Seriously. I cleaned all my guns and it was still going."

"The things I don't know about you, Sam."

He turned onto the driveway, the gate open for their arrival. "This place is too bucolic for Mr. Darcy. It could work for his friend's place—what's his name? The milquetoast who fell for the pretty sister?"

"Mr. Bingley."

"That's it."

"I must look terrible if you're trying to distract me by talking about *Pride and Prejudice*."

"Book's better than the movies. I read it in college, but never mind. You do look terrible. You've got that sunken-eyed look you get after jumping out a window into the snow. The choke hold and the blanket over my head I could take. Snow down my back..." He shuddered. "That's rough."

Emma burst out laughing. She couldn't help herself. High-testosterone Padgett shuddering over snow down his back was more than she could take.

He ground the gears downshifting, but he grinned at her as he pulled the car to a stop at the farmhouse's side entrance. "We want you smiling when you talk to your art thief."

But it was Finian Bracken who greeted them. He rushed to Emma and took her hand as she climbed out of the car. "Colin told me you'd been through a difficult experience. If only I'd been there. Emma." He kissed her on both cheeks. "Thank God you're all right."

"Thank you, Fin," she said, then introduced him to Padgett.

Finian brought them inside. "Oliver is in the kitchen arguing with Martin."

They went down a hall to a classic English country kitchen. Oliver was pacing on the tiled floor. Martin Hambly sat at a large wood table, a flower-decorated pot of tea in front of him. Oliver pointed at him. "If you'd died, Martin, a forensics exam would have been required. It would have confirmed you didn't fall on a rock, as you insist, but instead were hit by a sharp metal instrument, which is what I suspect happened."

Martin sniffed. "I suppose my death would have been more easily solved than my injury."

"If not for that rock head of yours, we would be getting your autopsy results right about now."

Martin stood as Emma, Padgett and Finian entered the kitchen. "Agent Sharpe," he said. "What a pleasure to see you again."

"Emma," Oliver said, with less enthusiasm.

They exchanged a few pleasantries, but Emma and Padgett both turned down tea and breakfast. "We'd like to see the dovecote where Martin was injured," she said, addressing Oliver. "Would you mind?"

"Of course not."

Hambly declared he was well enough to walk with them.

They went out through the kitchen, crossing a terrace to a stone path. Oliver led the way, with Padgett and Finian picking up the rear. The path took them through a perennial garden to a sodden lawn and a fenced field. They followed along the edge of the field to a narrow dirt track.

Emma breathed in the fresh morning air, feeling more herself again as they arrived at the dovecote. On any other day, she would have taken a moment to appreciate its history and architecture, the beauty of the setting. This morning, she asked Martin to point out where he'd left the package. Then she took a look inside the small building. Oliver joined her, but the other three men stayed outside.

She pointed to a locked door. "Your studio?"

"That's right. I'm shutting it down. The Saint Brigid's cross is to be one of my final creations. There's no sign of a break-in, if that's what you're wondering."

"I'm wondering everything," Emma said.

"It can be difficult to focus after an ordeal like yours." Oliver's pale green eyes settled on her for half a beat longer than was comfortable. He pulled away, dipping a finger into a clay pot on a workbench. "Needs water. It's an amaryllis bulb. Martin picked up two of them from a friend in the village before he ran into your colleague in front of the church."

Emma glanced around the potting area. Could Kavanagh have opened the package and stolen the cross when he was out here on Wednesday? Or could he simply have seen the package and left it alone, then made plans to intercept it when it arrived in Rock Point?

Naomi MacBride had been in the village then, too. Could she have walked out here without anyone having noticed? Then lied to everyone at the Plum Tree about it, including Kavanagh and Mike?

Warning herself against speculating, Emma followed Oliver outside. He led her around to the back of the dovecote. She paused, taking a moment to appreciate the sight of snowdrops blanketing a section of the hillside. If Hambly had fallen there, someone might have spotted him sooner—assuming anyone had passed this way before Naomi MacBride had wandered to the dovecote late Thursday morning.

Not exactly wandered, Emma thought.

"It's warmer here than Boston, anyway," Padgett said, easing in next to her.

Hambly walked past them and stopped a few feet down the wooded hill. "It wasn't an accident," he said, half to himself. "I was standing here...and I heard metal on metal. Then I was struck from behind." He placed his fingertips on his neck where he'd been hit. "I'd just returned from the village. I remembered the package and set it out for pickup. Then..." He turned to Emma, his face pale. "Someone was here, Agent Sharpe."

She glanced at Oliver. "May we take a look at the area?"

"By all means."

She went left and Padgett went right. The ground was soft, wet, with signs of spring here and there. Emma scanned the underbrush for footprints, anything that would confirm that someone had, indeed, attacked Hambly and could lead police to his attacker.

She came to the bank of the stream. It flowed softly over rocks and a coppery bottom. She could have sat there for hours, listening to the sounds of the water, breathing in the smells.

Not today.

She jumped onto a rock in the middle stream, steadied herself and then leaped to the other side. Her right foot settled into mud, but her left foot landed in a dry spot. She continued up the hill to a cluster of small evergreens. The ground behind the trees was stirred up, as if someone had staked out a spot for a quick nap or a night in the woods.

Emma returned to the edge of the stream and called to Padgett. "I've found something."

He and Finian took the same route across the stream, but Hambly and Oliver, in Wellingtons, walked right through the shallow water.

Emma nodded to the makeshift campsite. "It doesn't look like an animal's doing. Someone could have hidden here and spied on the dovecote, slept, had a picnic."

Oliver narrowed his gaze on the spot. "Bloody bastard."

Martin squatted down. Padgett touched his shoulder. "Best if you don't touch anything. Let's save it for the local police."

"What if I don't want to contact the local police?"

"Then I will on your behalf," Padgett said, matter-of-fact.

Emma squinted through the trees toward the dovecote. It wasn't a particularly good view of anyone at the dovecote or coming from the farm, but when she looked to her left, she could see the dirt track. Whoever hid here would have been able to see Martin Hambly walking to the dovecote with his amaryllis pots.

"This attacker feels chaotic, emotional, opportunistic," Oliver said. "Maybe not desperate, but not cold and calculating. Do you think this is the same person who attacked you, Emma?"

"I never said…"

"Please."

She nodded. "Yes."

Oliver looked grim. "A simple gift of sheepskins and a cross…" He took in a breath. "I'm so sorry. Martin. Emma. I had no idea."

Martin stood, unsteady. He reached for one of the evergreens but lost his balance. Padgett grabbed him and helped him to his feet. "I've no information to offer," the Englishman said.

Emma nodded. "I understand."

Padgett's eyes connected with hers. She could see he under-stood, too. They had to figure this out without Martin Hambly implicating Oliver as an art thief, because that wasn't going to happen. Martin would lie about what happened out here first, even to the local police—who could take him in for question-ing, arrest him. Emma and Padgett couldn't. They were on Oli-ver's property only with his permission.

"We don't need to dig into your affairs," Padgett said. "We're not here to bring in whoever attacked you. We're here to find out who stuffed Agent Sharpe into a trunk and then locked her in a shed without food and water."

Oliver raised his eyebrows. "Wouldn't want you to sugarcoat it, would we?"

Martin gasped. "There it is," he said in a hoarse whisper, pointing to a spot by the evergreens. "The would-be murder weapon, I daresay. Blast. I swear I can see my blood on it from here."

Padgett stepped in front of him. "We need to leave it for—"

"For the police," Martin said.

Emma could see a pair of old garden shears lying in wet, brown leaves. The metal-on-metal sound must have been Mar-tin's attacker opening and shutting the blades.

"It could have been worse, Martin," Oliver said. "The bas-tard could have lopped off body parts." He sighed. "I'll ring the police myself. Just not right this minute." He turned to Emma. "Shall we make a quick visit to the village first?"

Finian stayed at the farmhouse with Hambly, who was clearly worn-out after their trek to the dovecote. Emma and Padgett rode with Oliver in his Rolls-Royce. He drove, Emma up front as he chatted amiably, pointing out sights. When they arrived at the pub, a waiter showed them to a table by an open fire near the bar. Breakfast in the next room was done for the day, but their table was set with bowls of cut fresh fruit, natural yogurt, scones and York farm's' own gooseberry jam.

"Ruthie, my housekeeper, called ahead," Oliver said. "A proper breakfast will do you good after your flight. You didn't eat on the plane, did you? Airline food is a notch above poison."

"I didn't think it was bad," Padgett said, but dug into the fruit and yogurt.

The waiter brought a pot of tea and two coffee presses. Emma had tea and then nibbled on a grape. She wished she'd had a chance to talk with Ted Kavanagh and Naomi MacBride herself before she'd left Maine, but getting here—talking with Oliver and Martin, seeing the dovecote—had taken on an urgency she seldom felt. Her work usually allowed, even demanded, that she go methodically, step-by-step, putting often disparate pieces together. Choosing, carefully, when and how to act. She'd had times when she'd had to rely on her instincts and act quickly, but not as often as the deep analytical work she did day-to-day. She'd spent many hours with the files on a serial international art thief who had eluded her and her grandfather for a decade.

Now here she was, across the table from him with a scone and gooseberry jam.

She'd figured her art thief for an intelligent, perhaps well-off man, but she'd never imagined Oliver York.

He tapped the tray of scones with his knife. "Help yourself, Emma. You need to eat."

"Oliver…"

"I'm right. Eat."

She gave in and tried a scone, cream and jam. He was right, of course. She did need to eat.

"There," he said, smug, and turned to Padgett. "Did you say you had a list of names for us to check?"

"I did, indeed," Padgett said, pulling out his phone. "It's right here. I put together names and photos last night at the airport."

They went through them, but Oliver only recognized Ted

Kavanagh and Naomi MacBride. He drew a blank on the other names and faces. He took Padgett's phone and called over the waiter, flipping through the list with him while Padgett stewed but kept quiet. The waiter pointed to Naomi MacBride, Ted Kavanagh and Reed Cooper. Nothing new there. All three had already admitted to being in the village.

"Cooper here—" Oliver tapped his photo "—picked up Mac-Bride on Thursday, after she found Hambly. Could he have driven in from London on Wednesday?"

"I didn't see him," the waiter said.

"And he didn't stay here?"

"I don't think so. I'd remember if I'd seen him. It's quiet this time of year."

Oliver thanked him, then got up and went into a small reception area to find the proprietors, a young couple who eyed Emma and Padgett warily. "These are friends of mine," Oliver said cheerfully. "Emma and Sam."

Emma could see Padgett was having none of that. Keeping quiet with the waiter had tested him, but no way was he going to be Oliver York's American friend Sam. He rose and introduced himself. "I'm Special Agent Sam Padgett and this is Special Agent Emma Sharpe. We're with the FBI. We're looking into an attack on an agent in the US."

"Whoever did it also attacked Martin with garden shears," Oliver added.

Padgett leveled a look at Emma that said he never should have gone along with delaying a call to the local police. But this was Oliver York. The frumpy, awkward Oliver Fairbairn she, Colin and Finian had met in Boston was also this man—cheeky, wily and able to turn on the charm when it suited him.

But Oliver's comment worked, and the properly horrified proprietors agreed to look at the names and photos. Oliver left it to Padgett and rose, motioning for Emma to join him. Padgett gave her a dark look, but he said nothing as she followed Oliver out the main door. They went across the green, ducks gathering in the stream, small children chasing each other on the chilly Saturday morning.

Oliver wore an expensive leather jacket open over a dark sweater. He walked with the confidence and poise of a man well-practiced in Tai Chi and Tae Kwon Do, his martial arts of choice, but Emma also felt his familiarity with this small English village. He led her up a lane, past a row of small attached houses that he explained were mostly owned nowadays by Londoners. It was clear he distinguished himself from weekenders, people with no roots in the area.

They came to the church where Martin Hambly had chatted with Ted Kavanagh. Emma breathed in the cool air, taking in the pretty surroundings. "I wonder if anyone witnessed the exchange, or saw Kavanagh meet someone else—or saw someone spying on them."

"We could knock on doors and ask," Oliver said.

"I can't."

He sighed. "Rules."

"Oliver…" Emma hesitated before she continued. "I didn't realize until this morning at the dovecote that Martin knows you're a serial art thief."

"You've infected him with your suspicions, I'm afraid."

"I only saw him that one time in London in November, and we barely spoke."

"Three FBI agents showing up at the front door? What was he to think?" Oliver glanced at her. "Do you expect me to confess?"

"No, I don't. You've had years to confess. It's been months since you've known we figured out you're our thief. No, Oliver, I want the two Dutch landscapes back in Amsterdam where they belong. I'm not a Dutch official, but that's what I want."

"And then sin no more?"

"It's been a while since your last heist. I think you've already decided to 'sin no more.' Or perhaps you've just lost a step."

"Lost a step? Well. There you have it. You didn't put Agent Kavanagh on me, Emma. You have bigger fish to fry than a British citizen you consider to be a harmless, washed-up art thief."

Emma rolled her eyes. "Give it up, Oliver."

He nodded up the lane, past the church. "Come on. I want to show you something."

They went into the cemetery adjoining the churchyard. He was silent, a slight breeze catching the ends of his hair as he took her to a far corner of the cemetery and the York family plot.

"Martin comes here regularly," he said, staring at the gravestones. "I come on Easter Sunday. One of my most vivid memories of my mother is her wearing her last Easter hat." He smiled. "It was horrid."

"I'm sorry for your loss, Oliver."

"It's been a long time. I just turned thirty-seven. It's time to absorb the past instead of fighting it, don't you think?"

"Is that why you invited Father Bracken here?"

He frowned. "Maybe. I told myself it was because we got on, but we have a tragic past in common, don't we?" Before Emma could answer, Oliver turned from the graves and winked at her. "And Aoife O'Byrne, of course, though I believe she'd take garden shears to us both if she could."

He spun away from the graves. The moment of insight had passed. Emma followed him back to the lane and the church.

Oliver buttoned his jacket. "MI5 is sniffing around. Do you know anything about that, Emma?"

"Anything involving the British Secret Service is not my doing."

"A fine-tuned answer. You don't think they could be responsible for stealing the package?"

"They'd have been tidier, don't you think? More professional."

He grunted. "You and Martin did survive your ordeals, that's true. If it'd been bloody MI5, we'd have never found your bodies. They're coming for me, Emma."

"Mythology, extensive travel, martial arts expertise, a master at breaking and entering." Emma shrugged. "You could do some good, Oliver."

"I'd want a 'double O' number."

"But of course."

"Apparently priceless Middle Eastern antiquities have been stolen by bad people and sold to bad people, and MI5 thinks I might know something about that."

"Do you?"

He turned to her. "If I do, it's because I'm a well-traveled mythologist."

"You have at least two perfect covers as a bored aristocrat and tortured mythologist."

"'At least two'? You believe there are more?"

"I wouldn't be surprised."

"Anyway, they're not covers. I *am* Oliver York, and taking a pseudonym for my Hollywood consulting work made perfect sense."

"I'm staying out of it. I doubt Agent Kavanagh's presence here involved MI5."

"What about Naomi MacBride's presence?"

"I can't say."

"Mmm. My point."

They returned to the pub. Padgett had set off on foot.

"You drive the Rolls," Oliver said. "I'll phone the police."

Emma hesitated.

He nudged her toward the driver's seat. "It'll do you good. Right back in the saddle after your ordeal."

She didn't argue. She knew he was right.

And the Rolls practically drove itself.

"Why the cross, Oliver?" she asked when they arrived back at the farm.

"Saint Brigid was an accomplished woman and she's a fascinating saint. I know you carry her in your heart. You're not fighting your past, Emma. Sister Brigid is a part of who you are now."

Emma smiled. "Yes, she is."

"And the cross is damn fine work. I'm proud of it. You can hang it above your front door and ward off fires. Think of the fires you face, figuratively if not literally. You come across as a thoughtful, analytical ex-nun who specializes in art crimes for the FBI, but it's not that simple, is it, Emma? You like your fires."

"I look forward to seeing this cross," she said.

He smiled knowingly as they joined Padgett, Martin Hambly and Finian Bracken by the fire.

28

Colin had gone out with Andy on his lobster boat early, catching the sunrise and a good view of the Plum Tree Inn and the lightkeeper's house. Mike hadn't been in touch yet, but Emma had. She and Padgett had arrived in the English Cotswolds and had confirmed that Martin Hambly had been attacked. Hambly and Oliver York were "more or less" cooperating.

An interesting thief, Oliver York was.

"Colin." Andy tapped their table at Hurley's. "Whoa. Where are you right now?"

He smiled. "Having bacon and eggs with my lobsterman brother."

"Think Mike knew we were out there catching the dawn light?"

"I wouldn't be surprised if they all knew."

"Naomi MacBride wants Hurley's to put grits on the menu. She and Mike…"

"Yeah."

"I'm glad my life is simple."

"Right. This from the man who hooked up with Julianne Maroney. When does she get back from her Irish internship?"

"Early May. She wants me to fly to Ireland with her grand-mother."

"You and Franny Maroney on a six-hour flight together." Colin grinned. "That's worse than Emma and Sam Padgett. Franny wouldn't sleep a wink."

"She's excited about seeing the land of her ancestors. I just want to see Julianne. She and Franny are tight. I'll figure it out." Andy nodded toward the restaurant's entrance. "You've got company."

Matt Yankowski joined them at their table. He'd flown into Boston last night and driven up to Maine early. He wasn't as thrilled about catching the sunrise. He ordered coffee, then glanced at Andy.

Andy grinned. "I'll let you guys talk FBI stuff." He got to his feet, grabbing his jacket off the back of his chair. "Good to see you, Agent Yankowski."

"Don't let me run you off," Yank said.

"I'm good. It's late by my standards. See you around."

Yank watched Andy cross the restaurant, then turned to Colin. "Ted Kavanagh lost a CI in Afghanistan. An Ameri-can who got mixed up with some rough people. Drug dealing, arms trafficking and money laundering. He was killed ahead of an operation to capture the bad guys. He wasn't supposed to be there. Two dealers were killed along with him. An American and an Afghani."

"The CI got burned?"

Yank nodded. "The bad guys knew about him and the op-eration. Naomi MacBride found out and warned the team they were walking into an ambush."

"Mike," Colin said.

"Yeah."

"She saved his life?"

Yank's coffee arrived. He took a sip. "She exposed herself in the process. Two months later, a couple of the bad guys who slipped the net grabbed her. Mike was part of the team that rescued her."

"Ouch."

"Yeah. Ouch. In my opinion, Ted Kavanagh is crispy, and he's been looking for someone to blame for his CI and Naomi besides himself."

29

Naomi grabbed her suitcase and set it on her bed, still made up—a reminder of where she'd spent the night. As if she needed one. She'd slipped into her room to shower and change clothes. She'd meet Mike downstairs. More guys were due in that morning. She'd clear out. She had no regrets about making love to Mike last night, but she'd opened herself up to him again and that she did regret. How could she resume her life in Nashville, knowing he was in his cabin out on the Maine coast, working, living his life—alone?

But wasn't she just as alone?

She hated being emotionally vulnerable. Loving Mike Donovan laid all her emotions bare, exposed her in ways she never allowed with anyone else.

She noticed a bulge in a side compartment of her suitcase. She couldn't remember what she'd put in there. Shoes? A belt? She unzipped the compartment, then eased one hand inside. She felt metal and couldn't imagine what it was.

She withdrew the object and saw that it was a cross. An Irish cross, she thought. It was made out of silver but was designed to look as if someone had twisted together reeds.

It couldn't have been in her suitcase when she'd left England. She'd have noticed the bulk in that compartment, the weight of the silver. She'd left her suitcase in her room at her Cotswolds inn while she was at breakfast and the York dovecote. She'd locked the door, but Ted Kavanagh and Reed Cooper, both of whom had been in the pretty English village, knew how to dispatch with locks. But why would they bother? Why would they slip a cross into her bag?

And how could she not have noticed until now?

She'd carried her suitcase to Reed's car and then to check-in at Heathrow. She'd picked it up at Logan. She'd carried it into the Rock Point Harbor Inn. Mike had carried it upstairs. It'd been in his truck while they'd had breakfast at Hurley's.

She shook her head. *No.* The cross hadn't been in her suitcase. Someone had put it there since her arrival at the Plum Tree.

Planted it.

She'd seen for herself how easy it was to get hold of a passkey.

"Naomi."

She spun around. Buddy came out of her bathroom. "It's okay. Sorry. I didn't mean to startle you. I wanted to talk to you. You left your door unlocked."

No, she hadn't.

"I thought…" He winced. "I don't know what I thought."

"Let's go downstairs and talk. I was going to take a shower and get dressed, but I need coffee."

"Where were you last night?"

"What kind of question is that?" Naomi waved a hand. "Never mind. As I recall, you drink your coffee with an inordinate amount of milk—"

"Whole milk. Fat is back." Buddy smiled but his eyes were on her, wary.

"You're not your usual devil-may-care Buddy self. Come on. Let's go. Coffee always helps."

"I know it was you in England, Naomi."

She stared at him. "What?"

"You pushed that Brit and then you saved him to take the pressure off you. It's okay. I know why you did it."

"Tell me, Buddy. Why did I do it?"

"Leverage. Oliver York is an art thief. But you know that. He's wealthy, and he's in possession of valuable stolen art. He's working with Emma Sharpe. If that gets out, it'll spew scandal all over the Donovans as well as the Sharpes. It would hurt Mike. It would hurt Reed. Ultimately, it would hurt you and good clients like your doctors."

"Buddy—damn. This is nuts." Naomi pointed toward the door. "Let's go talk it out, because you are as wrong as wrong can be. You spend your time digging around in cyberspace, which can be a giant garbage heap. You come up with theories and tidbits and all sorts of things, but you've said yourself that ninety-eight out of a hundred theories you have will be worthless. This is one of the ninety-eight."

He didn't seem to hear her. "This Brit—Hambly—didn't trip. He was attacked, and you attacked him, Naomi. I know you were there."

"The morning *after* he was attacked."

Buddy shook his head. "The afternoon before. *When* he was attacked."

"You're wrong, Buddy. I don't care. It happens. We're friends."

"You always try to do the right thing, but sometimes you cross the line. I saw it in Afghanistan. Now I'm seeing it with this thief and Emma Sharpe. I don't know if Mike's brother realizes yet how corrupt she is—I doubt Mike does. This will blow back onto you and Reed. Your clients don't want that kind of notoriety around them." Buddy eased a hand into his jacket pocket. "Let me help."

Naomi didn't like not being able to see his hand. "All right. Let's go and talk about my options. A jolt of caffeine will help me make sense of this."

He shook his head. He didn't budge from his position between her and the door. "I don't want to go downstairs."

"Right now, Buddy, I don't care what you want." She pushed back her fear. She had to be herself. She would stand a chance if he tried to hit her, but she didn't know if he had a weapon on him. "You're making leaps in logic and drawing conclusions that are so far-fetched—"

"Believe me, I know. It took me a while to figure out what you were up to. You're good at what you do, and you have the best motives." He pulled an assault knife out of his jacket. He looked almost sheepish. "I got it off Serena. Couldn't get near a gun. I'd have grabbed a paring knife if that was all I could get."

"Buddy..."

"It's for self-defense." He pointed the knife at the bed. "I found the cross in your suitcase, Naomi."

"Did you put it there?"

"Oliver York made the cross. He sent it to Emma Sharpe. It will prove she's a dirty agent and lead to proof that he's a thief." Buddy redirected his knife toward Naomi. "Reed can't hire Mike. Mike's too big a liability now."

"The cross didn't come from me. Where did it come from, Buddy?" She heard the fear in her voice. "Agent Kavanagh was in England."

"He's an FBI agent." Buddy stepped toward her. "Kavanagh didn't plant the cross, Naomi. You're in a tight spot. Mike and Reed are going to find out about all your shortcuts and shenanigans. How many times did you cover up? Things went bad on your last days in Afghanistan because you screwed up."

She hadn't screwed up. Buddy had manipulated her. All of them. Ted Kavanagh, Reed Cooper, Mike Donovan.

"Don't be afraid," he said, moving toward her. "I would never hurt you. I would never hurt anyone. I'm just a tech guy who sees things. You must know that."

"What do you want me to do, Buddy?"

"Did you find any stolen art when you were sneaking into the dovecote?"

She shook her head. "No."

"Frustrating for you. Going to all that trouble and then not finding anything. You wouldn't get the full value for stolen art, but you'd get something. You have the contacts to pull off a private illicit sale."

"Why do I have the feeling we're talking about you now?"

"I can get you out of this. Come away with me. Today. Now. Naomi…you don't belong with Mike. This can all work out. I have a beautiful spot in mind for us. No one will ever find us. It's paradise."

He was in a fantasy world. "Buddy, put the knife away. You don't want to hurt me by accident."

"You and Mike." Buddy seemed to be seeing her and the room for the first time. "Last night. You were together. Oh, Naomi. You're making such a mistake. I have bigger stuff going down than Mike and Reed and the rest of these guys can handle. It's not just the productivity app."

"I know, Buddy. You're the best."

"But I've always been a coward. I know that. I'm sorry. I got scared in Afghanistan. I made mistakes."

He hadn't gotten scared.

"I appreciate what you've done for me, Naomi," he added, almost whining now. "Don't think I don't."

There was a knock on the door. "Naomi? It's Ted Kavanagh. Open up."

"T.K.," Naomi yelled. "Buddy's got a knife."

She launched herself toward the door, away from Buddy, but he managed to slash her above her right hip. She collapsed onto the floor, and he ran, bolting to the balcony. Clutching her hip, she half crawled, half slid toward the door, but Kavanagh kicked it open and burst into the room.

"He went out the balcony," she said, not sure if Kavanagh could make out her words. "That lying bastard."

"Easy, kid." Kavanagh sat on the floor next to her, using the heel of his hand to put pressure on her wound. "I can't leave you."

She gasped, feeling the pain now. "It was Buddy in Afghanistan three years ago. He played both sides. Ours and the bad guys'."

"Yeah. I see that now. I trusted him. I gave him a chance when no one else would. I paved the way for him to kill people."

"It was Buddy in England, too. He attacked that Brit."

Kavanagh held her. "Try not to move. Buddy won't get far. He doesn't stand a chance with Reed and Mike."

"Mike..."

"Yeah. You two. Damn."

Naomi smiled. "T.K...thank you."

30

Mike went out to the parking lot and shoved his duffel bag into the back of his truck. He didn't know how long he'd hang around but he wasn't staying tonight. He wasn't going to complicate Naomi's life and she wouldn't let him. Nothing had changed in three years. Reed could find someone else to help with her volunteer doctors.

He looked at the line of rental cars. The Masons' was closest. He'd start with it.

They'd left it unlocked. He could understand. He'd left his truck unlocked.

He popped the trunk as Colin arrived, pulling in next to him.

"I don't need a warrant," Mike said as his brother climbed out of his truck.

"No, you need a get-out-of-jail-free card."

"We find evidence Emma was in one of these trunks—fibers of the blanket, hair, skin, blood—"

"I know, Mike."

He shut the trunk and turned to Colin. "Whoever took her didn't happen on her. He waited for her. He ambushed her. He took the cross, either thinking it's valuable or it's potential leverage."

"Or both," Colin said. "I'll find out who did it and I'll find a way to prove it."

"Go ahead. I don't have to prove it. I'm not a law enforcement officer."

"Let's go talk to your friends. Emma's been in touch. Hambly was attacked. It wasn't an accident. And Buddy Whidmore was in England this past week. He flew into Boston on Thursday."

"Buddy." Mike swore. "He said he was in Nashville."

"What's his relationship with Kavanagh and Cooper?" Colin asked.

"He ingratiates himself with them."

"Did he ever work with Reed?"

Mike shook his head. "Not directly that I know of. Buddy's a tech guy who likes to move around. He works for anyone who'll pay him. I always thought if he'd settle down, he'd do better, but he says he's made a fortune."

"So why was he in London and why is he here?" Colin let the question hang. "Kevin's on his way. We'll sort this out."

Mike texted Naomi. Lock yourself in your room. Stay away from Buddy. On my way.

He got his Glock out of its lockbox in his truck.

He and Colin headed into the Plum Tree. Jamie Mason was behind the front desk, slumped on a high stool, holding his middle. Colin drew his weapon.

Jamie looked up. "Buddy stabbed me. No warning. He's got my gun."

"Where is he?" Colin asked.

"Dining room. Go." Jamie shuddered, in obvious pain. "I'll hold on. Serena just left to pick up guys at the Portland airport."

Mike and Colin were already moving across the lobby. They edged into the dining room, staying out of sight. Up by the windows overlooking the water, Buddy had a nine-millimeter pistol placed against Reed's temple.

"This is self-defense," Buddy said. "You can't kill me for something I didn't do. I'm telling you. You've pegged the wrong guy. It's not me. I didn't do anything."

"The hell it's self-defense," Reed said, his voice clear and strong. "You attacked that man in England. You didn't care if he lived or died, did you, Buddy? You never do. Just like Afghanistan three years ago. You tipped off those guys that we were coming. You got them to turn on each other. Three died."

"All of them scum."

"You know better. You know one of them was ours. So long as you made out okay, you didn't care who else got hurt in the process."

Mike leveled his Glock at Buddy, but Reed was too close. The shot was too risky. He glanced at Colin, who nodded in agreement. They needed Reed or Buddy to make a move. Right now, so long as Buddy was talking, he wasn't shooting.

"What are you going to do, Buddy?" Reed's voice was calm. "Kill me? Kill us all?"

"I've always been a bug on your shoe, haven't I?"

"It's just you and me here. Go ahead and tell me the truth. Take credit for what you've done. You played us for fools, didn't you? All of us. You figured out Kavanagh had an informant. You didn't care. You let him get killed."

Buddy snorted. "He knew the risks. I didn't kill anyone."

"You made it happen," Reed said. "You didn't just not stop it. You made it happen because our guy combined with a successful mission would expose you for double-dealing. Kavanagh's been haunted by what happened. He hasn't been after a ghost for the past three years. He's been after you."

"I assessed the risks and took action. Isn't that what you all do? I'm no different."

Mike could see the spittle on Buddy's mouth.

Reed stayed under control. "Yeah, you are different, Buddy. You lie, you manipulate, you play both sides." Reed's voice took on more urgency, as if he were about to let his anger get the better of him. "You're a rodent, Buddy. Do you feel powerful when you manipulate us? Are you doing it for profit? Do you like the thrill of getting away with murder? All of the above?"

"Works for me."

"The Brits—Martin Hambly and Oliver York?"

"York is a criminal who's stolen tens of millions worth of art. Hambly protects him." Buddy kept the pistol at Reed's temple. "I steal ten bucks at a gas station, imagine what would happen."

"I don't know anything about Oliver York or an art thief. No one's afraid of you, Buddy. You've piled up a lot of enemies. There's only one of you and how many of us? You should have kept things simple."

"You're not paying attention, Reed. I'm winning."

"But you haven't won. Not until you're on a beach with a bottle of rum and no one looking for you. It's not enough to think no one will find you. Someone will."

"Emma Sharpe is locked up without food or water. She'll die if anyone tries to stop me. And Naomi…" Buddy's voice was high-pitched with emotion, tension. "She'll bleed out if she doesn't get help."

"Go, then," Reed said, as if he were tired. "Just go, Buddy. Take a car and get out of here."

Mike turned to Colin. "You've heard enough? Reed knows we're here. Trust me."

Colin nodded, and they moved together. "Buddy," Mike called—and Reed ducked in that same instant, giving them the opening they needed. Mike and Colin both fired before Buddy could get off a shot.

Reed was ragged, leaning forward, grabbing his knees and breathing hard when Mike got to him. "Mike, hell. Thanks." He stood straight. "I wondered how long you two would leave me with that madman. Damn. And I always felt guilty for not liking him."

"I need to find Naomi."

Reed waved a hand. "Go. Both of you. I'm good." He pointed at the door. "Another Donovan has arrived."

Kevin entered the dining room. "Naomi called 911. She used Kavanagh's phone. She could reach it. He couldn't and still hold on to her. She's in her room. Ambulance is on the way."

Mike took the stairs, Colin behind him. The door to Naomi's room was ajar. They went in, and Kavanagh looked up at them, holding on tight to Naomi's middle. "I'm doing the best I can but she needs a doctor."

"I've got her," Mike said, taking over from Kavanagh.

Kavanagh, Naomi's blood on him, staggered to his feet. "Mike, you're a fool if you don't grab love while you can. The kind of love she has for you doesn't come around often, or at all for a lot of us." He sucked in a breath and turned to Colin. "Buddy?"

"He's done."

Naomi sank into Mike. "It was Buddy in Afghanistan. Buddy at the dovecote. I hate him."

"He wanted to best the alpha guys," Kavanagh said. "I'm not one myself. Maybe that's why I fell for it."

"Pretty alpha there when you stopped me from bleeding to death." Naomi winced in pain. "Go home to your ex, T.K. Repair your marriage. Make up for being a driven ass. She makes a good paycheck? Because you're going to need it when the FBI fires you."

Kavanagh had tears on his cheeks. "Maybe my son will let me bunk with him. He's a college senior. He's already getting job offers. Another techie. He'll make a fortune."

"I'm taking up sewing," Naomi said in a hoarse whisper. "I swear."

Mike held her. "Easy, Naomi."

"The paramedics are here," Colin said.

Mike could hear them in the hall. "I'll go with her—"

"You can't, Mike," his brother said. "Naomi and Jamie Mason will both be in good hands."

Mike didn't want to let her go, but when the paramedics entered the room, he transferred Naomi to them. He was reassured when he recognized one of them.

When they left with her, Colin touched his shoulder. "Come on. Kevin and his guys are going to need to talk to us."

31

Nobody had expected Buddy Whidmore to explode into violence. Colin could see why.

"I never saw it coming," Ted Kavanagh said.

They were gathered in the kitchen at the Rock Point Harbor Inn. Kavanagh, Yank and all four Donovan brothers. Naomi MacBride was in surgery. Jamie Mason was getting stitched up. Reed Cooper and Serena Mason were with them at the hospital. Mike kept checking his phone. Colin knew his older brother was champing at the bit to get to the hospital himself.

"I wanted to believe my guy in Afghanistan got caught in the cross fire between bad guys killing each other," Kavanagh said, half to himself. He and Mike had both changed out of their bloody clothes. "But it was Buddy. He turned those guys on each other. I bet when we take another look at that day, we find out that Buddy made a profit. Giving those guys advance warning wasn't just about saving his own skin. It was also about making a buck."

Yank nodded. "That's my guess, too. Buddy played both sides, illegal and legal, to satisfy his ego and his need for an adrenaline rush and cash. He thought he was smarter than everyone else."

"He was doing all right financially until last fall," Colin said. "His productivity app didn't work out. He was broke."

Kavanagh had a faraway look. "Living a lie. It caught up with him. He came to me after Reed went out on his own. He predicted Reed would recruit you, Mike. He couldn't poach on his old outfit—he needed his own guys. Buddy prompted me to look into the Donovans and Sharpes. Naomi was doing the same thing, on her own. Buddy used that as leverage, too. The son of a bitch played me like a fiddle, as the saying goes." Kavanagh drank some of his water. "Or is it a harp? Flute?" He swore under his breath. "I'm losing it."

"You need some rest," Yank said. "You did well today, Agent Kavanagh. I can't speak for the past, but today—you saved Naomi MacBride's life."

"And I'm never going to let her live it down." But Kavanagh's humor didn't reach his eyes and faded quickly. "Buddy didn't make mistakes. He misled. There's a difference. It took me too long to figure that out. He was always in control, even when he seemed reckless and out of control."

"He got to the Cotswolds about the same time you and Naomi did," Colin said. "I heard from Emma. She and Padgett have tracked down a witness who saw Buddy in the village—the grandson of the farmworker who came to Martin Hambly's aid after Naomi found him. He recognized Buddy's photo."

"He knew computers inside and out," Kavanagh said. "He would latch on to something and try to get me to bite. It was what he did. Point out stuff he'd figured out. He always thought what he had was solid. Sometimes it was."

Colin could feel his fellow agent's anguish at being duped. "After Buddy attacked Martin Hambly on Wednesday, he drove to Heathrow and stayed overnight at a hotel there. He took a flight to Boston the next morning."

"In time to pick up York's package here in Rock Point and ambush Emma." Kavanagh sank against the back of his chair. "Leverage, profit, adrenaline. Violence. What Buddy did always made sense to him. He was good when he was good."

Mike, standing in front of the kitchen sink, didn't argue. "Reed didn't expect violence but he suspected something was up. When Buddy surfaced, Reed invited him to the Plum Tree. You, too, Agent Kavanagh. Reed never saw Buddy as someone capable of violence and betrayal. He figured he could handle whatever agenda Buddy had and was open to the idea he might have something to offer."

"Your instincts about Buddy were right, Mike," Kavanagh said, clearly exhausted.

"He played people to feel sorry for him."

Reed Cooper arrived, coming in through the back door. "I sent the guys who were arriving today home. They're keeping Naomi overnight but she'll be fine. Waking up soon. She'll be stuck in Maine for a little while, anyway. You can break it to her that she won't see grass for months."

"We have an ocean," Colin said.

Reed managed a thin smile at the three FBI agents. "Feel free to call me personally anytime the FBI needs extra hands. I mean for Cooper Global Security to be the best of the best."

Yank made a polite comment that he'd be sure to call. Mike said nothing. Colin could feel his older brother's restlessness. He nodded to him. "You don't have to stay here, Mike."

Kevin agreed. Mike grabbed his jacket and left.

He would be where he needed to be right now—at Naomi MacBride's side.

Colin wasn't surprised when his mother invited Ted Kavanagh to stay at the inn, her treat. He accepted with thanks and allowed Colin to pour him a whiskey. They'd moved into the living room with Yank and Kevin. Andy had gone to explain what he could to Franny Maroney, who knew finding Emma's phone hadn't boded well.

"Buddy was right," Kavanagh said, still processing the events of the past week—and the past three years. He drank some of his whiskey. "I underestimated him. I never considered he knew how to use a weapon. He was good with that knife. Naomi was lucky to survive."

"You thought he was a geek who wouldn't think of using violence," Colin said.

Kavanagh gave him a ragged smile. "You Donovans don't mince words, do you? But you're right. It's taken me a long time, but I was duped and manipulated by that weasel. Mike, Reed and Naomi are good guys and you and Emma aren't up to anything. The only mess to clean up is my own." He sank deep into the couch cushions. "I'm not a bad guy."

"You never gave up on your guy who was killed in Kabul," Yank said, pouring whiskey for himself. "We like our dogged sons of bitches."

"Buddy wasn't a skilled operator or marksman but he was dangerous. His particular gift was in manipulating. He got those guys to commit violence on his behalf. For his benefit. You were right about me, Colin. I had the blinders on. I'm burned-out. Not cut out for this job anymore."

"You need that vacation," Colin said. "Director Van Buren will be glad she doesn't have to explain a rogue agent."

"Just a dumb one. You bastards went through my life, didn't you? Did you search my apartment? I hope you found the cufflink I lost. My grandfather gave me a set of cufflinks when I graduated high school."

"We didn't go through your life," Yank said.

Colin grinned. "Should have, maybe."

Kavanagh drank more of his whiskey.

Yank turned to Colin. "Emma needs a few days before she

flies back here. Van Buren wants you to take a break before you go under for HIT."

Colin stood by the fireplace with his whiskey. "Telling me to go to England, Yank?"

"England or wherever Emma ends up. We'll talk when you get back." Yank heaved a long sigh then shook his head at Kavanagh. "Have you noticed that Donovans don't do anything the easy way?"

"I'm beginning to," Kavanagh said.

The senior FBI agent swallowed more of his whiskey. "Their poor mother, my wife says."

Colin rolled his eyes. "My mother met my father after she got everyone out of a bank that was being robbed."

"You made that up," Yank said.

Colin thought he saw Kavanagh smile but he kept his attention on Yank. "Are you going to Boston or Washington from here?"

"Boston," Yank said, then shook his head. "Lucy bought an espresso machine."

32

The Cotswolds, England
Saturday, 9:00 p.m., BST

Finian could see that Emma was exhausted. Sam Padgett had declined an invitation to stay at the York farm, and he only shook his head and sighed when Emma told him she would stay. He left in time to make a late flight back to Boston. "I'll take the car," he told her. "You don't need to be driving. The air's out of your tires, Emma. Take a few days. Mop up here. Work with the locals. They like you."

Finian poured Yellow Spot, one of the few Irish whiskeys Oliver had on hand. He had three glasses—for Emma, Oliver and himself.

"Only a little for me," Emma said.

"I'll have a dram," Oliver said. "Or a *táoscan*, I suppose, since it's Irish whiskey."

A welcome diversion to serious matters.

A fire crackled, burning hot in the front room fireplace. Martin Hambly had retreated to his cottage for a nap. The police questions and the certain knowledge, now, of his close call had taken their toll. But he'd promised he would be "right as rain" in the morning.

Ruthie Burns had brought a tray of fruit, cheese, nuts, honey and biscuits.

Oliver helped himself to a bit of Cotswolds cheese. He'd unearthed a small watercolor painting and set it on a chair across from him, as if it were an invited guest. It was a moody landscape depicting three crosses on Shepherd's Head in the tiny village of Declan's Cross on the south Irish coast. Storm clouds swirled overhead and stirred up the Celtic Sea. Finian's reaction was visceral and immediate—an unbidden, unexpected stirring of nostalgia and homesickness, of faith and hope and inexplicable, timeless love. He was a simple whiskey man and priest. To elicit such emotions was for poets and artists—for a brilliant painter like Aoife O'Byrne.

The painting was unsigned, but this was her work, he knew.

It was one of three paintings Oliver had stolen on his first heist a decade ago, when he'd slipped into the O'Byrnes' run-down seaside house in Declan's Cross. He'd returned the two Jack Butler Yeats landscapes in November. Anonymously, of course.

"I'm convinced it's an early work by Aoife O'Byrne," Oliver said. "I can't say for certain where I got it. But it's lovely, isn't it?"

Emma made no comment. Finian handed her a glass of whiskey, then one to Oliver.

"I need to go back to Declan's Cross," Oliver said, not taking his eyes from the landscape. "One last time."

"Yes, you do," Emma said.

Oliver stared into his whiskey. He made no secret that he was deeply unsettled by the recent events here on his farm and in Maine. Finian understood. Martin Hambly could have been killed. Oliver's alternate life as an art thief could have been more broadly exposed.

"This Buddy Whidmore didn't want Martin to see him,"

Oliver said. "He didn't care if Martin lived or died. He hit him to protect himself. Then he lay in wait at the rectory for the package—and for you, Emma."

She seemed to make an effort to smile. "All's well that ends well."

"A simple package. Sheepskins and a handcrafted cross. Look what happened." Oliver shifted to Finian. "Life's uncertainties, eh, Father Bracken? Is that why you and Declan went into the whiskey business? To cope with the unknown, or to embrace it?"

"Perhaps both," Finian said.

"Well, then. On to the next challenge." Oliver raised his glass. "It's good to have friends in the priesthood and the FBI. Cheers, my friends."

Finian wasn't positive Emma returned the toast, but she did drink some of her Yellow Spot.

In his chair by the fire, Martin swore he ached more now than he had in the first hours after Buddy Whidmore, computer genius and master manipulator, had attacked him. At least it was quiet now. No FBI agents, no local police, no curious villagers. No Ruthie. He'd shooed her out for what he hoped was the last time an hour ago. "I'm *fine*," he'd told her emphatically.

When a knock came at the door, he considered pretending he was dead.

"Hambly," came Oliver's voice. "Open up."

Martin struggled out of his chair. He opened the door.

"You look ghastly," Oliver said, stepping into the cottage. "Shall I phone for an ambulance or just bring whiskey?"

"A good night's sleep will do the trick."

"Good. Emma and Finian are discussing her upcoming wedding. I'll give them a few minutes and then engage them in an intellectual discussion of Saint Brigid and the Celtic goddess Brigid."

"I'll be dead to the world by then, I hope," Martin said. "What can I do for you?"

"I miss those two old dogs we lost in December."

"I do, too, but couldn't this wait—"

"A puppy will aid in your recovery. I'm putting you on the search. I'm not fussy about breed, but I know you probably are—which is fine, because you'll do most of the training."

"You've been into the whiskey cabinet, haven't you?"

"Finian found the one bottle of Irish. Good stuff. But it doesn't affect anything. A farm needs a dog." He took in a breath. "A puppy will help me, too, Martin. In my recovery. If it's not too late."

"It's never too late."

Oliver's pale green eyes caught the light from the fire. "Have you always known?"

"I suspected. Vaguely. Then more than vaguely."

"I'm so ashamed."

"As well you should be. You've returned the art in good order. That's a start."

"Only a start, alas." Oliver pulled his gaze from the fire, any melancholy—real or feigned—gone now. "MI5 will come calling any day. They think I might know something about stolen Middle Eastern antiquities."

"Do you?"

"Of course. I suggest you walk in the countryside and enjoy whiskey and do extra push-ups. I've amends to make, my friend."

"You've a country to serve with your unique capabilities, insights and contacts."

"That, too. A puppy, Martin?"

"A brilliant idea. I'll get on it straightaway."

"Good man," Oliver said, then disappeared back out into the night.

Martin shut the door, latched it and returned to his chair. As stiff and miserable as he felt, he smiled as he shut his eyes. Yes. It was time again for a puppy on the farm.

33

Mike was surprised when Naomi asked him to crack the window so she could hear the ocean. He'd picked her up from the hospital and brought her to his parents' inn, getting her settled in the room at the top of the stairs. It would be a week, at least, before she was cleared to fly. The drive to the Bold Coast was almost as bad, ruling out his cabin, at least for now. Reed had brought her things from the Plum Tree. He was returning to Nashville as soon as possible.

"The perfect room to recover from a knife wound," Naomi said, bandaged, tucked under her comforter. "I swear I can smell the ocean."

"You can stay here as long as you want," Mike said. "Then I'll take you home to Nashville."

"We can have barbecue and bourbon at my favorite hangout."

"We can," he said with a smile.

"I'm not going to let that bastard Buddy ruin it for me. Damn,

Mike. He stabbed me. His eyes…" She fingered the comforter. "I bet we're going to find out he killed those guys in Afghanistan himself."

"The FBI can find out." Mike turned from the window. Her color was decent, but she looked worn-out, emotionally spent if still her indomitable Naomi self. He'd never met anyone tougher. "Anything else you need?"

"You next to me? Or would your parents flip?"

"They're leaving for Florida in the morning. Visiting friends."

"How convenient." Naomi smiled, but her eyes were sunken, her wound and the strain of the past twenty-four hours taking their toll. "Will they leave a pie?"

Mike winked. "Apple. And my father is making muffins."

"Retired cops make the best breakfasts. It's a rule or something."

But tears formed in her eyes, and as much as she tried to fight them, they spilled out and down her cheeks. Mike sat on the bed next to her. "Cry all you want, Naomi."

"Your kindness isn't hard to take." She sniffled, touching his hand. "And it's not unexpected."

He kissed her on the forehead. "Get some rest. We have time."

"Don't you have work waiting for you on the Bold Coast?"

"Nothing that can't keep waiting."

"You live in the real world. You're not hiding. But you never planned to live that far down east forever, did you?" She glanced around the pretty room. "This is home. Rock Point. Where your family is. You can keep your cabin as a cabin—as the refuge it was always meant to be." She was silent a moment. "Am I babbling? I'm still on pain meds."

"You're doing fine," Mike said, not moving from her side.

"Reed could use you with my volunteer doctors."

"He can find someone else. Right now I'm here with you."

"It'll be a few months before they deploy," she said. "I'll be back to dancing on tables well before then."

"Have you ever danced on a table?"

"I could go snowshoeing again, or you could take me out into the wilderness to see a moose. There's a reason *wilderness* is in your job description, isn't there?"

He smiled. "There is."

She yawned, closing her eyes but still awake. "My mother offered to fly up here. I told her it's okay, I'm in good hands. She does great with my sister. They're more alike." Another yawn. "My sister sews."

Naomi dozed. Mike didn't move. He felt the cold air, tasted the ocean in it.

"Maine's growing on me," Naomi said, not opening her eyes. "I could get into life here. I think I'll like Emma. She sounds very centered. I'm not that centered."

"You'll like Julianne, too. She's not that centered, either."

"The marine biologist. I can't tell a porpoise from a dolphin."

"A lot of people can't."

"Mike…" She licked her lips, opening her eyes now. "I was dreaming about you when the rooster woke me in the Cotswolds."

"I'm not going anywhere, Naomi."

"I am a magnet for trouble, though. You were right about that. Seriously. Last time I saw you, I was in a stretcher. Then yesterday…another stretcher."

"You're a woman with a tough job that needs to be done."

"And I trusted Buddy Whidmore," she said.

Mike squeezed her hand gently. "Get some rest. I'll come up and check on you in a little while."

"Is Reed still here?"

"I think so."

"He can take care of my doctors while I recover. I've done most of the heavy lifting already. He just has to follow the plan and do his thing."

"You're the brains."

"Damn straight. I'm going to laze around here and read about puffins and wild blueberries. Maybe your mother has a sewing machine I can use. I know how to sew. I'm just not as good as my mother and sister." She seemed to make an effort to smile. "I can make you a lumberjack shirt."

"You can show me the plans for your volunteer doctors first."

A light came into her eyes. "Mike…"

He kissed her softly on the lips. "I've loved you for a long time, Naomi." He stood up from the bed. "Heal well, okay?"

She smiled. "I'm highly motivated."

He laughed, remembering their nights together. Every one of them.

She caught her fingertips into his, then sank deep into her pillow, fast asleep.

Mike went downstairs. Reed had coffee made and muffins warmed on a plate. "Do we talk about Cooper Global Security, or do we talk about painting canoes?"

"We can do both."

34

Declan's Cross, the South Irish Coast
Sunday, 8:00 p.m., IST

The bar at the O'Byrne House Hotel was overflowing with Brackens. Declan was there with his wife and their three young children, and Finian, alone. The three Bracken sisters had decided to join their older brothers. Two were married and came with their husbands and a total of five more small children. The youngest sibling, Mary, who worked for Bracken Distillers, came on her own. Emma had met Declan before but not the Bracken sisters. Their laughter, ready wit and good cheer were the perfect antidote to a very long few days.

Black-haired, blue-eyed Kitty O'Byrne, Aoife's sister and the proprietress of the upscale boutique hotel, had pulled a bottle of Bracken 15 Year Old from her whiskey cabinet. Whoops of appreciation came from the Bracken crowd.

As Kitty poured glasses, Emma received a text from her grandfather in Dublin. The two Dutch landscapes had been returned without fanfare and now were hanging in the museum gallery where they'd hung for decades.

One last escapade for our thief.

Emma slid her phone back into her jacket. *How* had Oliver pulled that one off?

She and Finian had flown into Cork that morning. Oliver promised to join them in the evening.

There was time—if not a lot of time—to pop over to Amsterdam from England, return the paintings and then fly to Cork and drive an hour east to Declan's Cross.

Oliver must have had the operation planned well in advance, Emma thought. All he'd been waiting for was a reason to execute the plan.

She managed one sip of Bracken 15 before Oliver walked into the bar.

If Kitty and the rest of the Brackens knew he was the thief who'd broken in here ten years ago, they gave no sign of it. Finian welcomed his English friend and introduced him.

More Bracken 15 flowed.

Emma stayed on her bar stool by the window. Others would figure out that Oliver York and Oliver Fairbairn were the same person. He didn't hide it but he didn't publicize it, either. He and MI5 might have to deal with persistent rumors that he was a serial art thief, but they were up to the challenge. Not everyone was a Naomi MacBride or Buddy Whidmore.

Aoife O'Byrne came in through French doors that opened onto the patio and dark Irish night. Emma noticed the Irish artist's eyes scan the crowded room, and then her smile as two of the children ran up to her. The Brackens were singing and laughing, telling stories. Kitty had abandoned her whiskey pouring and now was arguing with Sean Murphy, her Irish detective love—who knew as well as Emma did that Oliver York was the thief who'd slipped into the O'Byrne house ten years ago.

Finian looked at Emma and smiled, a lightness about him that was unmistakable.

Aoife spun off from the little ones and flirted with the Brackens' master distiller, a good-looking Irishman who obviously had no idea she was an artist—which seemed to please her.

Oliver plopped onto the bar stool next to Emma. "Perhaps there's a sexy MI5 agent in my future."

"Maybe she'll speak Dutch."

"Ah. You heard about the mysterious return of the landscapes. Wendell texted me earlier. The Heineken must be flowing in Amsterdam. By the way, your grandfather has invited me to the open house of the new Sharpe Fine Art Recovery offices in Heron's Cove. I wouldn't miss it. He says you and Colin have a guest room." Oliver smiled. "Why do you think I sent you three sheepskins? One for the guest room. I hate cold feet."

He spun off with a glass and the Bracken 15 before Emma could tell him he wasn't staying in her guest room. Finian joined him by the fire. His friendship with Colin had already been established when he and Emma met, and he'd been friends with Sean Murphy since the garda detective had investigated the tragic deaths of Sally Bracken and her two small daughters.

Perhaps, Emma thought, Oliver was another dangerous man Father Bracken counseled.

Aoife slipped away from her whiskey man and sat on the stool Oliver had vacated. "I heard you've had a difficult few days, Emma. I thought you should know that I went to London last week because I knew Declan and Finian were there, and I wanted to see Oliver." She smiled. "I think I'm a bit obsessed with those two. But not in the way I was last fall. They're friends."

"I'm glad," Emma said.

She lasted a few more minutes before she left the party and slipped out of the lounge to head up to her room. She and Colin had stayed in the same room in November. She remembered making love in front of the fire. A few days later, he'd proposed to her in Dublin.

She pressed her engagement ring to her lips, as if it brought him closer to her.

Aoife was right, Emma thought. She had definitely had a difficult few days. She decided to indulge herself and take a luxurious bath in her quiet room.

When she got out of the tub and wrapped herself in a thick robe, she saw she had a text message from Colin. I'm about to get on a plane to Ireland.

Perfect.

See you soon, babe. We'll have a few days to ourselves.

And then what? Mina Van Buren, Yank, the Washington meetings...

All that could wait. In a few hours, Colin would be here, and they would once again make love by the fire.

★ ★ ★ ★ ★

AUTHOR'S NOTE

I hope you enjoyed *Keeper's Reach*, the fifth novel in my Sharpe & Donovan romantic suspense series. Many readers have asked me about Mike Donovan. Now we know more about him, but I have a feeling he has secrets yet to be revealed, don't you? Emma Sharpe and Colin Donovan continue their adventures, and Finian Bracken takes another step in his journey since the tragic loss of his family.

It's exciting, challenging and fun creating a world for this cast of characters. Oliver York's family "farm" in the Cotswolds was inspired by my own trips to this beautiful part of England. Joe and I didn't get knocked on the head, but we had a few adventures. I've put some of the photos we took onto my website. Take a look!

Ireland, of course, continues to inspire and fascinate me. As I write this note, Joe and I are preparing for another trip to the southwest coast and Saint Declan country on the south coast. We look forward to chatting about whiskey with our friend John Moriarty, who has been so gracious in answering my questions about everything from sheep to the proper pronunciation of *táoscan*.

And Maine... I love New England in spring, summer, fall and winter. In *Keeper's Reach*, we get a taste of the Maine coast in winter. I swear I almost got frostbite writing some of the scenes! One of my favorite winter activities is to strap on snowshoes and head into the woods—followed by hot chocolate by the fire!

I'm deep into planning my next Sharpe & Donovan novel. To stay up-to-date and get sneak peeks on all my books, and for photos and ultrashort videos that will give you a taste of the Sharpe & Donovan world, please visit my website www.carlaneggers.com and sign up for my eNewsletter. And enjoy the recipes! Scones, for one. How could I resist?

Thanks and take care!
Carla